TWO BITES TOO MANY

The rising decibels of the mutterings in the room indicated the natives were getting restless. Her mother had joked that nothing could start without Lance, but it wasn't like Maybelle to keep people waiting.

Sarah checked her phone to see if she had a message from her mother.

None.

Commotion near the door used by the council members caught Sarah's attention. Bailey, the loan officer, stood in the doorway. This time he wasn't burdened down with a pile of papers when he scurried into the room toward the dais. If it was possible, Sarah thought his face was even paler than before. Although he went straight to Anne Hightower, who sat erectly next to Lance's empty chair, instead of quite facing Anne, Bailey was intently scanning the audience. He froze when his gaze met Sarah's.

"It's Mr. Knowlton. He's dead!"

Not sure if she'd heard right, Sarah maintained an unbroken stare with Bailey. Only when he repeated "he's dead" and added "your mother" did she break the linkage of their gazes to push her way out of her row and the auditorium . . .

Books by DEBRA H. GOLDSTEIN

ONE TASTE TOO MANY

TWO BITES TOO MANY

Published by Kensington Publishing Corporation

TWO BITES TOO MANY

A Sarah Blair Mystery

Debra H. Goldstein

KENSINGTON PUBLISHING CORP.

www.kensingtonbooks.com

KENSINGTON BOOKS are published by

Kensington Publishing Corp.
119 West 40th Street
New York, NY 10018

All Kensington titles, imprints, and distributed lines are available at special quantity discounts for bulk purchases for sales promotions, premiums, fund-raising, educational, or institutional use.

Special book excerpts or customized printings can also be created to fit specific needs. For details, write or phone the office of the Kensington sales manager: Kensington Publishing Corp., 119 West 40th Street, New York, NY 10018, attn: Sales Department; phone 1-800-221-2647.

First printing: October 2019

10 9 8 7 6 5 4 3 2 1

ISBN-13: 978-1-4967-1948-5
ISBN-10: 1-4967-1948-4

Printed in the United States of America

Electronic edition:

ISBN-13: 978-1-4967-1951-5 (e-book)
ISBN-10: 1-4967-1951-4 (e-book)

For my children and grandchildren
who drive me crazy and keep me sane

ACKNOWLEDGMENTS

Each book or story I write is different. The differences include the ideas expressed, the emotions evoked, where I write the piece, and what music I listen to while the work is in progress. What doesn't change is my reliance and appreciation for those who help me on the journey.

My husband, Joel, encourages my writing. Consequently, he puts up with many lonely hours while I am, as he says, "labbing it." Friends Fran and Lee Godchaux and author T. K. Thorne repeatedly drop their own activities to beta read for me. Edie Peterson did the same for proofreading. Editors Lourdes Venard and Barb Goffman squeeze me in when I don't quite keep the schedule I should have. Both make me think of things that never crossed my mind but need to be worked in to strengthen the manuscript.

Susan Mason, George McMillan III, Meredith McMillan, Andrew Larkin, Stuart Stone, April Deal, and Jean Felts were generous with their time and knowledge to teach me about restaurants, cooking, convention bureaus, and cats. Any errors are my own.

A special thanks to my agent, Dawn Dowdle, who yanked me from the unagented pool of writers and represents me with skill, kindness, and a keen eye to what can improve my final submissions. Finally, my appreciation to John Scognamiglio, Editor-in-Chief of Kensington, who has the vision to see where the Sarah Blair mystery series and my writing career can go. When John tells me a manuscript is cleanly written, I happy dance all day.

CHAPTER ONE

"I don't care if you own this house. You aren't the one in charge!" Arms crossed, Sarah Blair stood in the middle of the carriage house's living room, straining to hear her hiding cat over the car horn blaring outside. Her mother was the nonstop honker.

"RahRah, where are you? I've got to get going!" She listened again, but the only thing she heard was the horn—short staccato beeps this time.

A soft rustle under the claw-scratched couch caught her ear. Dropping down on one knee, she pushed her curtain of hair back and peeked under the leather sofa. Two sparkling blue eyes stared back at her. Slowly, Sarah reached for RahRah. Her Siamese cat didn't shy away. Once she had a firm grasp, she gently eased him out from under the couch.

She cuddled RahRah's soft body to hers as she carried him into the kitchen. "Your food and water bowls arc full. I'd rather stay here with you, but Mom and I are seeing Mr. Knowlton at the bank before we go to the city council meeting."

A toot jarred their moment together.

"She's a little persistent with that honking, isn't she?"

RahRah didn't squirm, even when Sarah's loose brown hair touched his sides as she bent to put him on the floor. "I sure wouldn't want to be Mr. Knowlton today. Not with Mom on the warpath."

The horn sounded again. This time, one steady blow, as if a body lay collapsed on the steering wheel. Sarah glanced toward the front of the house, then focused back on RahRah. "I don't know why Mom insists I go instead of your Aunt Emily. After all, it's Emily's loan application the bank has denied."

She could have sworn RahRah tilted his tan head in her direction before he shook his body, sauntered across the linoleum floor, and stretched out in a patch of sunshine. She wondered if he understood her reference to her twin sister, Emily.

Probably. RahRah commandeered the same spot on the kitchen floor during all her discussions with Emily and Marcus about their plans following the fire that destroyed their restaurant. Sarah wouldn't put it past her cat to know the details of how the two chefs wanted to convert their damaged location into an upscale pub and, in partnership with Sarah, open an upscale restaurant in the big house Sarah owned.

Satisfied RahRah would be fine while she was gone, Sarah closed the kitchen door behind her, cutting RahRah off from the rest of the house. She grabbed her purse and keys from the table by the front door and hurried outside. As she locked the door of the carriage house, she realized the honking had stopped. Instead, a harsh male voice carried on the wind.

Whoever it was, she doubted anything could drown him out.

Uncertain which direction the voice was coming from, Sarah peered down the driveway, toward Main Street. Her mother's car was parked next to the property's big house, the driver's door flung open. No one lay dramatically on the steering wheel. Instead, her mother stood at the edge of Sarah's lot line with George Rogers, Sarah's across-the-street neighbor. It was his voice she'd heard.

Neither his stance nor apparent tirade changed when Sarah approached them. Her mother glanced toward Sarah and rolled her eyes.

Sarah picked up on her mother's cue. "What's going on, Mr. Rogers? Did something happen?"

Mr. Rogers broke off his rant midsentence. He turned so his bow tie and pince-nez glasses faced her. "I'll show you what's going on." Using the tip of his cane, he gestured toward the section of her wrought iron fence facing Main Street. "Look at what they did to your fence."

Sarah gazed at where his cane pointed. Several of the decorated fence spikes near the driveway were askew. Someone had taken a baseball bat or other blunt object to the sharp-edged finials topping her fence rods. Although a few of the decorative pieces dangled precariously, at least four were completely severed.

"They got my fence last night, too."

"Who?"

"Hoodlums. That's who. The same riffraff and

gangsters we're going to have in this neighborhood all the time if your rezoning plan goes through."

"Now, Mr. Rogers, if we get approval for my sister and her boyfriend to open an upscale restaurant in the big house, it's only going to attract high-class patrons."

"That's what you think. If this neighborhood becomes an entertainment district, it means bars and lowlifes. Look at your fence and mine. Who knows how deadly their malicious mischief will be next time? As it is, I can't find Fluffy."

"Fluffy?"

"That little white mutt that's been hanging around the neighborhood. For the past week, I've tried to get close enough to bring her into the house, but she won't let me. The best I've been able to do is get her to come around like clockwork for the food and water set out on the porch."

Mr. Rogers waved his hands again toward the fence. "Fluffy didn't touch her food today. If these hooligans you want to overrun our street didn't hurt her, they certainly frightened her."

Sarah bit her tongue. Her opinion on rezoning the neighborhood was diametrically opposed to Mr. Rogers, but they'd agreed to disagree without being unpleasant to each other. Seeing how upset he was about their fences and Fluffy, she forced herself not to fire back a retort. Instead, Sarah offered her help looking for Fluffy if she was still missing when Sarah got home.

"Thanks. If I haven't found her, I'd appreciate that." There was no divergence of opinion between them when it came to animals and their well-being. An entertainment district was another matter, entirely.

Mr. Rogers continued to rant about the gangster element that could invade their homes and property if Main Street was rezoned. Sarah tuned him out. She reminded herself that his reluctance for change reflected more than what he was verbalizing. Keeping the neighborhood exactly as it was perpetuated the memories he and his late wife created from the time they built their home across the street, well before Sarah was born.

No matter which view Sarah or any of her other neighbors held on rezoning Main Street, they all agreed Mr. Rogers was their neighborhood watch, eccentric, and historian rolled into one. Most also acknowledged his ever-present cane and bow tie represented an era no longer in fashion.

Sarah ran her hand over one of the damaged rods. "Considering the damage, I'm surprised I didn't hear anything last night."

"Well, the carriage house is set back quite a distance from this fence." Sarah's mother bent and picked up a metal finial lying on the ground. She turned it over in her hands.

"Sarah," Mr. Rogers said, "I called my nephew, Clifford. He's going to come by and fix my fence. If you want, I can send him your way, too."

Uncertain what to do, Sarah looked at her mother, who imperceptibly shook her head. Her mother slipped the finial she held into her oversized purse.

"That's very kind of you, George, offering to have your nephew help Sarah. But after she and I finish at the bank, we'll stop by Gus's hardware store. He owes me one, so I'm sure he'll tell us what we need and send someone to fix it at a discounted rate."

Sarah swallowed hard, watching her mother bat her eyes at Mr. Rogers.

She held her laughter back until her mother and she were safely in the car. "How is it that you live in Birmingham, but you still know everyone in Wheaton and everything about them?"

"Don't be so silly. Your dad did so much business with Birmingham and Wheaton folk, I got to know them all. You'll be the same way by the time you get to be my age."

"I doubt that. But tell me, what do you have on Gus?"

Her mother threw the car into reverse and looked in all directions behind her before releasing her foot from the brake. "I have nothing on Gus. He simply owes me a favor. Besides, it's always better to use a non–family member for house repairs."

Sarah held her next question until her mother eased out of the driveway and pulled the car from the middle of the street back into her own lane. "Even if the family member is a neighbor's, not yours?"

"Especially. It avoids problems."

"Good point. Mom, speaking of problems, Emily and I have been meaning to talk to you about this name business. It's one thing to insist your friends call you Maybelle, but having your daughters use your given name is simply weird. Considering our relationship, we think Mom, Mother, or Mama is more appropriate."

Maybelle leaned forward, checking for cars as she

rolled through a four-way stop. "Nonsense. My name means lovable. When I was at the spa, my guru told me the only way to obtain the best possible positive energy in my personal zone is to simplify everything. That includes the name I go by."

She gestured toward her open car window. "Like the birds that fly or smoke rising from a fire, using only one name opens my energy flow."

"There's no one more energetic than you, Mom."

"We're talking about my positive energy flow. Because the intensity of my flow translates into a force I use to help other people, I need you to call me by my given name, too."

"You answered to Mom this morning."

Maybelle glanced quickly at Sarah and then focused back at the road. "Only because George was so upset. I didn't want him to think we were minimizing his concerns. That would negate his energy flow."

Her petite mother maintained a tight grip on the steering wheel in the ten and two positions.

Sarah repeated the name, Maybelle, to herself. It felt as funny rolling around her brain now as it had four months ago, when her mother came home from the spa announcing everyone should address her simply as Maybelle. Considering how upset her mother was when she learned about her daughters' involvement with murders and murderers, neither Sarah nor Emily challenged their mother's demand. They figured it was the Maybelle fad of the week.

Surprisingly, unlike so many of the ideas that possessed her mother, it hadn't passed. Maybe it really was something to do with positive energy, but Sarah was pretty sure it might be tied to the difficulty Maybelle was having accepting this was the year she qualified for Medicare and her twin daughters turned thirty.

Then again, Sarah wasn't sure she felt too good about the upcoming big three-o, either. She questioned what she had to show for thirty years of living. Unlike Emily, Sarah's professionally trained chef and restaurateur twin, all Sarah could claim was marriage at eighteen, divorce before twenty-eight, employment as a law firm receptionist, an active social life only if the cats and dogs at the animal shelter were included, and recently moving from an efficiency apartment to the carriage house her cat inherited.

"Mom, I mean Maybelle, wouldn't it have made more sense to take Emily with you today? After all, she knows all the financial stuff related to Southwind's fire-insurance settlement and its reopening as a pub. She also has a better handle on the details of the fine-dining restaurant Marcus and she want to open in the big house."

"That's not today's main issue."

"It isn't?" Sarah wrinkled her brow. She thought this visit was generated by the bank turning down her sister's loan request.

"No. Today's goal is to remind Lance Knowlton of the long-standing relationship between his bank and your dearly departed father and how, as RahRah's guardian, you're now an important customer, too."

Sarah thought better of pursuing this or any discussion while her mother eased her car into the one spot open in front of the bank. It was touch and go for a moment, but at least, this time, Sarah was relieved Maybelle didn't use either the car in front or behind to determine the boundaries of her parking space. She only hoped her mother's confrontation with Lance Knowlton would be less deadly than her driving.

CHAPTER TWO

Inside the bank, Sarah lengthened her stride to stay even with her mother's quick pace across the lobby. Her mother was on such a mission to reach the bank president's closed door that she barely acknowledged a wave from one of the tellers as they passed. Sarah certainly didn't envy what the next few minutes would bring for Lance Knowlton, but she wished her mother would slow down. She preferred strolling through this bank's lobby to the clip her mother was setting.

Unlike the feeling she got in modern banks with their faux columns, glass windowed cubicles, and modular gray steel furniture, the almost one-hundred-year-old décor of this branch always lulled her with its sense of security. In her mind, the wood-paneled offices, polished furniture, and comfortable leather chairs, strategically placed throughout the lobby—so each had a view of the open vault door and the guarded safe deposit boxes—was what a bank should be. The only thing marring the historical feel of the building was its modern security cameras.

Lance's secretary, Eloise, intercepted Maybelle and Sarah before they reached his door. She guided them to two small chairs situated to the left of his office. "I'm sorry. He's running a few minutes behind. May I get you a cup of coffee or a soda? The matter he's dealing with just came up, but he should be finished momentarily."

When they declined, Eloise returned to her desk at the right of Lance's office. Its placement always made Sarah think about how secretarial desks were positioned at the beck and call of the boss in 1950s sitcoms. Sixty plus years later, except for Eloise and her ever-present intercom, bosses and secretaries communicated by email, rarely seeing each other.

Sarah's pondering of the furniture and Eloise's role in the bank was interrupted by an angry string of profanity, accompanying the words coming from inside Lance's office. "Lance, you had no right to call my loan. I swear I should kill you."

As she focused on the closed wooden door, trying to make out more of the shouted words, it crashed open with such force the doorknob banged into the wall.

A scowling man, whose plaid shirt contrasted with his tanned face and tousled blond hair made Sarah think "Paul Bunyan meets Surf City," stomped by her. He stopped almost even with where Sarah sat open-mouthed. His presence squeezed the air from her space, making her feel she might as well have been invisible.

Lance's voice brought her attention back to where he stood in his doorway, "Cliff, I'm sorry."

"Not as sorry as you're going to be." Without

glancing at Lance or her staring at him, he crossed the lobby and exited the bank.

Although the tension outside Lance's door immediately dissipated, Sarah looked toward Lance to gauge his reaction. As she glanced in his direction, he stepped closer to Eloise's desk to let a second man leave his office.

She wrinkled her brow in confusion. It was Jacob Hightower, a Southwind line cook. "Jacob?"

He acknowledged Sarah and Maybelle with a quick smile and wave but hurried past to catch up to the blue-jeaned windswept hunk. Sarah couldn't help wondering what about a loan being called generated such angry words or the need to barge in on Lance without an appointment.

Knowing Jacob, she bet it involved a development deal. Even though he was the son of the wealthiest Wheaton family and recently had been burnt in more ways than one, he remained one of the biggest promoters for establishing a new entertainment district. Unfortunately, his chief opposition was the rest of his family.

Sarah's thoughts were interrupted by Lance. "Maybelle, Sarah, how good to see you. Sorry you had to wait. Please, come in."

With one hand gesturing in welcome, he pulled a big white handkerchief out of his pocket with the other and dabbed his forehead.

Sarah let her mother step into his office ahead of her. As she followed, Sarah glanced back and realized Lance had stopped to talk with Eloise.

Maybelle pointed to a small door at the rear of the

office. "See that door? When your daddy was alive, that's the only way we came in or went out of this bank. Your daddy didn't believe in going through the main lobby. He liked using the alley entrance to keep our banking business private."

Maybelle stopped talking as Lance came in and settled himself into his high-backed leather chair. "My apologies again. I try to keep my job as president of this bank separate from my responsibilities as president of the city council, but on days like today, when our council meeting is only a couple of hours away, that's hard to do. Someone always seems to want something at the last minute."

He pointed to a stack of papers on his desk. "These papers are the ones going to the meeting, and they're only half of what I read each week to keep up with city issues. By the way, Sarah, I was pleased when the council voted last week in favor of permitting your animal parade idea as a means of earning money for the shelter. It was nice to see everyone in agreement on something when they expanded your idea into being an entire YipYeow Day. Let me know what the bank can sponsor for five thousand dollars."

Sarah was thrilled to hear her pet project not only had the city's formal blessing with its promise to provide traffic control and protection and let the shelter use the park pavilion for free but now had a sponsorship commitment from the bank. In Wheaton, having the bank and power company as supporters guaranteed a project's success. "That's so generous of the bank and you. Don't forget, the organizational meeting is Thursday at six at my house. I hope you'll come."

"Thank you, but I have another commitment Thursday evening. Just remember, when your committee is doing its planning, you can count on this bank for five thousand dollars." He paused and smiled. "It's nice to sponsor a project the entire council is behind."

Sarah agreed. Her excitement at his offer was only dampened by his not saying the council was also in favor of Emily and Marcus using the big house for a restaurant.

"Now, what can I do for you two lovely ladies?"

That, Sarah realized, was all the opening her mother needed to spring into fighter mode.

CHAPTER THREE

Sarah sat back to watch the Maybelle show.

"Lance Knowlton, you can tell me when you lost your mind. How could you refuse to give my daughter, Emily, and her friend Marcus a bridge loan when you had full collateral for it? Considering the extensive history my husband and I had with you, and that most of our deals were done based on a handshake, I don't understand this."

"Well, Maybelle, I'm not quite sure which loan you're referring to, but you know banking regulations have tightened in the last few years. Things we used to do on a handshake can't be done anymore. Compliance is the name of the game."

"Hogwash."

"Maybelle, I'm sure Bailey, my loan officer, had a good reason for turning down the loan application. Restaurants are tricky businesses."

"But guaranteed loans aren't."

"Excuse me?"

Maybelle waved her hand at the stack of papers on his desk he'd previously shown Sarah and her. "Have you gotten so carried away with your city council position that you're ignoring your bank duties? The guaranteed terms offered on this loan were the kind you should have signed off on in your sleep."

Sarah was glad she'd taken the guest chair farthest away from Lance's desk. While he stammered about bank regulations and how Bailey reviewed every loan carefully, she could tell from her mother's rising voice level and increasingly flushed cheeks that her anger and attack on Lance hadn't yet peaked.

When Maybelle rose and leaned over his desk, Sarah knew it was only a matter of seconds before her mother made mincemeat of Lance. "Since when does your bank turn down a loan when one of your longtime customers offers to either cosign or put up one hundred percent collateral from personal assets for it?"

"Maybelle, there could have been any number of reasons Bailey turned down the loan. He may have found the collateral insufficient or felt items in the loan request weren't financially sound. You'd be surprised how many times these young borrowers want money for thousand-dollar light fixtures when hundred-and-fifty-dollar fixtures over the bar will suffice."

Maybelle straightened and placed her hand on her chest, under her neck. "Bless your heart, I do understand the problems your Mr. Bailey must encounter all the time. Horrible. Simply horrible when your loan officer has to weigh helping folks and our community against profitability."

"That's part of the stricter compliance laws."

"Except none of those considerations applied

here. My daughter wouldn't overspend for anything anymore than I would be so lax as to not know to the penny what money I have in your bank."

Sarah remained silent. After her daddy died six years ago, Maybelle was petrified of outliving her money. Only when Emily and Sarah sat her down and showed her in black and white that she'd need to live to about one hundred and fifty-two to run out of funds did she relax. Since that day, Maybelle accepted with gusto the twins' encouragement to be a bit of a madcap, spending on things she wanted.

Spa trips and searching for positive energy might be an essential part of her mother's free-spending existence, but keeping track of every cent was equally important to her. If Maybelle said there was more than enough money to guarantee the loan Emily and Marcus applied for, Sarah knew there was.

"Let me get Bailey in here to clear this up. I can assure you having happy customers is this bank's primary goal. If a mistake was made, I'll personally make sure it's rectified." He picked up the phone and punched in a few numbers. "Eloise, have Bailey come in here and tell him to bring the Southwind file, please."

While he made the call, Sarah watched Maybelle rest her large purse on Mr. Knowlton's desk and rummage through it. Maybelle placed the spiked fence topper, a pair of reading glasses, and an old-fashioned savings account passbook on the desk. She kept her smartphone in her hand. Once Lance looked in Maybelle's direction, she typed something into it and stared at the phone's screen.

From Sarah's vantage point, she wondered if it

might be more effective to turn the phone on, but that apparently wasn't important to either her mother or Mr. Knowlton. She stifled a giggle.

Her mother shot her a stern look before turning her attention back to Lance. "I noticed Jacob Hightower and someone who didn't seem very happy about a loan call coming out of your office while we were waiting. Tell me, Lance, how much of this bank do Anne and Ralph Hightower own?"

Sarah was surprised to hear her mother mention Jacob's sister and father. Not only were they two of the most influential people in the city but also the most outspoken in their opposition to creating an entertainment district. If they owned the bank, it was no wonder Emily and Marcus's loan application was rejected.

"Now, Maybelle. You know they're investors, not officers. They aren't involved with day-to-day operations and certainly had nothing to do with the Southwind loan. My loan officer conscientiously handles all those applications, but I'll look this one over again myself. I'm sure there was a valid reason for the denial, but if . . ."

A knock at the door and its immediate opening interrupted his string of platitudes. A middle-aged man stood in the doorway clutching a thin folder. His dark hair, dark suit, and dark-rimmed glasses blended together in sharp contrast to his pasty white skin. Sarah wondered if he ever went outside before the sun went down.

"You wanted the Southwind file, sir?"

Lance took the file from him. "Thank you, Bailey." Gesturing toward Maybelle and Sarah, Lance did introductions. "They're inquiring about why the Southwind loan was rejected."

Bailey raised his hands, palm up, directing his answer to Maybelle. "I'm sorry. I don't know off the top of my head. Ms. Eloise said Mr. Knowlton wanted the file immediately, so I didn't review it before bringing it in. And, well, we process so many loan applications that I don't really recall the details related to Southwind, but, Mr. Knowlton, as you know, my reasons are always fully documented on the second page of the file."

He held his left hand out toward Lance for the file. "Mr. Knowlton, would you like me to go through this for you? It will only take a few minutes."

Lance glanced at his watch. "No, that won't be necessary. I'll personally look the file over. The council meeting isn't for an hour and a half. While I review this file, save me some time by taking this stack of papers over to city hall and getting things ready for the session."

"Yes, sir." Bailey combined bobbing his head and upper body in Sarah and Maybelle's direction with scooping the papers from the corner of Lance's desk. "Nice meeting you, Mrs. Johnson, Ms. Blair. Mr. Knowlton, I'm sure you'll find everything in order, but if there is anything else I can do, please let me know. If you need me to run back and explain anything, you or Eloise can reach me on my cell."

As Bailey juggled the papers and reached for the doorknob, Sarah leapt from her seat and opened the door for him.

"Thank you, Ms. Blair."

"No problem." Closing the door, she glanced back at her mother and Lance.

Lance opened the file. He shut it and dropped it on his desk near the finial without examining any of the documents. "Tell you what, Maybelle, I want to give this file the attention it deserves. We receive so many applications, Bailey may well have erred on the side of conservatism. I promise I'll review this before day's end."

Maybelle put her cell phone back in her purse and tapped her finger on her passbook, which still lay on his desk, then used the same finger to point to his watch. "Lance, I think there's more than enough time before the council meeting to approve a loan or for a customer to decide to move an account to a more independent bank."

She slowly returned her reading glasses to her purse before picking up her bankbook. She turned it over in her hands, examining its back and front covers while holding it up in midair, so Lance and Sarah could clearly see it. "After all these years, I'd hate explaining to the sewing club why I moved my account to the bank down the street. What would your wife say?"

Whether it was the threat of Maybelle moving her account or telling his wife, Lance again used his handkerchief on his glistening forehead while she dropped the passbook into her purse. "Maybelle, there's no need to make a hasty decision. Based upon what you've told me, I'm sure this loan matter can easily be resolved."

"I think so, too, but considering the motion for re-zoning for their restaurant should be considered today, it would be lovely if you could give Emily and Marcus an answer before the council meeting."

Lance wiped the sweat beaded on his brow. "You know, Maybelle, the agenda is pretty full today and that's a hot topic."

"I understand, but wouldn't it be to everyone's benefit if people knew there are no financial barriers for rebuilding Southwind or establishing a second dining location if the zoning change is approved?"

"Definitely." Lance smiled in Sarah's direction. "Tell you what, why don't you two ladies go get a cup of coffee while I review the loan application before the meeting?"

Maybelle returned his smile. "Why, thank you, Lance. I have had a hankering all morning for a Buffalo Betty's chicken biscuit, but I didn't want us to leave here with this matter unresolved."

He leaned across his desk and patted Maybelle's hand. "Nothing better than a Buffalo Betty's chicken biscuit. Go enjoy one for me while I work on this loan. Don't you fret about anything. By the way, Sarah, how's that cat of yours? He playing the stock market yet?"

Sarah gave him a Cheshire cat grin. "He's more into fur balls, but he's just fine, Mr. Knowlton. Just fine."

Before either of them could say anything more about RahRah, the door from the lobby burst open.

The hunk who'd left with Jacob rushed into the office, trailed by Eloise and a football player–sized security guard. "Excuse me, but this can't wait!"

As Eloise grabbed for the hunk's shirttail and missed, Sarah pulled her mother out of the moving train's path. She couldn't keep the hunk's flying hands from knocking the various items from the desk onto the floor. The contents of Maybelle's open purse spilled at the hunk's feet.

"I'm sorry, Mr. Knowlton. I tried to stop him," Eloise said.

Lance waved her and the security guard, whose presence filled the room, away. "It's okay. I'll take care of this." He repeated himself until Eloise and the guard, still not looking fully convinced, left. With their departure, the room felt less claustrophobic. She released her grip on her mother but didn't step forward to help as the hunk haphazardly picked up the various items strewn on the floor and threw them back into the pocketbook or on the desk.

From behind his desk, Lance held his hand out for the purse when the young man finished scooping up its fallen contents. "I'll take that, Cliff. Why don't you go back outside and make an appointment with my secretary?"

The hunk growled something, but when Lance held his ground, he hung the pocketbook over Lance's outstretched hand. Grunting an apology to Sarah and Maybelle and another warning to Lance that this wasn't the end of it, he backed out of the office, but not before Sarah felt chilled by the gaze she observed him exchange with Lance. Interestingly, the bank president didn't seem nearly as upset as when Maybelle threatened to move her account.

Lance came around his desk and gently took Maybelle's arm, while handing her the purse. "I'm sorry you had to see that. Cliff gets a little hot at times, but he's a good guy." Lance glanced at his watch. "You two better hurry if you're going to get one of Betty's biscuits before the meeting."

Guiding Maybelle, Lance ushered her out of his office but stopped abruptly when she froze in place. Sarah stumbled behind him. As she tripped, she barely managed to squeeze around them. Regaining her balance, she peered at them.

Maybelle was looking at Lance with her best church-going look of serenity. Her honey tone matched the sweetness and light of her expression. "Lance, I was thinking about that young man who just barged in here. Maybe you should review his loan file, too? From the sound of it, you might find an error that's enough to keep you alive."

Without waiting for him to reply, Maybelle gently pushed past Sarah. "Come along, Sarah."

Following her mother, Sarah listened for anything else Lance might say, but all she heard was the firm click of his closing door, followed by a large guffaw from Maybelle.

"Well, I do believe round one went well," Maybelle said.

"Round one? How many do you anticipate in this battle?"

"Whatever it takes to get a knockout."

"Even if it's a technical?" Sarah pointed to the polished wood clock hanging on the wall behind the teller counter. "Let's get over to Buffalo Betty's so we can visit for a few minutes before I need to meet Harlan at city hall. I promised to touch base with him fifteen minutes before the meeting in case he came up with any questions preparing his presentation to the council."

"We'll have to visit another time. We're not going to get a biscuit this morning."

"We're not?"

"No. Round two is about to begin. I can assure you Lance and I will have the matter of the loan resolved before the meeting. By the way, it was a good idea to let Harlan be your spokesman at the council meeting. He's pretty unflappable."

Sarah agreed. Her boss, Harlan Endicott, was both a competent lawyer and an excellent speaker. Unlike how her emotions or the council members' questions might distract her from hammering home her point, Harlan would stay glued to his topic.

"First, though, call your sister. Before I go for the knockout, I want to make sure Marcus and Emily didn't get carried away and buy any of those thousand-dollar fixtures."

"I'm sure Emily didn't. You know how practical she is."

"I repeat. Call your sister. I need my ducks in order before I circle back for the kill."

"Circle back?"

"Of course. You go on to city hall and meet Harlan while I visit a few minutes with Eloise. Then I'm going to use the door your daddy preferred to finish my banking. I want that loan approved before the council meeting and before I tell him I'm moving my account."

Sarah made a face but put through the requested call. Emily answered on the first ring and with equal quickness responded that neither she nor Marcus had ordered anything out of the ordinary for Southwind. There was nothing, Emily assured Sarah, in expenditures or proposed items that should have precluded the loan. Hanging up, Sarah shared Emily's comments with her mother.

"I didn't think Emily would have done something stupid. It will be interesting to see what Lance says once he reviews the file."

"If it was an honest mistake and he apologizes and approves the loan, why move your account? Won't that be a nuisance?"

"Because my reason for dealing with this bank was tied to your father and the relationship we built with Lance. While Lance was working his way up, he always provided us with excellent service. Now that he's on top, he's either shirking his responsibilities, enjoying people flattering him, or simply not keeping tabs on what his underlings are doing."

She pointed at Lance's closed door. "I'm afraid Lance's other activities have gone to his head. He's spending way too much time giving speeches and cutting ribbons to be an effective banker. He acted like he never signed off on this loan rejection, but his name was on the rejection letter Emily received. If he did know the details of the loan and still disapproved it, he's simply a louse. Either way, I don't want him as my personal banker, and I certainly don't want to deal with Bailey after he already rejected a loan request from our family. Now, get going, and if we're a few minutes late, remember the meeting can't start without the council president."

CHAPTER FOUR

Like Lance's office, the council room had two entrances. Most people entered at the top and walked down the steep steps in the auditorium-styled room to find a seat. A few feet in front of the first row, two unadorned long tables, each with three matching oak chairs, flanked a podium with a microphone. These seats, like those above them, faced the horseshoe-shaped raised platform where the council members sat. The single door on the far side of the dais was pretty much used only by staff members bringing in documents or council members making grand entrances or quick escapes to their offices.

Today, Jacob stood just inside the top of the council room. Sarah was delighted to see him. Although she'd written him off as a rich pretty boy slumming in Marcus's kitchen when they'd first been introduced, she'd come to realize he was the real thing—a hardworking friend who rarely thought about the good looks he'd been blessed with. They'd easily fallen into the teasing roles of a big sister with a pesky, but devoted, little brother, who shared her goal of rezoning Main Street.

"Deciding whether to stay or waiting for someone?" she asked him, opting not to tell him how proud she was when Emily confided he'd helped Marcus after the fire by insisting his share of the continuing wage insurance money go to the other employees.

"Waiting for my friend, Cliff."

A perfect opening, Sarah thought, to find out who this Cliff guy was. Something about him nagged at her. She was unsuccessful at making any connection until she glanced toward the dais, where Mr. Rogers was engaged in conversation with Anne Hightower, Jacob's sister and vice president of the council.

Seeing Mr. Rogers, Sarah remembered Clifford was the name of the nephew who was going to repair his fence. Considering coincidences rarely happened in real life, she doubted there could be many men named Cliff or Clifford who fixed things, living in Wheaton.

"Is your friend Mr. Rogers's nephew?"

"That's right. Cliff's late mother was Mr. Rogers's sister. Sorry about his huffing and puffing at the bank. He's really a good guy. This bank thing really got under his skin."

Lance, Sarah recalled, also characterized Cliff as a good guy. She wondered why, if Cliff was such a great guy, everyone was apologizing for him. She also questioned, but so Jacob could hear her, how she'd never met Cliff until today.

"Your paths probably never crossed. His mom sent him to military school between her second and third divorce. Back then, we'd have been way outside the high-school aged purview of my sister, Anne, and you."

Sarah laughed, tossing her long dark mane. She

reached up and pushed an escaped strand behind her ear. "You're right. Back then, I wouldn't have recognized the existence of anyone from the junior high." She moved out of the way of someone trying to get around them.

"I've always understood that in this part of the world sending a boy to military school in those days was code for dealing with someone who needed straightening out."

Jacob squirmed. "Let's just say Cliff always stood up for what's right or at least he thought was right. Sometimes that meant he came across a bit impulsive or abrupt."

"You're kiddin'. You should have seen him when he came back to Lance's office. Abrupt wouldn't quite be the word for describing that encounter."

"He came back? When?"

"While my mother and I were having our appointment."

"I didn't know that." Jacob rubbed his forehead. "You know, he's a very talented contractor. Wheaton was the last place he expected to land back on his radar."

People fled Wheaton promising to never come back, but often did. Her sister, Emily, was a perfect example. She'd sworn when she left for culinary school she was done with Wheaton and Birmingham. Emily's journey had taken her to New York, San Francisco, and other exotic-sounding places, but she'd ended up right back where she started. "What compelled him to come back?"

"His brother needed help in Birmingham."

Sarah screwed up her face. "I'm confused. Does Cliff live in Birmingham or Wheaton?"

"Until recently, he worked exclusively in Birmingham, but he's had a place here for almost a year."

It didn't make sense to Sarah. How could someone live in a small community like Wheaton without her seeing him when he shopped for food, banked, or took advantage of other downtown services? "Considering how many times we've seen each other today, I can't understand how our paths never crossed."

"Because he's rarely been in town. When Cliff called and told me his brother wanted his help on a short-term project, I invited him to bunk with me. He accepted, but once he realized the Birmingham project was going to take a lot longer than he'd been led to believe, he moved out."

"He got a place in Birmingham?"

"No. He'd spent time hiking around Wheaton's outskirts and suddenly couldn't remember why he never wanted to come back here. Instead of renting a place in Birmingham or Wheaton, he stayed in a hotel room in Birmingham but bought land on the bluff. About a year ago, he ran utilities to a small trailer he put on it to live in while he built himself a regular cabin. Unfortunately, until he finished the Birmingham job, he only worked on the cabin in his spare time."

"I gather from the scene in Lance's office, that loan was important to him. After watching what Emily and Marcus are going through as small business owners, I can understand how having his loan called on even one construction job would make things difficult across the board."

Jacob peered around the lobby and lowered his

voice, almost to a whisper. "I shouldn't say anything, but it was the mortgage for his cabin rather than related to his construction jobs. Having it called made so little sense, I told him he needed to make an appointment with Harlan because he might have a claim of some kind. Cliff's not overextended and there's no problem with his stream of income. He doesn't do odd jobs. His are all well-funded and big."

Sarah was glad Jacob had referred Cliff to Harlan. She liked the idea of additional business for Harlan. She still felt guilty for the many hours he'd neglected his practice while getting Emily and her out of trouble four months ago. Then again, after listening to Lance's explanation about compliance and regulations and Bailey's assurance that every reason a loan was denied was documented, she feared there wouldn't be any cause of action. "What job is Cliff doing?"

"Right now, he's the contractor the strip center hired to reconstruct the part that burned, including Southwind. That alone is a large job, but Marcus and a few of the other tenants have also hired him to oversee their buildouts."

"I don't understand. Why would Marcus contract with him separately?"

"Because the shopping center only provides a shell or four walls. Anything else you see in a store or restaurant, like the fixtures and décor, falls on the tenant. That's why opening anything is expensive and risky."

Jacob raised his hand and waved over her shoulder. "There's Cliff, now."

Sarah turned back and glanced toward where Cliff was coming through the doors. As striking as he was in a rugged way, he appeared more disheveled now than he had been during the altercation at the bank. She lowered her gaze, uncomfortable with what she'd learned about him. When she looked up again, he was glaring at her while rubbing the knuckles of his right hand. He stuck his hand into his pocket, but the direction of his gaze didn't waver.

Sarah decided they should meet another time. Faking seeing someone she had to say hello to, she muttered a quick good-bye to Jacob and took off.

Committed to continuing down the steps, Sarah peered around the auditorium, hoping to spot a friendly face. The first person she saw in a row on the left was her ex-husband's bimbo, Jane. The sight of her made Sarah's skin prickle. Feeling no need for an unpleasant confrontation, Sarah searched for a seat on the right side of the council room. She was relieved when Emily, seated midway down on the right with Harlan and Emily's boyfriend, Marcus, caught her attention and pointed to empty seats in their row. Sarah waved back and made her way toward Emily's row.

As she neared it, she noticed a handsome man she didn't recognize seated next to Emily. Rather than climbing over everyone in the row to reach the empty seat on Harlan's far side, Sarah sat next to the stranger. She snuck a peek at him and almost laughed out loud. For the second time in a day, she mentally found herself labeling someone a hunk. This one was more her type than Cliff. He was handsome in a similarly rugged way, but this guy was Mr. Polished. He could be cast as Adonis in any play.

Emily leaned over, in front of the stranger. "Glad

you made it. Sarah, I don't think you've met Thomas Howell, the owner of the new Birmingham Howellian luxury hotel."

Sarah put out her hand. "Pleased to meet you. I've been hearing about your art collection, especially the cat-themed exhibit. I understand it's quite something."

"So, they say." He smiled at Sarah, showing perfectly straight white teeth. He'd had a great orthodontist or been as blessed with teeth that were equally fine as his other well-chiseled features. Either way, Sarah labeled him model material.

"I have a Siamese cat, RahRah. Since I inherited him, I've really learned to appreciate cats. I guess you fancy them, too?"

Sarah barely heard him comment about his mother starting the collection because of her love of cats and how nice cat ownership was. She was too busy berating herself for letting her mouth run wild. As memories of what she knew about his hotel, travels, and lifestyle came back to her, Sarah was sure she'd come across as a first-class idiot, but his words belied that.

"If you like, I'd be glad to give you a personal tour of the cat exhibit."

"That would be lovely," she stammered, excited at spending personal time with him. She glanced over to see if Emily was paying attention to their conversation. If she hadn't known Emily and Marcus were an item, she might have thought Emily's flushed face and general level of excitement, so like the mannerisms Sarah associated with their mother, also showed a personal interest in Thomas. Instead, Sarah realized he'd probably invited Emily to do something in his kitchen.

That made sense. Thinking back, Sarah recalled Emily showing her his card right after Emily won the Wheaton Food Expo competition four months ago. Thomas had been in the audience that day. He'd been so impressed with Emily's presentation and cooking talents, he'd stopped her as she left the stage, pressed his card into her hand, and invited her to participate in a future food-related event at his hotel.

"Your sister agreed to do a cooking exhibition at the Howellian. You're welcome to join her."

Before she could explain how cooking wasn't really her thing, Marcus let loose with a tart zinger. "Better be careful, Thomas. When Sarah finds herself too close to a kitchen, she and anyone around it are liable to get scorched."

Sarah played along. Better not to dispute what was being said about her kitchen prowess, especially because it was true. In her mind, the best way to keep a kitchen clean was to never turn on the stove. Then again, after surreptitiously examining Thomas for a few minutes, she concluded he was a man she might be willing to learn to cook dinner for. He not only was handsome, but she couldn't help noticing he had the type of hands, with long tapered fingers, that made her melt.

Taking a deep breath to steady herself and keep from again demonstrating she talked too much, she reminded herself her ex-husband, William Taft Blair, also had had those kind of hands and things hadn't turned out well. But, as her mother repeatedly advised,

"Sarah, you need to give men a second chance. They aren't all rats like Bill."

Stealing another peek at his hands, Sarah observed his watch. Like his hands, it was beautiful. Sarah wasn't sure what brand it was, but she knew it was expensive. Silver or white gold, it had a wide face easily read even from where she sat. She was surprised to see it was already past one. Glancing back to the top of the auditorium, the double doors were closed. When she'd last looked, Anne and only one other council member were seated, but now all the council members were in their places except for the council's president.

The rising decibels of the mutterings in the room indicated the natives were getting restless. Her mother had joked that nothing could start without Lance, but as punctual as her mother always was, Sarah knew Maybelle would have prodded him to be on time for the meeting.

Sarah checked her phone to see if she had a message from her mother.

None.

Commotion near the door used by the council members caught Sarah's attention. Bailey, the loan officer, stood in the doorway. This time he wasn't burdened down with a pile of papers when he scurried into the room toward the dais. If it was possible, Sarah thought his face was even paler than before. Although he went straight to Anne Hightower, who sat erectly next to Lance's empty chair, instead of quite facing Anne, Bailey was intently scanning the audience. He froze when his gaze met Sarah's.

"It's Mr. Knowlton. He's dead!"

Not sure if she'd heard right, Sarah maintained an

unbroken stare with Bailey. Only when he repeated "he's dead" and added "your mother" did she break the linkage of their gazes to push her way out of her row and the auditorium. Behind her, Anne Hightower postponed the meeting.

CHAPTER FIVE

With Harlan and Emily close on her heels, Sarah ran toward the bank. The three worked their way around the small group of bystanders already peering through the bank's glass doors and windows, as well as the ambulance and fire engine that blocked the front of the building. The security guard who'd been on duty earlier let the three into the lobby but stopped them from going beyond the entrance by using his body as if it was a solid wall.

"Alvin," Harlan said to the security guard. "What's going on?"

Still huffing from running from city hall, Sarah didn't wait to hear an explanation. She forced words out of her mouth. "My mother?"

Alvin pointed across the lobby toward Lance's office.

Sarah shuddered. "My mother is in his office?"

Shaking his head, Alvin again pointed. This time, Sarah looked to the left of Lance's partially closed door to the seats where Eloise had Maybelle and Sarah wait earlier that day. Her mother was seated in one chair. Eloise sat beside her, her head bent toward Maybelle. She encircled Maybelle's shoulders with one arm, while reaching across her lap with the other to clutch Maybelle's hand. Even from this distance, her mother looked fragile and small, but she was alive and seemingly uninjured.

Both Emily and she started toward their mother, but Alvin, using his bulk, prevented them from moving any closer. "I'm sorry." His gaze fluttered between Emily, Sarah, and Harlan and finally focused on Harlan. "The chief, crime tech, and coroner are all on their way, but until they get here, the chief ordered me to secure Mr. Knowlton's office and keep the media and everyone outside."

"But these are Maybelle's daughters and I'm representing her. Surely that makes a difference."

Sarah stifled a smile at perhaps the only amusing thing in this entire situation. As if to add credibility to his assertion, Harlan had pulled himself up to his full height. Whenever he did this with her, her being a few inches taller than him negated the move's impact. With Alvin towering at least three inches over her, any benefit from Harlan's power effort was completely mooted.

The bigger man softly chuckled. His wide grin showed two rows of matched pearly whites as he spread his arms and hands almost to the point of an embrace. "Look, Harlan, you know how it is with the chief. Right now, he's only got the job on a temporary basis. He's hoping things go right so he lands the job on a permanent basis. What happened today is the last thing he needed or wanted while he's being considered for the position. That's why he's trying to go by the book, separating witnesses and such. He isn't going to be happy with me letting you in before he takes statements, but Mrs. Johnson's pretty upset. She found Mr. Knowlton."

"That's what we heard and why she needs her daughters. Alvin, you can always blame my forcing my way in, insisting I'm representing Mrs. Johnson."

Alvin glanced down at his own bulky figure. "I doubt the chief will believe you forced me to do anything, but I don't think he can object to her representative being present." He came closer to Sarah and Emily and winked. "As for you ladies, he's not going to be pleased with you being here, either, but I think Eloise needs a break. Despite her being upset, Eloise has been mothering everyone. She's done the best she can with your mama. Still, I reckon if I were Ms. Maybelle, I'd prefer my daughters being with me now, too." He gestured in their mother's direction as if shooing them toward her.

Without giving him a chance to change his mind, Emily and Sarah ran across the lobby to where their mother sat embraced by Eloise. As the twins crowded into the space near their mother and Eloise, it dawned on Sarah that the smeared makeup of the two older women belied their jointly shed tears.

Eloise whispered something too quietly for Sarah to hear. She gave Maybelle a tight hug and relinquished her seat to Emily, who almost knocked Eloise over in her rush to embrace her mother and pull her close.

As Eloise struggled to keep her balance, Sarah placed her hand on the older woman's arm to steady her.

Eloise regained her balance. "Thank you."

"No. Thank you for taking care of my mother. I know this is a difficult time for you, too."

Eloise nodded. A tear escaped from the corner of her eye and rolled down her cheek. She reflexively raised her hand to brush it away but only succeeded in making her mascara run more. "It doesn't seem real. I keep expecting him to buzz me at any moment. It's hard to think, after thirty-four years, he won't ever call for me again."

With tentative strokes, Sarah patted Eloise's arm as another tear dropped but was ignored. She felt unsure how to comfort Eloise. Even ashen-faced with streaked makeup, not a hair of her helmet-like coiffure was out of place. Eloise gave off the scent of Chanel No. 5 mingled with a take-charge air. Perhaps that was how Eloise kept it together when she cared for Maybelle. Then again, maybe being busy kept her mind off her boss's death.

Sarah didn't think she'd have been able to do anything, let alone for others, if she'd just lost her long-time boss. Her feelings would be too raw. She stared again at Eloise, who was telling her to let her know if there was anything else she could do for any of them. Sarah couldn't believe how strong Eloise was, while her own mother trembled in Emily's arms.

After being assured they'd call on her if they needed anything, Eloise made her way across the lobby. She repeatedly stopped for a moment to touch or talk to any employee she passed. As Eloise paused to apparently exchange a few words and help the blond teller replenish the cup supply at the coffee table, Sarah was envious.

To be so caring didn't come naturally to her. For

Sarah, hugging was foreign and forced, even if she was deeply concerned about someone or something. She certainly couldn't imagine keeping up the behavior Eloise was exhibiting if she'd lost someone so important to her.

Watching Eloise frown and take the cups from the teller, Sarah let a random thought nag at her. Maybe what she saw as caring behavior in the face of a devastating loss was all an act? How many stories and crimes involved longtime employees who felt unseen and unsung? Realizing she was being ridiculous and demonstrating having read far too many mysteries, Sarah focused her attention back on where her mother and Emily sat. Harlan knelt next to them.

Bending, Sarah placed her hands over her mother's. They were as cold as ice. Sarah tried picking up on what Harlan was saying in an urgent whisper.

"Maybelle, we only have a few minutes. You need to tell me what happened."

"Lance, dead." Her mother looked at Sarah. "Someone killed him."

"How? Did you stay and visit with Eloise like you said you would?"

When her mother blinked but didn't disagree, Sarah pressed on. "After you killed time with Eloise, did you go around the alley and have Mr. Knowlton let you in the back way?"

Maybelle took a deep breath. Taking her hands from Sarah's, she grasped the sides of her chair. "I talked to Eloise for about ten or fifteen minutes after you left. By then, I figured Lance would have had time to review the file, so I walked around the building to the alley. When I got to the door to Lance's office, I was about to knock when I noticed the door was open."

She wiped her tear-soaked cheek. "In all the years I've gone in and out of that door, it's always been locked. Lance had to let us in."

"That doesn't sound like a normal security practice for a bank." Emily took her mother's hand again.

"In the old days it wasn't, but when the bank installed alarms and security cameras, they put one above the doorway so Lance could see who was in the alley or knocking on the door."

Harlan pumped his fist. "That's great."

Sarah stared at him.

"If there's a security tape of the alley and back door, we'll be able to see who, besides your mother, used the back entrance into Lance's office. Hopefully, the camera was angled in such a way we can demonstrate the door was already open when she approached it."

"You make it sound as if Mother's the prime suspect."

"She probably is. Your mother found the body in what, for all intents and purposes, will be considered by the police to have been a locked room."

"But it wasn't locked," Maybelle protested. "The door was already open when I got there. Anyone could have come and gone that way or through the lobby entrance. They certainly all came running in from the lobby when I screamed."

"Knowing the door was always locked, why did you go into Lance's office from the alley instead of reporting the door being open to the security officer?"

"Harlan, I never thought about security. When I saw the door was ajar, I pushed on it. It opened all the way."

"And you went in?" Sarah prompted. "Weren't you afraid someone was in the office?"

Her mother shook her head. "I could see the entire office. Lance was slumped over his desk, instead of sitting upright in his chair. With his head down, he looked like a schoolboy taking a nap. I would have chided him if it wasn't so close to the council meeting. That's why I knew something had to be wrong. I was afraid he'd had a stroke or heart attack. When I went in, I wasn't thinking about anything except Lance being in trouble."

Harlan leaned closer to Maybelle. "This is important. Tell me exactly what you did next."

"I walked across the room to him and touched his shoulder. That's when I realized his head and shirt were covered in blood." She paused.

Emily and Sarah simultaneously squeezed their mother's hands

"He was so still. I knew then that he wasn't sleeping."

Harlan pointed at Maybelle's pants. "How did you get blood on you?"

Sarah looked to where Harlan was pointing. Faint red streaks ran across the upper part of her mother's pants in the same dirty pattern Sarah often created when unconsciously wiping her hands on her jeans. She raised her gaze, so it met her mother's.

"I tried to find a pulse. There wasn't one. That's when I started screaming."

CHAPTER SIX

Any further discussion was interrupted by the sound of people coming across the lobby. Sarah immediately recognized the one lumbering a few steps ahead of Alvin as the desk sergeant, who only a few months ago kept Harlan and Sarah waiting for almost an hour in the police station's waiting room before telling them Emily was in an interrogation room twenty yards away. From the way Alvin was fawning over him, the mayor must have appointed the Keystone Cop to be Wheaton's acting police chief.

Sadly, appointing him made sense. Unlike bigger cities, like Birmingham, Wheaton didn't have a defined hierarchy of officers descending from police chief to patrolmen. Here, things pretty much were limited to a chief, sergeant, and one or two others who performed duties as assigned.

As the chief approached, Sarah glanced at Harlan and Emily and saw they, too, were aware of the approaching officer and bank security guard. With the grace of her former cheerleading days, Emily gave up her seat to Harlan and glided in the direction of where a coffeepot had been set up near the bank teller counter. Sarah couldn't be sure, but the way Emily felt about the acting chief after her last encounter with Wheaton's finest, Emily and Harlan probably wanted to minimize any connection between Maybelle, Emily, and Wheaton's police department.

Sarah consciously blocked the memories and feelings welling up in her. She could give in to them later, but, for now, the only thing that mattered was protecting her mother, since it appeared her mother wasn't in a state to do so herself. Sarah couldn't recall the last time she'd seen her mother subdued like this. She prayed for her real mother's quick return. This calm before the storm was frightening.

Sarah felt certain once the shock of Lance's death wore off, the Maybelle gale, like the winds of a hurricane or tornado, would destroy anything in its path. Hopefully, until then, Sarah's mother wouldn't say or do something that inadvertently harmed her. In the meantime, it was up to Sarah to buffer the officer's actions and her mother's inaction.

"Officer . . ." Sarah cut him off before any words came out of his open mouth. She searched deep into the recesses of her mind for his name but came up blank. Reading his name tag also proved impossible. His ample chest and the other items he'd pinned to his shirt caused the tuck of his pocket to block his name. She didn't think he'd take kindly if she called him one of the Barney Fife–type nicknames she'd associated with the first time they met. Much as she hated it, she realized things might go better if she got into the habit of calling him Chief.

"Chief," she began again.

He held up his hand.

She couldn't help but stare at it. Although he was a big man, his hand was smaller and pudgier than hers. If handshakes could be associated with personalities, she bet his was soft and limp. Compliant, Sarah waited, her hands pressed to her sides. She had no intention of confirming her hypothesis. Instead, she watched him scan the lobby and eavesdropped on his conversation with Alvin, who'd glued himself to the chief's elbow.

It wasn't clear to Sarah from the chief's queries and the guard's responses if the chief was getting his bearings for what to do next or simply taking stock of who was where. Sarah decided it was the latter when he told Alvin to keep everyone in place until he was ready for them. Apparently satisfied Alvin understood his instructions, the chief ignored her waiting presence and instead pushed open the door of Lance's office.

Interested and protective of her mother, Sarah watched the chief's every move. She was anxious for him to get on with it. Instead, he simply stood in the doorway. She couldn't tell if he was assessing the room or if his reluctance to cross the threshold mirrored her own distaste for looking at a dead body. If that was the case, the chief had gone into the wrong line of work. Then again, despite the incidents a few months ago, Wheaton wasn't a town where law enforcement officials frequently viewed people who died of anything except natural causes. It was more of a place where the police responded to calls to rescue a cat or the burglary in process was merely a door blown open by the wind. The town's high point, every Sunday afternoon, was the five minutes the police and firefighters turned on their sirens and lights to make sure their equipment still worked.

When the chief moved nearer to the desk, Sarah inched closer to the office to observe him better. He slowly approached the desk, keeping at least a two-foot distance from it as he examined the scene from various angles. She wasn't impressed. From his speed and casual approach, it appeared his visual inspection was exactly the cursory type she expected from him. Moreover, he hadn't covered his shoes or put on any gloves.

The longest the chief paused in his examination, and it wasn't much longer than he had from any other direction, was when he faced the back of Lance's head. His momentary hesitation staring at Lance's head seemed to indicate Lance had been hit from behind. She wondered if Lance had seen his killer? Was he surprised or for some reason had he chosen to ignore his murderer's presence? Considering the proximity of Lance's office to the lobby, was he killed by a bullet from a gun with a silencer or by being struck by a heavy object?

Sarah inched toward the door, hoping to see if there was an obvious weapon lying on the desk or floor, but the chief, apparently finished with his study of the crime scene, stood in front of the desk, his back to her. His spread-legged stance, as he pulled his cell phone from his pocket and made a call, blocked her view.

When the chief slipped his phone into his back pocket and turned toward the door, she backed away from her vantage point. She moved closer to her mother as the chief, with a final peek in Lance's direction, again brushed right by her as he made a beeline for Maybelle.

When the chief touched the brim of his hat and addressed "Miss Maybelle," Harlan moved forward in his chair, placing his shoulder partially between Maybelle and the police chief.

The chief flashed a look of disdain in Harlan's direction.

Harlan seemed oblivious to it as he addressed him using the relaxed good-old-boy persona he often used with his clients. "Chief Gerard."

Gerard. That was the Keystone Cop's name. Something Gerard. Sarah mentally repeated it until she remembered. Dwayne, his name was Dwayne Gerard. Pleased, she almost missed the next part of Harlan and the chief's conversation.

"I don't think I've seen you since the mayor announced your acting appointment. Congratulations." Harlan waved his hand toward Lance's office as he ignored the chief's grunt of acknowledgment. "Horrible about Lance."

"Yes, it is." With the barest movement of his thumb, Chief Gerard repeatedly thumped one of his suspenders. That, combined with his whiny drawl, made Sarah think of the southern stereotypical mayors and law enforcement folks portrayed in bad car-chase movies, but his words belied that impression.

"Harlan, stand down. All I want to do is ask Ms. Maybelle a few questions. After all, in case you've forgotten, she's the one who found Lance."

"And that's why she doesn't want to talk about it.

Emotionally, finding her old friend dead has been a real shock to her system."

Sarah moved closer to her mother. She put her arm protectively around her mother's shoulders. The chief took advantage of Sarah's postural shift to push himself into the space in front of Maybelle. Sarah realized from his new position he could maintain direct eye contact while speaking with her mother.

"Ms. Maybelle, I'm Chief Gerard. I'm know you've been through a shocking situation, and I certainly don't want to do anything more to upset you, but, as you can well imagine, time is of the essence in situations like this. It would be a real big help if we could talk for a moment. Any details of what you remember about finding Mr. Knowlton could be crucial."

He paused, keeping his gaze locked on hers.

Sarah wasn't sure if he needed to catch his breath or was letting his words sink in.

"If we're going to have our best chance to wrap this matter up quickly, I really can't delay finding out your impressions," he added.

Under her arm, Sarah felt her mother tense. She didn't know if her mother was reacting to her memories of finding Lance or something in the chief's words or tone. Even if he wasn't coming across as doing anything more than his job, Sarah was worried. She couldn't decide whether to compare his tone to the pouring of honey or molasses or simply consider it plain sap, but there was something about his demeanor that sat wrong with her. Probably because it was her mother on the hot seat. He might want to wrap this matter up, but she wasn't about to let him run roughshod, no matter how sweetly, over her mother.

Speaking up, she clung to Maybelle more protectively. "I don't understand your insistence on taking her statement right now. You already know my mother found Mr. Knowlton. Rather than badgering her, shouldn't you have a crime tech or the coroner examining the scene and the body? I bet their findings will give you a lot more than trying to talk to my mother in her shocked state."

"Don't worry. The tech and the coroner are on the way, but this isn't a television show. Good police work dictates I obtain her statement while everything is fresh in her mind. I realize you've had prior dealings with criminal matters, but for everyone's own good, especially your mother's and yours, why don't you leave this one to the professionals?"

Harlan, hands on his hips, squared off against the chief but kept his gaze centered on Sarah. "Although I agree with you that Sarah should leave the investigation of Lance's murder to the professionals, I think you're overdoing it a bit. Let me make it clear. Ms. Maybelle is not up to being questioned right now."

"Now, Harlan, when did you get your medical degree? I thought you were a lawyer and speaking of that, to my knowledge, Ms. Maybelle doesn't have a representative because there's nothing here to represent."

"Representing her is why I'm here."

Sarah wasn't sure if the chief was responding to Harlan's tone or the situation was starting to get out of hand, but his relaxed body position was replaced with a more rigid stance. Instead of picking at his left suspender, the chief now held it taut, like one would do with a slingshot.

His right hand rested on his gun holster as he stretched Harlan's name to three syllables. "Ha-ar-lan, my understanding is Ms. Maybelle hasn't asked for counsel." He removed his hand from his gun and pointed toward the coffeepot across the lobby. "Perhaps Sarah and you should get yourselves some coffee while Maybelle and I sit here and talk. It would be a shame for Judge Larsen to get the impression you've become an ambulance chaser."

Harlan didn't retreat. "Ms. Maybelle?"

Sarah's mother shifted her body forward. Sarah strained to hear what her mother would say. Her mother's voice came out at its usual loud level, and Sarah was relieved. Maybelle was back!

"I don't know where you're getting the idea Harlan's not my counsel. He represents me in everything. You may be the acting chief, Dwayne Gerard, but I've known you since you were a little boy. You're not going to bluster me. You already know what I know."

Maybelle shook Sarah's arm off her shoulders, stood, and moved herself into the chief's personal space. She used the tip of her forefinger to emphasize each of her points into his chest. "Lance's back door was open. I found him facedown on his desk. Although there was a ton of blood, I checked for a pulse and got some of his blood on me. When I realized he wasn't breathing, I screamed. From that point on, everyone ran into Lance's office."

"Do you remember who some of those people were, Ms. Maybelle?"

"Eloise was first. I can't remember if one of the tellers, that blond-haired one, or Alvin came next. After that, the comings and goings blur, but there were a lot of people in and out of Lance's office. They probably trampled any evidence that might have existed. If you want that as a formal written statement, I'll give it to you tomorrow. Right now, my girls and I are leaving. Harlan?"

Harlan smiled. "Chief? Don't you think at this point it would be the wiser course of action for me to take Ms. Maybelle home to rest? She's had a shock today, and well, you can see, she's made her position clear. Unless you're arresting her, it seems to me it would be the better course of action to wait until tomorrow when she'll be glad to come to your office and voluntarily give you a signed statement."

CHAPTER SEVEN

Before Chief Gerard answered, a young man, laden down with cameras and other equipment, entered the bank. Sarah didn't recognize him, but from all the things he carried, she presumed he was either a reporter for the college paper or the department's police tech. Based upon Alvin's earlier comments about Chief Gerard wanting the press kept out of the bank, she decided this gangly kid must be the department's crime tech. Once he reached them, the real giveaway was his uniform. Although it was a different color than the police chief's, the emblem sewed to his sleeve identified him as part of Wheaton's police force.

Chief Gerard confirmed her hypothesis when he introduced him. "Dr. David Smith is our department's crime tech, forensic investigator, and coroner rolled into one. David, this is Harlan Endicott and Ms. Maybelle Johnson. Ms. Johnson found the deceased. Mr. Endicott is her lawyer. He wants to take her home, but I was just about to explain to him that, under the circumstances, I'd like you to swab her hands and get some pictures now."

Her mother glanced at Harlan, who gave her a slight nod. "All right, but after that I'm leaving. Harlan, if Dwayne tries to stop me, can you file something because he's holding me against my will?"

When her mother laughed, everyone joined in, the tension of the moment receding. Still, Sarah noticed Chief Gerard's thin-lipped smile didn't reach his eyes. They were cold and hollow, scaring her and immediately making her think, even as Dr. Smith placed his gear on Eloise's desk, set up, and swabbed her mother's hands, that nothing was going to be different than the last time Emily and she dealt with the Wheaton Police Department.

Once it was obvious Dr. Smith was finished with Maybelle and ready to move on to the actual crime scene, the chief stepped away and talked to him for a moment. Coming back, Chief Gerard addressed his remarks directly toward Maybelle. "Ms. Maybelle, you're free to go. I expect to see you in my office at eight."

"Chief," Harlan interrupted. "Ms. Maybelle lives in Birmingham. She came over to Wheaton today to spend time with her daughters and handle some errands. You can't expect her to stay here tonight. Considering she'll hit rush-hour traffic from Birmingham at eight, why don't we make it a little later in the morning?"

The chief nodded. "Harlan, this is a criminal investigation. In case you didn't notice, a leading citizen—our bank and city council's president—has been murdered. I don't have time to waste solving this crime nor do I want to take the chance of another one occurring."

"That's true." Harlan lowered his voice, so his tone was soothing. "But other than finding the deceased, my client had nothing to do with this horrible event. She's obviously going to be more comfortable in her own bed, fifteen minutes down the highway. She'll gladly agree to be at your office tomorrow morning at ten to give you a written statement. Right, Maybelle?"

"Right."

"Then I think we'll be going now." Harlan put his hand on Maybelle's elbow and guided her toward the door.

The chief didn't stop them, but when Sarah waved, catching Emily's eye and signaling her they were leaving, he stopped them in their tracks. "Where do you think the two of you are going?"

"To take care of our mother."

"Not until I get your statements."

"But we weren't here. Emily and I were at the council meeting."

"Then it won't take long for you to give your statements. If you'll sit back down where you were, Officer Robinson will take your statements as soon as he finishes with the tellers." He pointed to the chairs she and her mother vacated.

Sarah looked around for Officer Robinson. Even though there were quite a few people in the bank, she wondered how she'd missed another police officer. "Officer Robinson? Could you point him out to me? I don't think I've ever met him?"

Chief Gerard raised an eyebrow in her direction. "You were talking to him earlier."

"You must be mistaken. I'd know if I'd been talking to a member of the Wheaton police force."

Chief Gerard looked across the room to where Alvin was talking to the blond teller, who'd waved at Sarah and Maybelle earlier.

"Alvin?"

"That's right. He's out of uniform because he was moonlighting today as a security officer for the bank, but when he's on duty, he's our newest officer."

"I thought Doctor Smith was your newest officer."

For the first time, Chief Gerard cracked a smile. "Smith looks so young he makes all of us feel old, but he's been the department's forensic expert and medical examiner for just under five years. Officer Robinson had prior experience on an L.A. squad, so I thought he'd be a good fit when our recent vacancy occurred."

"He moved here from Los Angeles?"

"No, lower Alabama." Chief Gerard chuckled. "Sarah, I really don't want to keep you from being with your mother, but I'd like to get quick statements from your sister and you. With Mr. Bailey and Ms. Eloise being so upset and needing to give more detailed statements, I'll get started with them. Officer Robinson is just about finished with the last teller, so if you'll just give us a few more minutes, I'm sure he'll have you out of here quickly."

As if on cue, Alvin, carrying a large pad and pen, approached Sarah as the chief walked away. Emily joined them.

Emily turned to him. "Why do Sarah and I need to give statements? We weren't even here."

"I know." Officer Robinson sat in the chair vacated by Maybelle and motioned for one of them to sit down.

"We'll make this fast." Emily took the empty chair. "Personally, I don't think the chief knows what's right."

He shrugged. "That's not for me to say. Ms. Johnson. Mrs. Blair, while you wait, if you'd like some water or coffee, there's some on the table over there." He gestured to the table on the far side of the lobby on which a coffee urn and water dispenser sat. Earlier, Sarah had seen Eloise talking to Amanda Taylor as she placed extra cups on the table.

"That's okay." Sarah looked around the lobby. She figured there would be less chance of him being distracted if she stayed on his radar while he interviewed Emily. "Why don't I just sit right over there at Eloise's desk until you're ready for me? Chief Gerard mentioned he was going to interview her now and she's not at her desk. I assume he's interviewing her somewhere else."

When he nodded, Sarah felt pleased with herself.

"By the way, Officer Robinson, where is Eloise? She was with my mother when we arrived. I saw her talking with Amanda Taylor and adding cups to the coffee table, but I haven't seen her since just before the chief got here."

"It's Alvin, and she's in the vault."

Emily and Sarah turned their heads in unison to peer at the open vault door. Simultaneously, both said, "Excuse me?"

"Eloise was pretty broken up," Alvin said. "She started working for Mr. Knowlton right after she graduated from high school. They were both at the bottom of the totem pole back then. She kept it together while she was helping your mother and making sure everyone else was okay, but then it hit her. The little safe deposit room in the vault area was the only private place I could think of that wasn't being used."

Sarah gave him her chair. He immediately clicked open his pen and asked Emily to correctly spell her name. Rather than waiting across the lobby, Sarah opted for Eloise's desk chair. Because Dr. Smith hadn't closed the door to Lance's office, Sarah could see what he was doing. Moving Eloise's rolling secretarial chair, she positioned herself to get the best view possible.

In contrast to the chief, Dr. Smith had put on gloves, booties, and something over his hair to avoid contaminating the scene any more than it already was. Unlike the television shows she watched, he wasn't doing anything with the body. Instead, he had a camera hung around his neck and a video camera in his hands and was working the office from the outside in. He snapped pictures and took videos of the doorway, carpeting, walls, and around the desk from every angle. When he reached the desk, he focused the camera on the back of Lance's head. From the number of shots he took, she again was sure this was where the fatal wound was.

After Dr. Smith finished with his photos of Lance, Sarah expected him to put his cameras away. Instead, he aimed his still camera at the floor behind the desk. Sarah couldn't see what he'd spotted, but whatever it was made him photograph and videotape it carefully. Finally finished with his recording of whatever it was, he pulled a clear plastic bag from his pocket and bent to retrieve the object. He held it up in front of him to get a better look at it.

"I'm ready for you now," Alvin said.

Sarah didn't respond. She was staring at the object in Dr. Smith's hand. She was sure it was the same fence finial her mother placed on Lance's desk earlier in the day.

CHAPTER EIGHT

Officer Robinson gently touched Sarah's shoulder. She jumped in her seat and swung her head around to look at him.

He stepped away from her. "I didn't mean to startle you."

"You didn't. Well, I mean you did. I'm sorry. Lost in thought, I guess."

"No problem. I said I was ready for you." He motioned toward the two empty seats where he had interviewed Emily.

"Emily?" Sarah looked around the lobby.

"She said she'll meet you at Harlan's office. Your mother texted she was there." He gestured for Sarah to go ahead of him to the chairs.

Sarah pulled her cell phone from the pocket of her purse as she sat. There was a text from her mother.

Meet me at Harlan's. Forgot to bring an allergy pill to be able to deal with RahRah.

Sarah laughed. Her mother claimed to be deathly allergic to cats, even to the point that a cat's mere presence earlier in a room set her off. That was why this morning her mother had stayed outside honking for Sarah. The irony was that her mother exhibited no symptoms if Sarah and RahRah visited her home when she was out. In fact, a few months ago, when her mother was in Mexico at the spa, becoming "Maybelle," Sarah and RahRah stayed in her mother's home for several days. During that time, Sarah gave RahRah full run of the house. They were gone, as were RahRah's food, toys, and litter box, before her mother got home; and, surprise, the new and improved "Maybelle" had no problems from the cat's visit. Of course, Sarah knew, it wasn't worth mentioning their visit. Her mother either wouldn't believe they had been there or would suddenly have a delayed allergic reaction.

When Alvin opened his notepad to a clean page, Sarah steeled herself for his first question. Her hopes of giving her statement as quickly as Emily were dashed when she realized Chief Gerard was standing behind her chair.

"Mrs. Blair, there have been a few developments, and I think I'd like to take your statement." With a wave of his hand, he motioned for Officer Robinson to vacate his seat.

Sarah didn't say anything. Instead, she kept her eyes on Alvin's face. She had no doubt Alvin was as surprised by this change of plans as she was.

"Thanks, Robinson." Chief Gerard squeezed into the narrow guest chair. Like Alvin, Sarah noted, the chief had to sit forward in the chair or risk its arms pinching his sides or blocking access to his holster.

She needed to focus on what was happening, but the random thought of whether they both needed seatbelt extenders on planes went through her mind.

"Mrs. Blair."

Sarah corrected the chief. "I've been divorced for so long and, now with Bill dead, I prefer Ms. Blair."

"I understand, Mrs. Blair. Oh, I'm sorry, I meant Ms. Blair."

She didn't think he was sorry, but she had to admit, he didn't seem as thick as he had four months ago. Maybe it was being in the running for the new job or simply being in charge instead of having to answer to someone.

"As you can well understand, I'd like to get this matter wrapped up as quickly as possible. Luckily, it appears we've gotten some breaks in the case."

"Breaks?"

"Yes. It seems, as you well know, there were some earlier altercations before someone returned and killed Mr. Knowlton."

"If you're talking about the run-ins Mr. Knowlton had with Mr. Rogers's nephew, Cliff, I'm sure they were more bluster than anything else."

"I'm inclined to agree with you. After all, I understand from other witnesses that in both instances, people were in the room with him and Mr. Knowlton when he blew off steam. In fact, I believe your mother and you were there when he burst in the second time."

"That's right." Sarah was about to say something more when she realized she was giving Cliff an alibi but leaving her mother dangling without a witness who could swear the bank president was already dead when Maybelle returned. If somehow Chief Gerard already had tied the finial, which Sarah believed was the murder weapon, to her fence and had her mother alone in Lance's office, she understood why the chief thought he might have an arrest before dinner. He was treating it like a game of Clue. Maybelle, in the office of the bank president, with the decorative fence post top.

"I think before you take my statement, I'd like my lawyer, Harlan, present."

"Now, Sarah, you're being a bit melodramatic. You're not under arrest. You're simply giving me the facts as you saw them. There's no need to have Harlan present, or, for that matter, to drag him back over here."

Sarah's back stiffened as she willed herself to keep any sign of being a mouse in abeyance. "Having Harlan with me is the only way I'm going to give a statement."

"Then I guess you better call him and have him meet us at the station."

CHAPTER NINE

Sarah looked around the interrogation room as she waited for Harlan. The room, with its dented gray gunmetal-colored table and chairs, was unchanged from when Emily was in the hot seat four months ago. That time, Harlan dragged Sarah down the hall behind him, declaring to Officer Gerard, who had desk duty, that Sarah was part of his legal team. She wondered if he'd bring Emily with him in the same way today.

Unable to sit still, she paced over to the wall and tried to determine if she was being observed through a one-way mirror. It felt like hours since Chief Gerard handed her his cell phone to call Harlan, but her watch told her that wasn't the case. She'd made the call and then Chief Gerard immediately brought her back to the station and led her to this room.

Unless he drove from his office, which Harlan never did when going to the courthouse or any of the buildings in the city square, it would take him ten to fifteen minutes from her call to walk here, and that didn't count whatever time it took to convince her mother to stay behind until he returned. As much as

Sarah would like her twin to be at the station house with her, it would be better if Emily remained with their mother.

Unless Harlan hadn't told her mother why he had to leave the office, she could just imagine how agitated her mother was. Maybelle didn't suffer fools lightly. Once she'd found her tongue this afternoon, her mother had made it obvious she didn't have a high opinion of Chief Gerard. Sarah feared this would eliminate her mother's ability to be civil to him. The mind games she was playing stopped with the opening of the door.

"Harlan! I'm so glad to see you."

"Yeah. Remind me, I have to stop meeting members of your family like this."

His words stunned her until she realized it was his attempt at humor. "We've got to do something. I'm afraid they think Mother murdered Mr. Knowlton."

"My impression is the chief does." Harlan sat next to her and put his briefcase on the table. He opened it and extracted a pen and pad. Clicking the locks shut, he placed the briefcase under the table and turned to face her. "Sarah, Chief Gerard is going to be in here in a few minutes. He may think he's solved this case, but I've already talked to your mother about her two visits to Lance's office, and I think we can poke holes in his theory."

"But I think the murder weapon may have her fingerprints on it."

"What are you talking about?" He made a few notes on his pad as she told him about the finial from her fence and what she'd observed Dr. Smith doing with it.

"That complicates things a bit, but I think your mother has told us the truth. I'll just have to work a little harder on her behalf if things get that far. Do you remember when you last saw your mother with the finial?"

"Not exactly. I know, when she rummaged in her purse for her passbook, she took the finial, her phone, the passbook, and a bunch of other things out of her purse and laid them on Mr. Knowlton's desk. I wasn't watching which things she put back in her pocketbook before Cliff knocked her bag to the floor. Nor did I see what he picked up when he tried stuffing everything back into her purse. The finial could have been left on the floor at that point or it might have been one of the things he threw back on the desk instead of in her pocketbook."

"Well, let's hope the good guys, like Dr. Smith and Officer Robinson, but not you, come up with something forensic or investigative that leads to someone other than your mother."

"Harlan, this is my mother you're talking about. We can't simply sit here and hope the good guys will do something. We've got to—"

"Do nothing except let the professionals do their jobs. In the meantime, Chief Gerard will be in here in a few minutes. Answer the exact questions he asks without elaborating. Tell the truth and your mother will be fine."

Sarah wished she could believe him. One thing she was certain of, she wasn't going to leave it to the good guys to make sure other leads developed. It hadn't been that long since she'd seen what happened when she left it to the professionals. Nothing.

For the moment, though, she needed to play the game with the professional who'd just entered the room. "Chief Gerard, Harlan's here."

"I see. Ready to give your statement?"

She smiled at him. "Of course. Not being a law enforcement professional, this whole thing simply overwhelmed me. That's why I knew I'd feel more comfortable with my lawyer present."

Harlan gave a mock salute. "Present and accountable."

"Then, let's begin." Chief Gerard pushed one of the two chairs on the opposite side of the table from Sarah and Harlan toward the wall and pulled himself up to the table in the remaining chair.

Harlan frowned in Sarah's direction.

She ignored him. "Whatever you say, Chief Gerard."

The chief put a small recorder on the table. "Unless you have an objection, we'll tape and prepare a written transcript of your statement."

Sarah started speaking, but Harlan firmly interjected himself into the conversation. "Sarah has no objection to her statement being taped. Of course, we request a transcript."

Chief Gerard recited the preliminary information, including the date, time, location, and Sarah's name. Hearing him style the statement "In the matter of Lance Knowlton," Sarah shuddered. It was unreal—like having an out-of-body experience in which she could see him talking, but she wasn't the one he was about to question. She reminded herself she could handle this. She'd survived after Bill left, and while she wasn't the best receptionist and secretary in the world when Harlan hired her, she'd managed to improve and hold onto her job. She willed herself to listen and respond to Chief Gerard's questions.

The first ones weren't difficult. Name, birth date, address, and the reason for their meeting with Lance.

"But, I don't understand why, if the denied loan was for your sister, your mother took you?"

"I didn't understand it at first, either, but then I realized Mother was trying to show Lance he was neglecting or ignoring long-standing customers or customers with money."

"And how did you fit into that? I seem to recall, like most of us, you work because you need to."

"That's right, but I'm the trustee of a fairly large estate and real estate owned by RahRah, my cat."

Harlan interrupted the chief before he asked his next question. "Chief, none of that really matters. Ms. Blair wasn't anywhere near the bank when Lance was murdered."

"Her mother . . ."

"Found Lance, already dead. Ms. Blair has nothing to add because she wasn't there. Anything she heard from her mother or anyone else after the fact was hearsay. Chief, we believe the best evidence to resolve much of the confusion here is the tape from the alley camera. Have you watched it, yet?"

"No. We've had some technical issues with the tape, but I'm sure the lab will have them straightened out soon." He posed another question to Sarah. When Chief Gerard finally leaned back, she looked at her watch and realized almost two hours had elapsed.

She glanced at Harlan. Although his pad was covered with copious notes, he hadn't said or objected to anything more while she'd given her statement.

"I think Sarah has covered everything. It's been a long day. Instead of her waiting for the statement to be transcribed now, why don't you get it typed up tonight? Tomorrow, I'll give it a quick review before you take Maybelle's statement. Sarah can run by and sign it at your convenience."

When Chief Gerard grunted but didn't say anything, Harlan continued, "You can't deny Sarah's statement, especially in conjunction with the other ones you took, demonstrated there were a lot of people in and out of the lobby and Lance's office today. Any one of them could have murdered Lance, but I'd stake my law license you'll find it wasn't Maybelle."

"Better be careful what you bet. Harlan, I'd hate to see you lose your livelihood."

CHAPTER TEN

From the town square outside the police station, Sarah looked at the slit windows that began a few floors above the interrogation room she'd been in. She took a deep breath. "I swear the air out here smells fresher than it did in there. I don't know how people tolerate being in that jail. Those windows barely let a sliver of light in. I'd be absolutely freaked out the minute they closed the door of my cell."

"Do the crime, pay the time."

"Harlan! How can you be so cynical?"

He shrugged and kicked an acorn off the sidewalk. "Some days it comes with the territory."

Sarah studied him. She hadn't noticed how dark the circles under his eyes were. "Are you okay? You don't seem as chipper as usual."

"Just tired."

"You're afraid Chief Gerard is going to railroad Mother, aren't you?"

He rubbed his brow. "A little. It's not something I think Dwayne is going to do intentionally, but he's in a bad position. He spent years as the department's number two, with no hope of promotion. Now, when circumstances finally give him a chance to grab the brass ring and become chief, the murder of one of the most beloved men in our community stands in his way."

"But that's not my mother's fault."

"True, but every hour that passes without Dwayne announcing a killer means more people talking about the murder and considering Dwayne in a negative light. Remember, he's filling a partial term by appointment. He'll need to run again next year. Dwayne may not always appear to be the brightest bulb, but he's smart enough to know if he doesn't solve Lance's murder quickly, he can kiss being chief on a permanent basis good-bye. Consequently, he's getting desperate."

What Harlan said about the chief's motivation made sense, but it was his characterization of Lance she zeroed in on. Considering how Lance had roused her mother's anger by his treatment of Emily and Marcus, she doubted everyone in town viewed Lance Knowlton in the same generous light. "Don't you think beloved is a bit much?"

"Not really. Think about it. Your mother may be annoyed with Lance today, but there was a reason your parents dealt with him for all these years. It's the same one that has so many folks up in arms about his murder. Whether at the bank or in his different roles on the city council, he made people feel he cared about them and their needs. More importantly, he repeatedly demonstrated he would go the extra mile to help them."

Sarah crossed her arms and planted her feet on the concrete walk. It sometimes unnerved her how

Harlan almost seemed able to read her mind. "He didn't exactly go the extra mile for Emily and Marcus."

"Lance didn't make the decision about their loan request." Harlan held up his hand, forefinger in the air.

Seeing this, Sarah braced herself for one of Harlan's professorial lectures.

"Lance told you Bailey made the decision. You can bet if Lance ever looked at the file, considering the people involved, there wouldn't have been a rejection."

"Exactly my mother's point. She felt Lance slacked off on his banking responsibilities because he was enjoying the benefits that came with being president of the bank and the city council."

"Part of that might be true, but the crackdown on banking regulations, especially the hoops banks must jump through to satisfy compliance requirements, changed the game's landscape. In the old days, which was only a few years ago, your parents would ask for a loan, and Lance, knowing them, would probably agree without a lot of formalities. Collateral and guarantees weren't as important as a good banker's gut-level reaction."

"And Lance had that as a banker and a politician."

Harlan nodded. "No question. But that's not the case in the world of finance today. Every 'i' must be dotted and every 't' crossed. The past leeway of decision-making for bank presidents has given way to an era of scrutiny. Lance proved himself an adaptable banker able to keep up with the times. He shifted responsibilities to loan officers, like Bailey, as a means of maintaining arm's-length relationships. His attitude and behavior probably are more relevant to today's banking world than your mother's."

"But it still seems strange he didn't know anything about the loan request, especially when my mother said the rejection was over his signature."

"You and I work closely in my office. Don't you have certain letters you send out with my signature without me reviewing them because they're standard? Appointment reminders or notices when clients are late paying their bills? And, do you think you know everything about every aspect of the cases I work on? I certainly wouldn't ever claim that I keep up-to-the-minute tabs on what you're doing."

"Perhaps not." Sarah didn't think it would be advisable to tell him a little sneak peeking at the paperwork and notes on his desk, reading through the correspondence she typed or filed, and making entries in the firm's business ledger gave her a better idea about most things in his office than he could possibly imagine. Some things a good secretary or receptionist needed to keep to herself.

Considering what Eloise had said about how long she'd worked for Lance Knowlton, Sarah bet Eloise knew where the skeletons were buried—the bank's and any personal ones Lance had. She made a mental note to follow up with Eloise in the next few days to see how she was doing after today's tragedy, especially if Chief Gerard insisted on making Sarah's mother his main person of interest. No matter how beloved Harlan might think Lance, Sarah believed every white knight had a chink in his armor.

"Excuse me, Harlan. What did you say? I'm afraid my mind was wandering."

"Where?"

"Where?"

"Where was your mind wandering?"

"Oh, I was simply wondering how Emily is doing with my mom."

"Probably fine, but why don't you call and check up on them? If everything is okay, let's sit down on one of the benches here in the square. I'd like to talk to you privately before we join them at the office."

Sarah studied Harlan's face. Whatever was bothering him enough to want to talk in the open town square rather than back at his office must be serious. She couldn't see a hint of a smile on his lips or in his eyes. Still observing him, Sarah reached into her oversized purse and rummaged around until her hand touched the protective shell encasing her phone. It felt colder than anything else in her purse. She pulled the phone out and turned it on to check her texts before she called Emily.

"I didn't know you were an Alabama fan," Harlan said.

"Excuse me?"

He pointed to her telephone.

Emily followed his finger and realized he was looking at the houndstooth case she'd put on her phone. "Oh, that. I didn't think about the significance of the houndstooth pattern to Bear Bryant and the Crimson Tide when I bought the case. I wanted to protect my new phone. This was one of the cases in the five dollars or less sales bin."

Harlan laughed.

"You better be careful. Your clients might get the impression you're no more a sports fan than I am." She glanced at the face of her phone and saw a highlighted text from Emily. Sarah clicked it open and read it.

"I hope you didn't need to talk to my mother again today," she told Harlan.

"No. I'd covered almost everything for tomorrow with her before you called me to come over to the station."

"Good. Mother decided she's had enough of this fun. She went home to sleep in her own bed."

"I'm surprised Maybelle didn't stay in Wheaton long enough to make sure everything was okay with you."

"You don't know my mother. She has full confidence in you."

"That's nice to hear, but I'm not sure I can always guarantee the result she wants."

"Well, apparently, she thinks you can." She glanced at her phone again. "She said to tell you she'll be at your office at nine in case there's anything else she wants to discuss with you."

Harlan chuckled. "I gather that's an exact quote?"

"Yup. Though I'm sure if there's anything you want to interject, she might give you a few minutes."

"I love your mother. She's wild."

Sarah didn't know if she should smile or frown, which was the feeling she often had when dealing with her mother. "You might say that. Because Mom went home, Emily went to Southwind to help Marcus. She asked me to meet them there when we finished."

"If you want, text her back. I won't keep you long, I promise." He sat on one of the redwood benches that dotted the town square and patted the seat next to him. "It really is a beautiful day. That's why I thought we should take advantage of having the square almost to ourselves to talk."

Sarah sat and looked around. She hadn't realized how empty the square was this late in the day. Without its usual bustle, she could really take in its quaintness. Although there was no mistaking it had the planned essence of a traditional Southern small cobblestone town square framed by community services buildings and the main library, someone, in the last decade, convinced the city council to make it more inviting for people to hang out in. Benches and picnic tables, as well as a children's play area near the library, had been added to the original plan. The play area consisted of intertwined metal hoops children climbed and crawled through and the pièce de résistance, a fountain set into the ground with heads randomly shooting water at different heights and angles.

Nice as the square was, Sarah knew sitting there or in a park wasn't Harlan's normal style. "Harlan, is there something wrong?"

"What could be wrong? With everything that's been happening during the past few months, we've been so busy we haven't taken the time to simply sit and talk."

For wanting to talk, she noted he was quite silent, almost seemingly preoccupied by the one child playing in the fountain. She pointed at the child. "I don't think you have to worry about him splashing us. We're not close enough."

"Wasn't even thinking about that."

Observing his focus remained on the child, Sarah waited.

When he finally spoke, he still didn't look at her. "Sarah, now that your circumstances have changed, have you thought about your future?"

She stared at him, uncertain what he was driving at.

Whenever her ex-husband, the now-dead rat, opened a conversation in this way, she'd learned it meant criticism was coming her way. But Harlan wasn't like that.

Still, had she failed to enter a check in the ledger? Perhaps she'd missed a deadline on getting something in the mail or failed to type something he'd dictated. Maybe she'd been a little too snippy with the card-playing ladies who'd come in to see Harlan the other day without an appointment? Come to think of it, she had been a trifle exasperated by them not understanding, even if one was his aunt, they still couldn't see him on the spur of the moment, especially when he was out of the office in court. Could his aunt have demanded he fire her? No. His aunt drove Harlan too crazy for him to give in to one of her whims. That might get her a mild reprimand, but it wouldn't be enough for a termination.

Sarah tried to calm herself by tightly grabbing the bench's metal armrest. She was jumping to conclusions. Harlan might not be mad at her at all. Maybe he simply wanted to talk friend to friend. She kept her gaze on him, but he still watched the child playing near the fountain.

"It's been a few months since RahRah and you came into your inheritances. Now that you're financially secure and have options open to you, have you given any thought as to what you might want to do long-term and with whom?" He turned and looked at her.

She averted her eyes and concentrated on the child squealing when the wind blew water at him. What was Harlan asking her? He'd always been there for her— a true friend. Had she been so wounded she'd missed some subtle signs? She looked at him. She had to think, but she couldn't now. Not while she sat on this bench next to him.

"It's been nice moving into a bigger place and knowing I have a little financial security, but, Harlan, my job at your office is still very important to me. I understand helping Mom and me wasn't good for business today, and I'll be glad to pay for your time."

"That's not necessary."

"Well, I will. I'm just so sorry this is happening again. I don't know what to say."

Harlan cut off her nervous babbling. "Sarah, relax. I'm not trying to fire you."

"That's a relief. I was worried."

Harlan laughed. "I thought we'd put that topic to rest. You're doing a good job. Believe me, if you weren't, you'd know it."

Sarah puzzled over how, while she'd grown in her position and confidence, she still had moments of insecurity or inadequacy, but Harlan had no complaints. Either he was clueless, or she was too hard on herself. She released the armrest. Raising her hand to push her hair back, she noticed a red mark creasing her palm. She hadn't realized how tightly she'd been holding the bench. She looked at him again. "Well, in that case, maybe this would be a good time for me to ask for a raise?"

Harlan immediately opened his eyes wide while denying her request in a monotone. She couldn't help but laugh. She was glad to see the realization she was kidding prompted a fleeting smile before he addressed her with an air of earnestness.

"My concern is whether, with the change in your

circumstances during the past few months, you've taken the time to give any thought to your future?"

She shook her head. "Between everything that has happened with Southwind and RahRah, Mother being upset when she got home and found out how much danger we'd been in, settling in to the carriage house, and waiting to see what the city council does with our proposal for the big house, I've been taking it one day at a time."

This time he met her gaze. "You're talking about things relating to everyone else. I'm talking about you."

Sarah glanced away. She appreciated his concern but wasn't sure what was prompting it or how to react to his attempt to have a serious discussion. "It's all interwoven. I own the big house, so the council vote impacts me, too."

"I understand, but let's zero in on you. Would you want to work with Emily at the pub or the big-house restaurant on a daily basis in the future?"

"Not really. Cooking and restaurants are the last things that interest me. That's not to say I won't take shifts serving or cashiering during holidays or if they have a big party, but I can't see myself involved in day-to-day operations. I don't live and breathe that world like Emily and Marcus do."

He laughed. "Yeah, I remember the Jell-O in a Can recipe you demonstrated at the food expo. So, we'll scratch that off your wish list, but what's on your list? What about going back to school?"

"Getting a degree is something that interests me." She didn't tell him about the brochures she'd shoved under her bed shortly after her divorce. "You know, I enrolled at the community college after I graduated from high school so I'd be in the same town where Bill worked, but before I ever went to my first class, he convinced me there was no need for us to wait four years to get married. Back then, I thought a Mrs. degree was the only thing I wanted in life." Sarah stood and walked a few feet away from the bench.

Harlan scrambled to follow, but before he reached her, Sarah stopped and looked back over her shoulder at him. "Things don't always turn out the way one thinks they will, do they?"

He stood perfectly still. "No, they don't. You've been through a lot during the past few months. Things that can change a person."

Sarah frowned. "I don't disagree with that. In some ways I feel like I've lived four years instead of four months."

"In a way you have. It changed you. You aren't the scared woman who'd had the rug pulled out from under her who I originally hired."

"I simply hide my knees shaking better." She shook her head, causing her hair to flow over her shoulders. "No. I shouldn't say that. I've changed, but I'm still learning who I really am."

"That's why I'm asking these questions." He took a step closer to her. "You're young and can do so much, especially now that you have financial stability."

"Are you sure you're not trying to fire me in a graceful manner?"

"Absolutely not. I'm simply concerned about you." He scuffed his shoe on the path but kept his gaze focused on her face. "What about your personal life? What do you want for that? And don't tell me it's to work for me, volunteer at the animal shelter, help Emily out with big gigs, and take care of RahRah."

"I haven't really considered that question. The things you listed keep me busy and don't give me much time to think about serious topics like that."

"But you owe it to yourself to take the time."

"I know, and I will if Chief Gerard does his job. Otherwise, I'm going to be busy developing some suspects for him, other than my mother."

Harlan jerked his head upright. "Sarah, have you forgotten what happened last time you got involved in an investigation?"

Now it was Sarah's turn to look away as she thought about how her meddling almost got her killed. It wasn't something one easily forgot.

"You've got to promise me you'll leave finding out who killed Lance to the professionals."

Surprised at the intensity of his answer, she faced him. Sarah knew Harlan was only trying to protect her, but if Chief Gerard refused to consider anyone besides her mother, she couldn't imagine simply sitting on the sidelines. Still, she could tell from the earnest tone of Harlan's voice and the furrows in his forehead how important this was to him. Keeping her hands to her sides, she slightly crossed two fingers. "Promise. Satisfied?"

Uncrossing her fingers, she started walking away from him again but stopped dead in her tracks at his next question. "How about dating? Have you thought about putting yourself out there again?"

She paused for a moment to give her words more emphasis. "I already have a special man in my life."

She smiled when he stuttered over his words.

"You . . . you do?" He took a step backward.

"Most definitely." She grinned but said nothing more.

"Well, um." He muttered something else she couldn't quite hear, but she didn't ask him to repeat it.

"Right now, RahRah is my special guy. He takes a lot of my attention."

Harlan rubbed his hand across his cheek. "I meant someone human."

Now, there was no question what he was getting at, but she wasn't ready to address it with Harlan or anyone, no matter how wonderful they were. "Sharing my life with someone again is far from my highest priority. I need to figure me out first."

He kicked another acorn. "You know squirrels plan ahead. They don't want to be caught without nourishment when winter comes."

Sarah reached out and gave his arm a squeeze. "Guess I'm lucky we have grocery stores. Thanks for caring."

CHAPTER ELEVEN

"Try one of these." Emily handed Sarah a bite-size appetizer, which she promptly popped into her mouth.

"Delicious. What is it?"

"A sweet potato puff. Grace and I wanted to do a play on the standard potato puff pastry bite."

Sarah glanced from Emily to Grace, her favorite Southwind line cook and Emily's right-hand person, who was holding out a plate with more of the same appetizers. Sarah took another one and bit off half of it. Swallowing, she tried to determine what they seasoned the sweet potato with. The filling's sweet taste was a nice contrast to its crispy outside.

"These really are good."

"Grace's recipe."

Sarah swallowed the remainder of the potato puff. "I've got to come around more for treats like these. I'm glad to see you, Grace. It's been too long. What have you been up to?"

"Not much. The new term at school started, so my schedule isn't fully settled, yet. I've only had a few hours a week to help out here. I guess our paths just haven't crossed."

Sarah nodded. She hadn't seen much of any of the line cooks since the fire because Marcus only had enough insurance money to assign them limited hours. She was glad Marcus was doing whatever he could to keep everyone on payroll. They were all such great people.

During the food expo, she bonded with several of them, especially Jacob and Grace. When Sarah had been forced into cooking during the expo, it was Grace who had been her rock. Many, observing button-down-shirted Sarah with the tall copper-toned woman with the full-sleeve tattoo and Afro, would not think of the two of them as associates, but in fact, there they were.

Grace held the plate out, offering her another sweet potato puff.

Waving her hands, Sarah begged off. "No thanks. I don't want to spoil my dinner. I've been looking forward to a Marcus-cooked meal all afternoon."

"Then you'd better have another puff," Emily said. "Between not getting the permits and being busy with the contractor this afternoon, Marcus still can't cook in this kitchen. The only thing we have to nibble on are the various appetizers Grace and I made at her place."

"If the other ones are anything like your sweet potato puffs, I'll be in heaven."

Sarah looked around the kitchen. Although some appliances had tags on them and not everything was in its final plugged-in position yet, even to her untrained eye, the kitchen appeared ready to use. The dining room, as she well knew from having helped hang pictures and unload and position chairs and tables, was ready to go.

"When I got here after Mom went home," Emily said, "I realized how annoyed Marcus was at still not having the permits and that he might be tied up all afternoon with the strip center owner and insurance people, so I slipped over to Grace's apartment. We've been playing with a few things, and this afternoon gave us time to work on them. We brought the finished product back here for Marcus to taste."

"Emily thought our appetizers might sweeten his mood, but he's been too busy to taste anything."

Sarah helped herself to another puff and glanced around the restaurant. "He's definitely missing out. Where is Marcus?"

"Outside. Tread lightly when you see him. Between the loan being denied and the postponement of today's council meeting, Marcus is fit to be tied. He thinks he's jinxed because there always seems to be another problem that may delay things, even if our Southwind permits go through at next week's meeting."

"What's the problem?"

"We're about to hear." Marcus came into the kitchen, with Cliff behind him. Marcus bent and gave Emily a quick kiss.

Sarah smiled. The contrast between Emily's blond cheerleader look, so different from Sarah's willowy dark look, and Marcus's sheer bulk, emphasized by his colorful billowing chef pants, amused her. Now that Emily and Marcus admitted being more than simply business associates, Emily maintained a professional reserve, even in front of Sarah, but Marcus made no attempt to hide his public displays of affection.

Both Marcus and Cliff took one of the sweet potato puffs Grace offered them. Giving the puff a thumbs-up, Marcus reached for a second one. He swallowed it in one bite. "These go on our pub menu, if this guy ever stops finding headaches to keep us from opening."

Cliff shrugged and held up his hands like a bad guy giving up. "I'm just the messenger."

"Messenger?" Emily asked.

"We got word today that one of your major equipment suppliers is experiencing a one-week delay."

Grace offered Marcus another pastry puff, but he declined. "Chef Marcus, at least look at it from the bright side. Hopefully whatever it is that still needs to be delivered will be here and installed by next Tuesday, so you can open immediately if the council approves everything."

"Ah, our Pollyanna. From your mouth to God's ears, but I'm afraid there's more to it than simply waiting for our ceiling hood to arrive. Cliff, explain it to them."

"The strip center had a surprise visit from the building inspector today, and, well, he has a problem with the ventilation for the ceiling hood Marcus is waiting on. The inspector insists the venting approved for the mall renovation is insufficient for that particular hood."

"What does that mean in terms of our budget?" Emily asked.

"It means we either come up with twenty-three hundred dollars for a ventilation modification from what the landlord is required to provide or we go with a different hood."

"But that's the best hood for our needs."

"Right. So, we're stuck with another twenty-three hundred we need to absorb into our portion of the build-out costs." Marcus opened a cooler sitting next to the bar. "Anyone want a soda or beer?"

Cliff shook his head. "No thanks. I've still got to deliver a message from the building inspector to the owner of Miscellaneous Shoes."

Emily took a sparkling water. "Cliff, is there any way Marcus and I can appeal the determination or ask for a variance?"

"Like I told him when we were outside, appealing will delay us further and cost more money than it would be worth. Besides, the odds of winning that kind of appeal are slim to none. Better to change the hood or come up with the twenty-three hundred."

After putting the almost-empty plate on one of the tables, Grace broke the momentary silence at Cliff's bad news. "Much as I'd like to, I don't think I have a way to give this a cheerful spin. I've got class tonight, so I'll think about it there."

"And while Grace is going, I'll take my leave to let the three of you stew on it." Cliff waited for Grace to grab her purse so they could walk out together. "Let's hope Slim at Miscellaneous Shoes doesn't shoot the messenger."

After Cliff and Grace left, the three sat at the table with the remaining sweet potato puffs. While Marcus kept turning his beer bottle around, the twins finished off the puffs.

"I'm bummed," Marcus said. "I expected we'd at

least get our kitchen permits today to allow us to take on catering jobs. Between the supplier, building inspector, and postponed council meeting, we're worse off tonight than we were yesterday."

Sarah was confused. She understood the problem posed by the $2,300 ventilation cost and that every day Marcus and Emily couldn't operate Southwind cost them money, but at this point, how significant was losing one more week's worth of business? She posed the question to Marcus and Emily.

He jumped on her inquiry. "Sarah, even if we can't operate the restaurant, we have a profit margin built into all of our catering jobs. I had to turn down handling the reception after Lance's funeral. Do you have any idea how much revenue and free advertising Emily and I lost refusing that funeral lunch?"

"Marcus, a man died. Money and advertising? How callous can you be?"

"I'm not being callous. Would you call a funeral home callous? We provide a service to people in sorrowful and joyful times. If we take the burden and worry off the family at a time like this, we're doing our job right, so I don't begrudge us making money, too. Handling the catering after Lance's funeral probably would have been one of our biggest jobs, outside of holiday catering, for the year. It would have paid for the twenty-three hundred overage and made up a portion of the loan his bank denied us. Equally important, people from Wheaton and Birmingham would have tasted our food and seen the Southwind logo there, so they would have filed the name of our business away for future use."

"Guess I didn't look at it that way."

Emily put her hand on her sister's arm. "How could you be expected to? You're not in the business. We're more sensitive because, with our loan being denied, not only does every dollar count, but so does getting our name out there. We can't afford to let people forget us for their future catering needs."

Marcus nodded. "People are fickle. If someone else steps up and does a good job, that's who they'll call next time. Every day we must make the public, our potential customers, understand the quality and service we offer is better than our competitors'. This job would have been nice and eased some of our burden, but I'll concede one job and one week isn't going to break us. My fear is how next week's council meeting will play out."

Sarah glanced from Marcus to Emily. "I don't think I understand. What are you worried about?"

"Marcus is worried about who will be appointed to finish Lance's term in office and whether Anne Hightower will be elected president of the council."

"Doesn't whoever fills Lance's slot automatically become president?"

"No. That person becomes a council member, and there is a new election for president. Considering Anne's views about downtown, if we don't get someone in there who is friendly to our stance, she'll easily be able to use procedural delays to keep our plans for using the big house for a restaurant from coming to a vote or she might have enough votes to shut us down completely."

"Who appoints the council replacement?"

"Normally, the mayor and council. Right now, names are being gathered for consideration. Whoever is appointed will have to stand for election next year when the term runs out."

"Have you given any thought on someone to suggest who might support our position for developing an entertainment district? How about Jacob?"

Emily shook her head. "That won't work. His name is Hightower."

"So?"

"It's simple. Even though his viewpoint is diametrically opposed to his father and sister's, the council already has a Hightower on it. Wheaton voters aren't going to want someone who they think might result in one family controlling the voting on all matters. The Hightowers have enough power as it is. Sarah, do you think Harlan would throw his hat in the ring? He's fair and well-respected."

"He'd be great, but he won't do it. I can't tell you how many times he's told me he swore after the stint he did on the Economic Council with Bill, he'd never hold public office again. He believes he can do more good being a lawyer for the people than a politician. Why don't one of you run?"

Marcus laughed. "Because we're chefs. I don't think I could hold myself in check for an entire meeting."

Emily rubbed his shoulder. "Nor would he have the patience to sit through committee and regular council meetings."

Sarah laughed. There were plenty of times she'd seen Marcus impassioned about something. "What about you, Emily? You have a sound business mind and you've always been civic-minded and good with people. Plus, I've seen how focused you are when you're cooking."

"That's different. After everything that happened with Bill, I don't think I ever want to be involved in political behind-the-scenes dealings. It's not for me."

"Well, I may not have any other ideas for the election, but I think I can see a way clear for you for the twenty-three hundred dollars."

"What?"

"Let me give it to you."

Marcus banged his bottle down on the table "Absolutely not. If you come in as a partner on the big house project because you own the property, that's one thing, but we're not going to let you use your money to bail us out."

"Why not? Emily is my sister and, even though I don't have an interest in Southwind, I am, like you said, going to be your partner in the new venture. Look, I can afford to do this for you and I want to do it."

"Sarah, restaurants are speculative businesses at best. You keep that money for you. Emily and I will find a loan or some other means of getting it. I don't want to be obligated to you in case something goes wrong. You need to use that money for something you want to do."

"I want to help the two of you."

He looked at Emily, who reached over and took his hand. "We appreciate your offer, but we can't. Don't worry. We'll find a way."

Sarah watched this exchange between them as she thought about how hard going to a bank was. "You know, I think you should try the bank again. Mom was sure you'd sail through because she'd offered to cosign or guarantee the loan with her own assets."

"We don't want to take her money, either."

"You wouldn't be. She's only guaranteeing you'll pay back the loan. At least that's what I understood when she let Mr. Knowlton have it when she took me to the bank today. From what he said and the look on his face, I think he would have reversed his loan officer's decision if he had lived."

Marcus ran his hand through his hair. "I had no idea Maybelle told the bank she'd guarantee our loan request. That was most generous of her."

"Mother is always full of surprises. That's why she was so mad when she found out your loan request was denied. So, if you won't take the money from me, I'm sure she still would do that for the two of you. If she does, you, not her, will be the ones paying back the loan."

"She wouldn't be out any money. I'd make sure of that." Marcus held up his bottle and Sarah clinked her soda can against it.

Emily ignored her bottle of water sitting on the table. "There is another solution, but things have been so crazy, I haven't had the chance to share my good news with either of you."

CHAPTER TWELVE

Marcus and Sarah stared at Emily.

"I was waiting to tell both of you once the details were finalized, but now seems like the perfect time to share my good news. Sarah, you remember meeting Thomas Howell this afternoon at city hall?"

"Yes. I gather he invited you to cook at an exhibition at his hotel."

"More than that. That's what I was so excited about, but with everything with Mr. Knowlton and Mom, I mean Maybelle, and then working with Grace, I didn't even get a chance to tell you, Marcus."

From the way Marcus tightened his grip on his beer bottle, Sarah gathered there might be something she didn't know about how he felt about Thomas Howell. "What news about Mr. Hotel didn't you share with me?"

"His name is Thomas Howell, not Mr. Hotel, and he not only invited me to be part of that event, but he made me a proposition that could be the answer to our money problems." Emily grinned broadly at Sarah and Marcus, but while Sarah forced herself to smile back, she observed Marcus's reaction was a frown.

He cleared his throat and took another swig of his beer. "Considering how things have been going, this sounds too good to be true. I'm glad I'm sitting down."

Tension zinged through the room as Emily made a face at his snide remark before blithely continuing. "But it is. Thomas Howell couldn't have been nicer when we were talking before you got to the council meeting. He told me he'd heard we'd run into some delays getting back on our feet since the fire."

Marcus leaned forward. "How much did you tell him?"

Now, it was Emily's turn to frown and wrinkle her brows, but in obvious confusion rather than anger. "The truth, of course. We haven't been able to open the restaurant or take any catering jobs, but that as soon as all the permits are approved, we'll be back in business."

"I'm sure that thrilled him to no end."

"He didn't say either way."

"What did he say?" Sarah tried to avoid a collision of opinions between Marcus and Emily. From past experience, she knew that both were stubborn and could dig in their heels. Better to defuse the moment, if possible.

"He told me that while the hotel is doing well, the restaurant has had some problems."

Marcus took another sip of his beer. "That's an understatement. It's well known that it's been floundering almost since day one. So what did he want from you? Our recipes and tricks of the trade?"

"Not at all. He acknowledged that since he opened, his restaurant staffing has been hit and miss. He's trying to start over and needs an executive chef. He offered me the job."

"You already have a job with Southwind. And you'll have a second one if our new restaurant gets off the ground."

"That's exactly what I told him."

Marcus relaxed into his chair and played with the label on his beer bottle. "Now that is good news."

"But, Emily, I don't see how what you told him helps Marcus and you monetarily."

"It doesn't. That is, until Thomas sweetened his offer. He understands my loyalty to Southwind, so he offered me a six-month executive chef contract. I'll come onboard and straighten out the kitchen while he continues looking for a new permanent chef. Whether he finds one in one month or six months, he'll pay me the entire amount of our contract. Thomas also said I can bring my own sous chef, so I can put Grace on his payroll, too. Between what I'll make and Southwind not having to pay Grace, we can easily handle the expense of the hood."

"Em, are you sure you heard Thomas right? That doesn't sound like the kind of contract Harlan would negotiate at our office."

Marcus crossed his arms. "No, it doesn't. What out clause does Mr. Hotel have?"

"I can't believe how cynical you're being. Thomas is willing to pay because he wants an experienced hand to help him start over."

"Maybe, but I guarantee you, Mr. Hotel will put something in the contract letting him fire you without paying you for six months. Once you straighten things out and give him our secrets for running a successful restaurant, he won't need you anymore."

"Don't be so silly, Marcus. Thomas isn't like that. What's even better is his hotel kitchen is permitted and meets all required codes. He understands the pickle we're in with the permits, codes, and rebuilding time, so because his kitchen is permitted as a commissary-approved kitchen for preparation and distribution, he's willing to let me make food there and bring it to Wheaton to sell at one designated location. Surely, once we're working together, he'll also let me use his kitchen during off times to prep for catering jobs until Southwind receives its permit."

Marcus took a few steps from the table but then returned and stood over Emily and Sarah. "Are you crazy? You really think he's going to let us cater our food out of his establishment? He wants our catering business for the Howellian. Who do you think stepped in when I couldn't accept the job catering the meal after Lance's funeral?"

Sarah agreed with Marcus. She didn't understand kitchens, wouldn't know a walk-in refrigerator from a walk-in freezer until she opened its door and felt how cold it was, but she understood business competition. She typed complaints and answers every day in Harlan's office stemming from disagreements. Wouldn't commissary-delivered food driven in from Birmingham in a hotel-owned temperature-controlled truck have packaging bearing the hotel's name? Why would Howell let food from his kitchen be associated with Southwind? Surely, he'd want it to be an advertisement for the Howellian and his other businesses.

Glancing at how excited her twin was at having

found a partial solution to their monetary woes, Sarah was sure she hadn't thought beyond the dollar signs. As Emily continued prattling about how kind and warm Thomas was, Sarah wished her sister would rein in her enthusiasm. From the way Marcus bent forward over the wooden back of a new chair, his hands pressed flat into the table, she doubted he'd be able to control his temper and tongue much longer.

"Are you stupid or simply naïve? Don't you realize his customers will associate our cooking and recipes, if you make them, with the Howellian rather than our restaurant? As long as you're there, they'll flock to you. When he's done with you and has your recipes, he'll fling you aside to come back to Southwind, but the damage will have been done. The public won't associate your food with you. You'll always be the one who prepares food like they do at the Howellian. If they can get the real thing, why should people drive fifteen minutes for a knock-off?"

Seeing two dots of red contrasting with the heightened pallor of Emily's cheeks and the right tilt at which she held her neck, Sarah waited for Emily to explode. She didn't. Instead, Emily stood and picked up her purse.

"I think you need to cool off. You're not thinking rationally. We've got a problem, and this is an honorable way out of it. In six months, everything you're saying can't possibly happen. Come on, Sarah. Let's go to your place and let this blowhard calm down."

Emily stomped out of the restaurant. Sarah stood, torn. She couldn't help but agree with Marcus. After being married to a rat, Sarah had too much practical experience in observing situations like this. She thought Emily did, too. But her sister was her sister and, like the old saying, "blood is thicker than water."

"I'll talk to her," she assured Marcus as she followed Emily from the restaurant.

"Please."

When she looked back, Marcus was again seated at the table, the beer bottle pushed away from him, his face engulfed by his big hands.

CHAPTER THIRTEEN

"RahRah," Sarah called as Emily and she threw their purses and coats on the couch in the carriage house. Hurrying to the kitchen, she opened its door, but RahRah didn't dart out of the room. She peered inside the room, and her heart almost stopped. He was in the same position he'd been in when she left. Crossing the room in three steps, she repeated his name.

This time, he stirred. Assuming she woke him from a deep sleep, she didn't try to touch him until he was fully awake. Instead, she picked up his water bowl and went to the sink. While she refilled it, she kept up a running patter. "Were you dreaming? From the looks of your water and food bowls, it looks like you had a good meal while I was gone. Did you decide to take another nap after you ate?"

"Yup."

Sarah spun around at the low purring response only to see her twin, convulsed with laughter. "Got you!"

"No, you didn't."

Emily repeated her gravel-voiced response.

Rather than denying the truth, Sarah gave in to her sister's assertion. She watched Emily open and immediately close her refrigerator. "Well? Find what you were looking for?"

Emily nodded. "Other than more nail polish and spaghetti, I see you haven't added much to your food stock since I last spent the night."

Sarah placed RahRah's water back on the floor. Returning to the sink, she used a watermelon-decorated glass from a mismatched set her mother had given her after her divorce for a glass of water for herself. "I've got enough to get by. Between work and spending extra time at the shelter playing with the animals, I'll admit the fridge is a bit bare. Do you want something to drink?"

"No thanks. And, I know, you're planning a grocery run for this weekend." Emily pulled a chair out from the kitchen table.

Sarah joined her sister at the table. "Exactly. Well, maybe not. This is my Saturday to walk dogs at the shelter. Speaking of which, if you really take this new gig, are you going to help me with the people and animal treats for YipYeow Day or should I start practicing with brownie mixes?"

"Don't worry. You know I'll work it out, and I'm sure Marcus, and probably Grace and Jacob, will help, too. Just let me know what the date turns out to be. Speaking of dates, would you join me for lunch tomorrow at the Howellian?"

"Are you buying?"

"No, Thomas is. He wants to take me on a tour of the kitchen and hotel. You can come, too."

"Shouldn't you take Marcus rather than me?"

"I think it was clear he wants nothing to do with Thomas Howell and the Howellian. Forcing Marcus to go would only cause more tension between us. That's the last thing we need right now."

"Em, why then are you even considering accepting Thomas's job offer?"

Emily looked at RahRah, who had sauntered over to their table and plopped down on her feet. "When you're short on money, you find a way to make things work. This is our best temporary solution."

"But you have other alternatives. I'll give you the money."

"Marcus and I won't take it from you." Emily pointed at Sarah's glass. "You've gone without so long, you deserve to be able to buy things you want instead of settling for hand-me-downs."

Sarah grabbed Emily's hand. "It's no big deal. I have enough money now that making you a short-term loan won't keep me from doing anything."

"Restaurants are tricky businesses, and with all the delays and snags we've hit, we won't take a chance on not being able to pay you back quickly. Look, I've seen the catalogs under your bed. I know you want to go back to school. If we take the money, that will delay you even longer. I don't want that on my conscience."

"Now you're being melodramatic. Because you saw a few catalogs lying around doesn't mean I want to enroll in classes. I have plenty of cookbooks, and I have no desire to cook."

"Okay. I'll grant you that, but we won't take the money from you. The subject is closed."

"Then why not let Mother lend it to you or guarantee a bridge loan for Marcus and you?"

"We'll see. But there are still no guarantees. Remember, we apparently tried that route and it didn't work."

"But it should have. If you'd been in Mr. Knowlton's office, you would have seen him realize it was a loan that should have been approved. Neither he nor I had any idea why it was denied. If he'd lived, I bet he would have approved it before the council meeting began."

"If he'd lived." Emily rubbed her neck. "Right now, Mom has enough on her plate. She doesn't need to worry about Marcus and my finances. So, will you come with me to lunch tomorrow?"

Sarah wanted to refuse, but one glance at her sister made her decide to go. This invitation was so out of character for Emily, it was a sign a twin couldn't ignore. She didn't want Emily to cut her out of her trust loop. Last time that happened, things blew up in deadly fashion. Who knew what might happen if Sarah blew this invitation off? She couldn't take the chance. Besides, maybe, if Sarah was there, Emily would let her be the voice of reason Emily seemed to be ignoring.

"I'll come. Em, one thing I don't understand is why Thomas is bothering bringing a commissary concept to Wheaton. Doesn't he have enough on his platter?"

"I think there's a family relationship between him and some of the Wheaton families. This is his way of paying back their investment in him."

"Investment in him?"

Emily nodded. "At a crucial point, before Thomas broke ground for the hotel, he ran into money problems. Via the bank, Thomas found a group of investors from Wheaton who got him over the hump. The commissary is something Lance and he worked out."

So Thomas was tied to Lance, too. Perhaps there was something in their relationship that would make Thomas Howell a suspect, too. Sarah hoped not. He still was someone she wouldn't mind getting to know better.

"Thomas promised to fill me in on everything over lunch. If you have any questions, you can ask him then."

Sarah wondered exactly how much Thomas would tell Emily tomorrow. It seemed unlikely he would share more than basic financial facts with a potential executive chef and her tagalong sister.

CHAPTER FOURTEEN

The next morning, Harlan was already setting up the office coffee maker when Sarah arrived for work. She dropped her purse into her bottom desk drawer, hidden behind the partial wall separating her workspace from the cozy waiting room, grabbed her coffee mug, and joined him.

"Good morning," she said, as they both waited for the coffee to brew and drip through the machine "You came in early today."

"I wanted to get a few things done before Maybelle gets here. Just so you know, except for when Maybelle signs her statement, I'll be in the office all day."

"Thanks for telling me. Obviously, I'll be here in case someone comes in while the two of you are at the police station, but would it be okay if I take a slightly longer lunch break today? I'll stay late to make up the time."

"Sure. It isn't every day you have the opportunity to spend time with your mother."

Sarah placed her mug on the counter and reached in front of him for the almost-empty sugar holder. She pulled a box of raw sugar packets from the cabinet above her head and refilled the holder while deciding how much to confide in Harlan. Finished fidgeting with the sugar, she faced him. "That's not it. I'm hoping she'll be gone well before lunchtime."

Harlan raised his right eyebrow in the fashion she knew meant more information was necessary immediately. Without further prompting, she filled him in on Thomas Howell's offer, Emily's and Marcus's reactions to it, and her fear of what might happen if she didn't join Thomas Howell and her sister for lunch because Emily wasn't thinking like Emily.

"I agree you need to be there. Also, why don't you tell Emily I'll be glad to look over any contract before she signs it."

"Thanks." She held out her hand. "Give me your cup. I'll bring you your coffee when it's ready."

"Perfect." He handed her his mug and went into his office.

Sarah put his cup on the counter near hers. While she waited for the fresh brew, she picked up a stray magazine someone had left on one of the four guest chairs. The headline for an article on magicians and escape tricks caught her eye and she thumbed to it. She always marveled how magicians got out of sealed tanks and freed themselves when their hands and feet were tied. According to the article, it was a cinch. The key was to keep yourself from being tied too tightly by tightening your muscles or causing a gap between your wrists by bringing your knuckles together while pulling your hands back to your chest. She wondered if the situation Emily was getting herself into would require having a secret way to escape.

Hopefully, Sarah would get a better understanding

at lunch. For now, she neatly arranged the magazine with the others on the table where Harlan kept reading matter in case a client had to wait. A few months after she began working for Harlan, when cash flow was a little tight, she suggested he cancel his numerous office magazine subscriptions to cut expenses. After all, most clients killed time reading digitally. Harlan rejected the idea not only because many of his clients weren't tech savvy, but he believed print magazines gave the waiting room a homey ambiance. Now that she had worked for him for a while, she agreed with him.

When the coffee was finally ready, Sarah filled their mugs and dutifully delivered Harlan's to him. Returning to her desk, she saw Mr. Rogers approaching the front door. She buzzed him in. Before she could get good-morning greetings out of her mouth, Mr. Rogers rapped his cane on the floor and demanded to see Harlan.

"He's getting ready to leave for an appointment, Mr. Rogers. Could I help you or make you an appointment for later today?"

"No. I need to see him, now." He marched toward Harlan's office.

Sarah came around from behind her desk and cut him off. "I'll be glad to make an appointment for you."

He stared at her and shifted his cane in a manner that made her think he might use it for something other than a walking stick. "I told you, it's an emergency. It can't wait until later."

"What seems to be the problem, George?"

Harlan stood in the open doorway of his office. He nodded at her. Sarah stepped out of Mr. Rogers's way, but rather than walking past her, he stood where he was, shaking his cane.

"It's that blasted nephew of mine. I've given him everything he ever wanted and more, and this is how he treats me. This time he's gone too far!"

Harlan held his hands up to slow Mr. Rogers's rant. "George, start at the beginning. I don't know what you're talking about."

"It's very simple. My nephew wants me locked up in one of those places where they throw the key away."

"Now, George, why would he want to do that?"

"Because he wants my house and property, and I won't give them to him." His bow tie quivered against his Adam's apple.

"You don't have to give him anything, ever," Harlan said.

"That's exactly what I told him, but when I made it clear I would cut him out of my will, he started talking about how I need to be in one of those senior community retirement homes. Said it would be in my best interests now that I'm getting on in years."

Sarah thought about how much upkeep there was on her property. Mr. Rogers easily had the same responsibilities. "Maybe he's suggesting it for your well-being?"

"The only one's well-being that boy ever thinks about is his own. He can suggest from here to doomsday, but I'm staying put until they plant me. You're not going to see me in one of those places, where they give you three lousy meals and a choice between playing checkers, watching the other inmates, or staring at television until you wither up and die."

Sarah was impressed Harlan could keep a straight face when he said, "I gather you told him that."

"Dang straight, I did."

Harlan smiled. "And what did he say?"

"He laughed. Said it wouldn't be up to me in the end. Harlan, that's why I need you to draw up some kind of paper to keep him from doing anything. Apparently, he's gotten tired of waiting for me to croak."

"Surely not." Sarah clamped her lips shut when she caught the stern glance Harlan threw in her direction.

He gestured Mr. Rogers toward his office. "George, relax. Let's go in my office and talk about this some more. Believe me, your nephew is not going to do anything while you're here."

Harlan put his arm around George's shoulders and guided him the rest of the way into his private office. From the bang the door made closing, she knew Harlan had given it a firm push.

This was one of those times Sarah wished Harlan and she had some type of intercom system or maybe, since no one was in the office, she could simply hold a glass against the wall. She desperately wanted to eavesdrop. In all the time she'd known Mr. Rogers, she'd never seen him this emotionally overwrought. He was the kind of person, as she'd seen in his neighborhood dealings, who used analytical arguments to get even. Whatever Cliff was up to, he'd obviously pushed his uncle's buttons beyond Mr. Rogers's limit.

Her mother at the door made Sarah hope Harlan could help Mr. Rogers, but quickly. Maybelle wouldn't be happy waiting long for Harlan to review whatever list of points she'd brought to discuss before she gave her statement.

Once cleared to enter, her mother bustled in. Instead of Maybelle's usual makeup and flamboyantly colored attire, today she wore a simple blue shirtwaist dress and little makeup. Her hair was combed back, anchored by a cloth headband that was the same shade of blue as her dress. "Hi, honey. Where's Harlan?"

"Tied up with someone in his office. What's with the outfit?"

"Nothing."

Sarah stared at her mother.

"Oh, okay. Considering Officer Fife seems to be convinced I did it, I thought I should go with an innocent look."

"Officer Fife? Do you mean Chief Gerard?"

"He may be Chief Gerard to everyone, but all I see when I look at him is a bigger version of the deputy from *The Andy Griffith Show.*" Her mother drummed her fingers on the counter separating Sarah's desk from the waiting room. The glint from her diamond solitaire reflected against the counter's metallic finish. "Why don't you tell Harlan I'm here?"

"I'm sure he'll be ready for you in a few minutes."

"He better be. We need some time to talk. I thought of a few more things for him to think about saying when we go to sign my statement."

Sarah hoped her smile and calm attitude about how soon Harlan would be free was more convincing than she felt. Maybelle picked up a magazine from the table, then threw it back on the other ones lying there. "We're not going to have time to talk if he doesn't hurry. I don't understand why he's meeting with a client now. He knew I'd be here early for a last-minute review before we went to the police station."

It was nice not being the target of her mother's ire. She couldn't help baiting her, though. "Maybe he thought there wasn't anything else worth discussing."

Sarah kept a straight face while her mother rustled the magazines irritably before plopping into one of the guest chairs with a *Vogue*. Giving up, Sarah addressed her mother's annoyance. "Tell me how you really feel."

Maybelle tossed the magazine back on the table. "I would have thought Harlan would have wanted to go over some legal precedent or argument applicable to the chief's narrow-minded focus on me."

"He still might. Harlan came in early and was working on your case when something neither of us expected came up."

Maybelle sat up straighter in the chair. "Whatever distracted Harlan from our scheduled meeting better have been important."

Sarah assured her mother Harlan must have deemed it urgent or he would have rescheduled or more quickly wrapped up the unexpected matter. Both Sarah and her mother looked up at the sound of Harlan's office door opening.

Harlan and George Rogers came into the waiting room. Simultaneously, the two said, "Maybelle, sorry to keep you waiting."

"Ditto," Sarah and Maybelle said simultaneously. Both then burst out laughing while Harlan and Mr. Rogers stared at them.

Sarah quickly regained her composure. "Ditto is

something our family always shouts when two of us say the same thing at the same time. Old habits are hard to break. Right, Mom?"

"Almost as hard as educating a child to say 'May-belle.'"

Now it was Harlan and Mr. Rogers's turn to laugh. Harlan still was chuckling when Maybelle slid by him into his office while Harlan said good-bye to a calmer George.

Returning to what she'd been working on when her mother arrived, Sarah listened with one ear to Mr. Rogers's cane tapping the floor in rhythm to his step as he crossed the room. When the beat abruptly stopped before she heard the door open, she raised her eyes and glanced in his direction. He stood five feet from the door staring at her.

"Is something wrong, Mr. Rogers?"

Shoulders slumped, he shifted his weight back and forth in the same way she did as a kid when her mother caught her with her hand in the cookie jar. She waited for him to speak.

"I'm sorry if I came across as rude. I know I barged in without an appointment and raised my voice to you, but this whole matter with my nephew is unsettling."

"That's okay. It sounded like you had a right to be angry. I hope Harlan was able to help."

"I think so. At least, I feel better knowing Harlan thinks there are ways to thwart what my nephew wants to do." Mr. Rogers smiled, then frowned. "It's just painful to think I've been there for him for all these years, and now he shows his true colors. I know he's had financial problems, but . . ." His voice trailed off and, for the first time, Sarah thought he looked his age. "I only hope Harlan can put a stop to this nonsense."

"I hope so, too. Do you need me to make you another appointment?"

"No. Harlan said he'd call after he talks to my nephew. Well, I better be getting along. Gotta put out some fresh food for Fluffy."

"Did you find her?"

"She still won't come to me, but she came back to eat last night."

"I'm so glad."

CHAPTER FIFTEEN

Sarah whipped her car between the arched columns of the Howellian Hotel. If she could quickly figure out where the restaurant was, she might be on time.

Between her mother lingering in Harlan's office, providing a full report of what transpired while she signed her statement at police headquarters, and Harlan needing a motion typed and filed before Sarah could leave for lunch, the cushion of time she intended to leave in case there was traffic was almost nonexistent. An accident closing one lane of Highway I-65, a few exits before the one she needed for downtown Birmingham, destroyed her hope of being early.

At least the hotel's valet parking offered quick service. A young man, who looked like he was playing hooky from high school, immediately opened her door, presented her with a ticket, and directed her in the direction of the restaurant and art galleries while she fumbled with removing her valet key from her fob. She said a little prayer of thanks when the elevator door opened, delivering a passenger, at exactly the instant she was about to press the button to summon it. As the doors closed and the elevator rose, she glanced at her watch. She was just on time. A stop to use the ladies' room or examine the artwork lining the hallway walls would have to wait until after she'd been at the table.

From the hostess desk, she saw there was a formal dining room and a more casual terraced bar area. People were eating in both locations; either she'd arrived before Emily and Thomas or they were hidden from her view. Sarah wondered if they could be seated in a private dining room rather than the informal wicker-and-glass terrace or the gray-and-black-accentuated white-cloth room.

"Mr. Howell's table, please."

The hostess, whose gray-and-black uniform blended with the dining room, peered over a pair of oversized eyeglasses at her. "Ms. Blair?"

Sarah nodded.

"This way, please. They're waiting for you." Dropping the menu she'd picked up back onto her stand, the hostess ushered Sarah across the dining room. Although Sarah wanted to assure her, "I'm not late," she simply followed the hostess to a corner table tucked into an alcove in the main dining room. Because of the table's careful placement in the room's nook, she hadn't been able to see it from the hostess stand.

After she exchanged greetings with Thomas and Emily, she slid into her chair and looked around to get her bearings. Their table not only offered privacy from the eyes in the room, but both her seat and Thomas's were situated in the L of where the two rooms met, giving them perfect sight lines between the pillars into the two rooms. She couldn't help wondering if the placement of this table in the alcove had been deliberately designed or simply happenstance.

The one thing she was certain of was that Mr. Thomas Howell still was a hunk. He was formally dressed in a navy business suit, and she couldn't help but notice how the combination of his pink shirt and cornflower blue tie highlighted his blue eyes. She wanted to say, "You look lovely" but settled for "Your hotel is lovely."

"Is this your first time here?"

"Yes. I can't wait to look around a little more. I understand, in addition to the cat exhibit, you have a sculpture garden, dog photo room, and a full art gallery."

Emily put her napkin in her lap. "Sarah is a sucker for sculpture gardens."

"Guilty as charged." Sarah smiled at the hunk.

"Then, before you leave, I'll give you a private tour. Of course, besides the sculpture garden, I'm very proud of our other collections, too."

"I've read about them—especially the cat exhibit."

"Sarah owns a cat," Emily said. "Or, maybe I should say the cat owns her."

"Cats have a way of doing that. My mother was a big cat lover. We always had a few in the house when I was a kid."

He turned so his gaze was focused on Sarah. "I remember you told me your cat is a Siamese."

She was pleasantly surprised he remembered. "That's right. What kind of cats did your mother have?"

"Anything that strayed her way."

"I know your hotel has been written up for its cat

motif and artwork collection, but do you actually permit cats here at the hotel?"

"No. Between guests who might be allergic to cat hair and health restrictions in the kitchen area, I thought it best to stick to paintings for the cats and photos for the dogs."

He glanced at his watch. "Tell you what, before we have lunch, let me give you the royal tour. Emily, I know you've seen the kitchen area, but I don't think you've taken the grand tour?"

"I haven't."

Thomas signaled the waiter, who, by how fast he arrived at the table, must have been keeping an eye on them. Unlike the valet, the waiter was an older gentleman who Sarah recognized as having previously waited on her when, in the old days, Bill took her to their favorite high-end Birmingham restaurant to celebrate her birthday or their anniversary. It had been years since she'd been to that restaurant or he'd waited on her, but she would have known him anywhere. If he was working lunch service here, tips must be good, which would speak to the volume of customers or the food prices.

"Hi, I'm Ned. I'll be serving you today. May I bring you something to drink?"

"Ned, I'm going to take these lovely ladies on the Cook's tour of the hotel. Please hold our table for us. When we come back, we'll need to place our orders."

"That won't be a problem, Mr. Howell." Ned reached to pull out Emily's chair while Thomas did the same for Sarah. As they walked from the table, Ned neatly folded their napkins over the backs of their respective chairs.

Fifteen minutes later, Sarah had to admit there wasn't another hotel in the Birmingham area comparable to the Howellian. The wine-tasting area, teaching kitchen, statue garden, art gallery, shops, conference rooms, and cat and dog exhibits were all impressive, but it was when they went through the kitchen she could see why Emily was itching to work there. Shining workspaces, multiple refrigerators, freezers, ovens, and even two dishwashing stations were to die for. Even with the limited knowledge Sarah had of restaurant kitchens, she knew this one was top of the line. Sarah couldn't imagine what it had cost to put together. What she, and she bet Emily, couldn't understand was why, with a facility like this, there was any problem with any aspect of the restaurant's operation?

Returning to their table, they were barely in their chairs when Ned reappeared to take their drink orders. After Sarah and Emily ordered water and Thomas asked for water and coffee, the three stared at their menus. When Ned returned with their drinks, they ordered: a Shrimp Louie salad for Sarah, Howellian chicken salad for Emily, and a hamburger for Thomas. Orders completed, Thomas turned the discussion to Emily's employment.

"Emily, at least for six months, more if I can twist your arm, the kitchen we just walked through would be totally yours. You'd be responsible for all food preparation for this restaurant and the hotel's room-service menu under the hotel's Howellian signature name and you'd oversee Monday to Friday delivery of food to our Wheaton commissary. Of course, I don't expect you to do this alone. We have some line cooks who, from what I understand, you can probably whip into shape, but I'll be glad to put a sous chef of your choosing on payroll."

"That sounds wonderful, but I was wondering if I could also use the kitchen, during off hours, for a limited amount of catering jobs?"

He waved his hand in the direction of the main dining room. "That's a no-brainer. We already have a catering operation through which you can handle any jobs that come your way."

Recognizing Emily and Thomas were talking about two different things and, that for some reason Emily wasn't speaking up, Sarah interjected herself into the conversation. "Emily isn't referring to catering under the Howellian name. She's talking about using the kitchen to prepare the food for some jobs contracted by Southwind customers."

Realizing she might not have phrased it in the correct terms, Sarah looked to Emily to clarify what she was trying to say. "Em? Did I explain that right?"

Emily nodded before hastening to assure Thomas it wouldn't be many jobs and only until the Southwind permits came through. Her words tumbled together as she rushed to explain how Marcus and she weren't allowed to make anything in the Southwind kitchen for public consumption until the permits came through. She concluded by declaring that the Howellian kitchen, which was approved for everything, would be a big help.

Thomas sat quietly for a few seconds and then threw a quizzical look in Emily's direction. Sarah listened to him but kept her gaze on Emily's face.

"You want to run catering jobs for two places from here?"

"Only occasionally and only until Southwind's permits come through in the next few weeks. These wouldn't be big jobs that competed with the ones the Howellian handles, only a few small dinner parties or gatherings. As you can imagine, if you permit us to do a few jobs using your kitchen, it would certainly help cash flow until Southwind reopens."

Thomas crinkled his perfectly shaped brows, causing his eyes to narrow. "It seems slightly irregular having an unrelated restaurant cooking out of my kitchen, but it's something I'm willing to consider once you take over."

Although Emily appeared satisfied with his response, Sarah wasn't. It sounded to her like catering for something other than a Howellian enterprise wouldn't get off the ground. "Will the commissary location in Wheaton also operate under your signature name and, if I may ask, won't it take more effort and time for it to be profitable than if you did something similar here in Birmingham?"

"Some." Thomas didn't reply to her first question. "But Lance and I already identified a well-trafficked location to put it in in Wheaton."

Sarah was perplexed. While trying to get the big house zoned for restaurant use, Harlan and she had been keeping tabs for the past few months of any restaurant-related applications filed in Wheaton. There wasn't one she could think of with Thomas Howell's personal or hotel name attached to it.

"Where do you propose putting this restaurant?"

"At the bank."

"Excuse me? I don't remember seeing any space approved for a restaurant in the bank building."

"It's not a restaurant. A commissary is the way office building owners often provide quick food access for their tenants. State regulations allow us to sell the food we make here in this restaurant and at one other location, without jumping through a million hoops. Although something might need to be warmed using a microwave or conveyor oven, the commissary only serves prepared things like salads, sandwiches, and yogurt and fruit cups. Nothing is cooked on-site."

"And you're going to put that into the bank?"

"Yes. Several office buildings have been built near the old bank during the past few years, including the large one that abuts the alley, but no restaurants were added to the area. Before he died, Lance and I identified a perfect spot in the back of the bank building, which had been intended, but never used, for storage. Without much modification, we decided the space would work well for a small commissary operation."

His voice rose with excited animation. "We figured low labor costs because of only needing one or two employees to man the operation. Our outlay for equipment also would be minimal: one refrigerated display case for the day's salads and sandwiches, beverage dispensers, and a one-stop counter space where customers order, pay, and pick up napkins and silver. Best of all, because the space already offers security camera–controlled access to the back alley and the bank's lobby, our only structural modifications are framing and Sheetrocking a firewall and installing another set of street doors to bypass direct entry from the lobby."

Now it was Emily's turn to be skeptical. "If I understand you correctly, you expect me to order, prepare, cook, package, and deliver, as well as handle inventory control, for all of your operations from the hotel? But what about day-to-day operations in Wheaton? Who is responsible for filling in if employees don't show up for work or the power goes out?"

"You. Of course, if you think you and Marcus aren't up for the challenge, then I guess our discussion is over." He reached for his water glass.

"It isn't the challenge. You simply added more than I thought you were proposing, so it will take some additional planning, but I think Marcus and I can handle this."

Scared her sister was setting herself up for failure by forgetting she was only one person, Sarah decided it was better to raise her concerns now instead of after the fact. "Maybe I'm butting in here, especially because being in a kitchen frightens me, but this still seems like a big undertaking to me."

Emily laughed, but, to Sarah's ears, it sounded forced. "Sarah, people run different restaurants all the time. Isn't that what Marcus and I are looking to do in Wheaton? It's simply a matter of organization and delegation."

Sarah stared at Thomas, who steadily met her gaze. "But other than the sous chef, you're not providing more personnel, are you?"

"That's where the partnership with Southwind and its employees comes into play."

This was beginning to sound to Sarah more and

more like Marcus's prediction. Southwind would do the work and Thomas would take the credit. "Will the food at the commissary location be labeled as coming from Southwind or under the hotel's logo?"

Emily leaned forward to catch Thomas's response to Sarah's question.

He cleared his throat and frowned. "I'd planned on doing it under the Howellian logo, but I guess, with what you pointed out, we'll have to design a new joint logo."

Sarah glanced at her sister. Despite his hesitation and sidestepping, Emily still bobbed her head in full agreement with him. She seemed to be having no problem with any of the red-flag issues bothering Sarah. Perhaps Emily was too excited at the opportunity to help Marcus or to have a chance to prepare food in this state-of-the-art kitchen. Or maybe it was Sarah who was overreacting. Em might simply be comfortable because, being in the business, she knew the things that seemed odd to Sarah were standard operating procedures.

In the face of Emily's positive attitude, it was difficult for Sarah to be defensive on her sister's behalf. It was even harder balancing a sense of wariness of Thomas's comments with the desire to become better acquainted with him. She had a feeling it would be nice if his flashing a smile was directed only at her. She willed herself to focus on the discussion. Her purpose for attending this lunch was to be her sister's advocate, not to snag a date.

"Wouldn't it simply be easier to use the Southwind logo at this location, too? After all, it has a respectable following in Wheaton."

"True, but restaurants go in and out, have fires, and, if Southwind's quality or popularity diminishes, it could and would impact the commissary. Better to come up with a new logo incorporating a reference to the Howellian, too."

Sarah couldn't resist pushing back at his argument. "But don't hotels change ownership, go up and down in the rankings, and lose popularity as they age?"

"That's not going to happen in the class the Howellian falls into. Multidiamond or star establishments strive to maintain their achievement levels."

Sarah couldn't help sparring with him. "We all strive for things but don't always accomplish them."

"But that's when one most needs to redirect one's efforts. We received a wonderful star rating for our hotel accommodations, but our restaurant needs improvement for us to attain the rating I want." Thomas reached out and put his hand over hers, while glancing at Emily. "Sarah, I know you have your sister's best interests at heart. I do, too. Trust me. This arrangement will be a win-win situation for all of us."

"I hope so."

"I know so."

Sarah didn't move her hand, but she glanced around the restaurant rather than at him. She hadn't realized both rooms had filled up with customers. Here and there she recognized familiar faces. Her gaze stopped at a terrace table where Jacob, his sister, and Mr. Bailey, from the bank, were engrossed in conversation. She couldn't imagine the three were good buddies, so she wondered if it was bank, development, or city business bringing them together today. Seeing

Mr. Bailey also reminded her she needed to find a time to check on Eloise.

Thomas's abrupt removal of his hand from hers brought her attention back to their table.

A shadow loomed over it. She looked up. Cliff's hulking presence filled their alcove as he bent forward and thrust his finger into Thomas's chest. "I should take you outside and beat the crap out of you."

CHAPTER SIXTEEN

Thomas pulled back. "Are you out of your mind? Can't you see I'm having lunch with these lovely ladies?" He glanced at his watch. "If you want to meet me in my office in an hour . . ."

"No. This can't wait. We need to talk about Uncle George now." Cliff spread his legs in a wide stance as he moved closer to Thomas's portion of the table, his fists clenched.

Although his tight blue jeans and suede-elbowed sports coat should have made him blend into the lunchtime crowd, the way he inched into Thomas's space went against the cultivated image of the restaurant. Sarah shuddered as Thomas abruptly stood, almost clipping Cliff's nose.

The two men scowled at each other. With slight body shifts, they danced around in the alcove's limited space, much like boxers prepping for one to throw the first punch. While Sarah debated whether to intervene verbally or physically, using her body as a buffer between the two men, she stole a glance at her twin. Emily's mouth was slightly open, and her hand was braced on the table. Sarah bet the same thoughts she was having were going through Emily's mind, but neither said anything.

Turning away from Cliff, Thomas dropped his napkin on his chair and rearranged his features from scowling to smiling. "Ladies, I apologize. I don't know if you've had the pleasure of meeting my brother."

Sarah opened her mouth, but nothing came out. Cliff Rogers and Thomas Howell were brothers? It didn't compute. She finally sputtered out a few words. "You're brothers?"

Thomas grinned in Cliff's direction, but Sarah noticed neither Cliff's expression nor his clenched fists had changed. "Sons of a different father, but we both claim the same dear mother, for whatever good that did either of us."

Sarah glanced at Cliff. He reminded her of a firecracker about to blow.

"As you can see," Thomas said, "Cliff's the more emotional one. If you two will excuse me, I'm afraid I need to deal with this interruption."

Thomas pointed to where Ned stood just outside the alcove, having rested a serving tray with their food on a collapsible stand. "I'm glad we already took the tour. No telling how long this is going to take, but please enjoy the remainder of your lunch and walk around the hotel afterward as my guests. Emily, I'll call you later. I think we covered almost everything, but why don't you two continue to talk, and if you have more questions, we can discuss them then. Sarah, it was a pleasure getting to know you. I hope our paths cross again in the very near future. Now, please excuse me."

Thomas flipped his hand over in the universal

"after you" gesture. Sarah wasn't sure if Cliff was going to go peacefully, but he did. Once the brothers left, Ned promptly stepped into the alcove and placed Sarah and Emily's food in front of them. Sarah looked behind him to where he'd left Thomas's plated hamburger on the serving tray. She hoped it wouldn't go to waste.

Ned hovered at the side of their table. "Is there anything else I can get you now?"

Sarah looked at Emily, already tasting and analyzing her Howellian chicken salad. "No, thank you." She waited until Ned was out of earshot before poking around her plate with her fork while asking her sister how the chicken salad was.

"It needs seasoning and more chicken. Too much mayonnaise. How's the Shrimp Louie?"

Sarah took a taste and put her fork on the table. "This isn't something I'd order again. Besides feeling like it's a treasure hunt to find a shrimp, it tastes funny."

She pushed her plate toward Emily, who stabbed a bite.

After another taste, Emily passed the plate back to Sarah. "The shrimp not only is nonexistent, but it isn't fresh. In fact, I don't even think they fully defrosted what they used. Skimping on the main protein is guaranteed to produce unhappy customers. I can assure you that won't be the case when I take over."

"Whoa! Emily, don't you think you're jumping into this? I know finances are tight, but I'm getting a bad feeling about the things Thomas wants you to do."

"Sarah, I know you're worried about me, but don't be. There's nothing Thomas said that's any different than being an executive chef elsewhere. Lots of balls in the air."

"But it seems you have a lot of moving parts here. Between the pub and the fine-dining concepts for Southwind, the restaurant and room service here, and a commissary that is going to have to be handled without your direct supervision, I'm afraid you're spreading yourself too thin."

"For six months, I can handle it."

"What if you drop one of the balls? Won't that impact your name and Southwind? Aren't those your priority? And if you do succeed, won't that promote the Howellian name instead of yours? Maybe Marcus was right?"

Emily didn't answer.

Sarah tried again. "Look around this hotel. Despite its opulence, I get the distinct feeling Thomas Howell cut corners with his restaurant or it would be a success, too."

"Even the best establishments can have bad restaurants if everything doesn't jibe."

"But why put yourself in that position? You don't have to. You have so much going on in Wheaton, why take a chance of tainting it with this? Look, let's enjoy the parts of our lunch that are edible and take a quick peek into the jewelry store off the gallery before I go back to work. You can chalk this up as another life experience."

Emily put her fork down. "Sarah, stop. I'm going to do this. I think I can make a difference here that will reflect positively on Southwind and me in the long run."

Sarah stared at her sister. Emily seemed beyond

listening to reason. "At least will you let Harlan and Marcus, instead of me, attend further meetings with you and go over any contract Thomas proposes before you agree to anything?"

"That really isn't necessary. I told you. I can handle this. Sarah, I've seen enough restaurant employment contracts that I don't need to pay an attorney to review one anymore."

"I know you have plenty of experience, but Harlan offered to review any contract Thomas and you hashed out for free. Why not take him up on his offer? It would make me feel better. Pretty please?"

"What are we, back to being five? Pretty please with sugar on it?"

"If that's what it takes."

Emily laughed. "Okay, I'll let Harlan look at the contract."

Sarah debated whether to continue the conversation or simply give up. There were pros and cons to both sides, but, considering the reason she'd been invited to the lunch, she knew she couldn't simply look the other way. She had an obligation to play devil's advocate.

"Emily, it seems like you're leaving Marcus with more of a burden. I mean, he's going to have to deal with the rest of the buildouts, plus find financing."

Although Emily shook her head in the negative, Sarah pressed on. "You're the one who told me after you paid off the share of Southwind my ex gave Jane that Marcus and you were short of money to open the pub, let alone the fine-dining establishment."

"That was yesterday."

Sarah was confused. Where had she been to miss something this important? "Did Bailey approve your loan after Lance was killed?"

"No, but after a lot of talking and being talked to, Marcus and I were convinced to take in a minority stockholder late last night. This partner wants no say in the business, only repayment of the initial investment plus a set interest amount either when the pub is on its feet or when both establishments are profitable."

Remembering Marcus's choice of partners in the past included such winners as her ex-husband and his bimbo, Jane, Sarah immediately felt skeptical about this turn of events.

"Investors usually don't do things without definite payback dates or maintaining some control until fully paid back. You remember how it was when the rat was your partner? Have you checked this person out?"

"We didn't think it was necessary."

Sarah inwardly groaned. "Emily, you're a great cook, but I'm beginning to question your business savvy. Look, it's easy to make bad decisions when you're jumping from famine to feast, and Marcus and you have had a lot on your plates, but greed and business change people."

"Oh, I hope Mother doesn't change much. I'm just getting used to calling her Maybelle."

Sarah started to say something and then realization dawned on her. She cracked up and Emily followed suit. "You had me going, again."

"Yes, I did." Emily gasped between peals of laughter. "Mother or Maybelle sat us down last night and made it perfectly clear this was a business deal. A little loosey goosey, but her terms were simple: she wants her money back and she wants us to succeed. We debated it, but the reality is, she's the answer to our prayers."

"So why complicate things with this hotel job?

Emily stared at her hands. "I need it for me."

Sarah looked at her sister. All the years her sister had been the popular slender blond cheerleader, Sarah never thought Emily had a doubt in the world. For the first time, Sarah saw through the veneer. As accomplished as Emily was in the culinary world, she was as insecure as Sarah often felt. Understanding her twin was no different than she was, Sarah's concerns, other than the toll it might take on Emily's energy and time, evaporated. "Well, I guess I better help you with your research. Shall we order dessert?"

Chapter Seventeen

When Ned placed their desserts in front of them, Sarah felt a pang of calorie guilt. Normally, Emily and she skipped dessert or shared one, but because they were eating on Thomas's dime and Emily was ostensibly researching everything the kitchen put out, they splurged. Happily so. The desserts, in Sarah's opinion, were the best part of the meal. Apparently, Emily agreed with her. She told Sarah the pastry chef would stay under her new regime. They were both licking their forks when Thomas, sans Cliff, rushed to their table.

"I'm glad you're still here." He grabbed one of the chairs and turned it around so he could straddle it. He angled himself to primarily face Emily. "I'm sorry you had to see that little display of family discord. We haven't been seeing eye to eye on an extended-family matter, but that's not what I need to discuss with you. Another kitchen issue has come up and I wondered, or should I say hoped, you would help me out."

"What's the problem?"

Thomas looked from Emily to Sarah and down at the floor. "I didn't handle things too well."

The twins looked at him, waiting for more of an explanation.

With one of his perfectly manicured hands, he brushed an immobile piece of hair from his forehead. "I was so excited and positive after our lunch, I shared our potential plans with my acting chef and he up and quit."

"What? How could you say anything to your present chef when Emily and you don't have a deal yet?"

Thomas cocked his head downward. "I got excited and wasn't thinking. Besides, he was doing the job in an acting capacity, and, as I'm sure you tasted, it came across in his food." He raised his head and flashed them a sheepish grin. "My excitement at you joining the Howellian family, whether for a limited time or indefinitely, overtook my reasoning. Maybe I did get some of Mother's emotional genes."

He flashed his perfect white teeth in Emily's direction. "Anyway, I hope your ears were burning when I bragged on you, Emily. I said some very nice things about your cooking being Michelin level without really assessing how my words were coming across. By the time I realized he wasn't taking too kindly to the idea of being replaced, he'd quit."

"We don't have to go forward with my hiring. You're welcome to forget our discussion and go after him."

He waved his hand. "I don't want him back. You're the one who is going to take the Howellian to the next level."

Emily blushed.

"I know we haven't ironed out all the contractual details, but is there any possibility you could start today or tomorrow morning? We have several jobs on tap for the end of the week, and it doesn't appear he did anything to prepare for them."

"Of course."

"Em." Sarah tried to catch her sister's attention to slow down her acceptance. She wished she could make her sister understand his desperate need for immediate help gave them bargaining chips, but there was no stopping this train wreck.

Thomas was already on his feet pumping Emily's hand in agreement and appreciation. Other than catching that one of the jobs was Friday's meal after Lance Knowlton's funeral, none of the other functions mentioned for the next few days made an impression on Sarah. What did strike her was how fast Emily agreed to run home, change, and return in a few hours to take control of the kitchen without a second thought to Marcus, a formal employment contract, or her promise to make the refreshments for tomorrow's animal-shelter meeting. Sarah didn't know which one to worry the most about, but she hoped the people coming to the meeting would like brownies from a mix or her velvet chocolate pie.

"This is wonderful," Thomas said. "You're a life-saver. I've got to run to put out another fire, but have the front desk page me when you get back. Okay?"

Emily nodded as he left them for the second time. She immediately began gathering her things together to leave. Sarah didn't move.

"Sarah, don't you have to get back to work?"

"I do, but I think we need to talk for a minute."

"I really don't have time right now."

"Make time." Sarah pointed to the chair Emily had vacated, but Emily remained standing.

"Well?"

"Well, what's gotten into you? You remind me of a horse champing at the bit to start a race. You know how much that catering job meant to Marcus, both in terms of prestige and money, but rather than let it collapse in Thomas's lap or suggest a duo catering role, you're jumping in to save the day under what I'm sure is going to be labeled a Howellian job."

"Is that all you have to say? Thank you for your concern. I'll handle this. Let's go."

Sarah banged her hand on the table. "I'm not ready to go, yet. Don't you realize you're behaving like Jane used to at Southwind? High and mighty and not thinking of the feelings of others. What kind of morale do you expect to find in the kitchen if they know Thomas fired their boss for you?"

"Their boss quit. It happens all the time."

"Sorry, I don't buy it. Whatever bug Cliff got under Thomas's skin, I'll bet Thomas took it out on his executive chef. Most chefs don't quit in the middle of lunch service. This wasn't a normal parting of the ways."

"I don't care. Look, I told you I'm going to do this for six months. If getting Thomas Howell through this weekend with flying colors gains me some brownie points, I'm all in favor of it. Things go wrong in kitchens and some will go wrong under me, but if I have some goodwill in the bank going into one of those bad days, more power to me."

"But what about my meeting? If you're tied up here

starting today, how are Grace and you going to handle the refreshments? Should I go get a brownie mix?"

"Don't worry. We'll whip up a few things or I'll send you two recipes tonight for some really simple treats."

Sarah shuddered. She hated the word "simple" because she knew even a simple treat wasn't going to be simple in her hands. The guys had nailed it at the meeting. If there was a stove or oven involved with Sarah, people should flee for their safety or, at least, keep a fire extinguisher handy.

Emily stood. "I've got to run. Coming?"

"In a moment. I want to finish my coffee first. Love you."

"Love you, too. Even if you can be a Debbie Downer." Emily bent over and gave her sister a parting peck. She left smiling.

Sarah couldn't say the same about her own lips. She felt sure, as she reached for her coffee, they were pointed downward. Before she could bring the coffee to her frowning mouth, Ned refreshed it. Even with her sister and Thomas Howell gone, Ned was still on duty, attentive to her needs.

Drinking her coffee, she let her mind wander. Sometimes letting her brain go where it wanted helped her gain insight into situations she had no answer for. Hopefully, today would be one of those times. There wasn't anything she could do to change her sister's seemingly out-of-character spontaneity and odd behavior toward Marcus and Southwind. Thinking of those two made her realize that if Southwind came out losing because of Emily's actions, her mother, now being a partner, would also lose.

That was another strange thing. Her mother, who

usually ran over at the mouth, hadn't told her about the silent partnership, which was out of character. Maybe the moon or Mercury was in retrograde. The world definitely was out of whack. No matter, whatever Emily, their mother, or anyone else was up to, Sarah vowed to protect her mother.

Finishing her coffee, Sarah observed the terraced area and the dining room from the seclusion of her table one last time. To her surprise, she saw the third person at Anne and Jacob Hightower's table had changed. Bailey was gone. Thomas sat in his seat. Apparently, his burning fire had petered out. From the shared wine in their glasses and the ease with which they all were laughing, it didn't much look like work talk. In fact, Thomas Howell didn't appear to have a care in the world.

CHAPTER EIGHTEEN

Realizing she'd been gone from the office for almost three hours, Sarah hurried back to work. She felt a little guilty that there was no time today to stop at home to play with RahRah or to have made a little time to really look for Fluffy for Mr. Rogers. One of the advantages of living in a small town like Wheaton, where Harlan's office was only a few blocks from the carriage house, was the ability to go home for lunch.

Sarah knew most working pet owners left their animals home alone during the day, but she'd vowed as far back as her childhood to only have a pet if she didn't have to be one of those people. Instead, she'd announced to her family she would devote her extra time and love to shelter animals. She'd kept her promise until her ex-husband's mother died and made Sarah the de facto owner of RahRah. Now she couldn't imagine life without RahRah.

She still would have snuck home for a few extra minutes because Harlan knew this was going to be an extended lunch hour, but there were too many things she wanted to discuss with him. Unless he'd added an appointment, his calendar should be free for at least the next hour.

Happily, the office waiting room was empty and there was a faint twang of country music coming from his office. That was good, because it meant he was alone. He never played background music when he conferred with a client.

Hand up to knock on his door, she paused and listened to his music choice. She'd learned she could predict her workload by identifying what he was working on based upon the tempo of the music he played. He'd never admit it, but he was consistent in his musical choices. Harlan researched and wrote briefs to ballads and motions and shorter pleadings to more upbeat songs. Today's song was fast and peppy, which meant he would be less intense when she interrupted him.

She knocked and called his name through the door. Acknowledged, she turned the knob and walked in. "Harlan, why didn't you tell me Thomas and Cliff are brothers?"

"You didn't ask. Besides, I thought you knew. After all, you're the one who lives across the street from George."

"When I lived in the big house with Bill, we didn't have much to do with the Rogers family. I don't remember why or what it was about, but Bill was crossways with them."

"Sounds like your ex."

Sarah smiled while taking a seat on his leather couch. "Yeah, the rat was good at doing that. Anyway, other than saying hello to Mrs. Rogers and complimenting her on her garden, I rarely saw either of them or their guests. I moved into my studio apartment almost immediately after Bill asked for the divorce. By the time I came back to care for RahRah in the carriage house, I discovered Mrs. Rogers had died and Mr. Rogers was the neighborhood's darling eccentric."

"And the uncle of two nephews, Cliff and Thomas."

"That fact eluded me. When Mr. Rogers was here, I thought his rotten nephew was Cliff, but now I'm confused."

"Why?"

Sarah told Harlan what had happened between the brothers at the Howellian. "From how Cliff threatened Thomas, I'm not sure George was worried about Cliff trying to move him to a retirement home."

"He's not. George would have no problem if Cliff were his only nephew."

Harlan came around his desk and took his favorite wingback chair. He propped his cowboy-booted feet on the coffee table in the conversation area he'd created. "Although Cliff is a big proponent for developing Main Street, he has no desire to kick George out of his house. He probably can imagine a million possible uses for George's property, but he's made it clear he can wait for his uncle to voluntarily vacate the property with or without his boots on." He raised his feet from the table and wiggled the toes of his boots in the air.

Sarah groaned at his immature behavior. "For a guy who has his hands full in Birmingham, why does Thomas want to kick his uncle out of his home?"

"I could say it's because we're a growing bedroom community of Birmingham."

"You could, but you know the growth is going out Highway 280."

Harlan put his feet on the floor, which Sarah knew was a dead giveaway that he once again was Harlan Endicott, serious lawyer. "His hotel looks opulent, but it has been a money pit. He may have some ideas to sell it and go into a smaller venture, or he may be looking for more investors to bail him out."

"But he said they've had a great occupancy rate."

"He's telling the truth on that, but areas like the model kitchen, wine tasting, and restaurant aren't pulling their weight. He's playing a dangerous game."

"What's that?"

"In one breath, he's playing up to the redevelopment advocates, but his long-range goal, for developing his uncle's land and whether he can keep the How-ellian afloat, requires financing. He tapped out most financing resources building it, but he's managed to keep Lance's bank and supposedly a group of Wheaton investors behind him, up to now."

"So he was willing to do anything Lance wanted while Lance was alive, but now?"

"I don't know."

"What kind of relationship can he expect with Bailey by the Book?"

"I think Bailey has some leeway, but instead of Lance, he'll have the board and shareholders looking over his shoulder determining if the decisions he makes are good for the bank."

"The way you explain it, I can understand him kow-towing to Bailey, but if he wants to develop his uncle's land, why would he be courting the Hightowers?"

"What do you mean?"

"After he left us, he joined Anne and Jacob at their table. The three looked quite chummy."

"I haven't heard anything about him trying to partner with any of the Hightowers, but I wouldn't be surprised. He's not one to let grass grow under his feet. Maybe he's trying to court Anne's vote for any future development he makes in Wheaton, especially if she wins the next mayoral election."

"That makes sense. Jacob was at the table, but my impression was Thomas was playing up to Anne." She filled him in on what she'd observed in the Terrace room. "Tell me, though, why do you think the Hightowers were having lunch with Bailey?"

"Probably to discuss banking business. He has been named the acting president of the bank."

"What?" She thought for a moment. "Maybe that's why he looked so bad. I swear he was even paler than the last time I saw him."

"Could be. He's got a lot on his plate. Not only is he in charge of the general operations of the bank, but he's still handling most of the loans. I'm sure, like our acting police chief, he wants to make good."

"Does Bailey have competition?"

"Sarah, everyone has competition. Though, in the bank, after Lance, Bailey probably is the most knowledgeable. He's been handling the loans and most of the big deals and customers since Lance got so busy with the city council. With our bank being a community bank rather than part of a larger group, its board is extremely sensitive to the opinions and feelings of its investors and patrons. After finding out Lance was murdered in his supposedly locked office, they know a lot of folks are skittish. That's why the board decided it would be a good move to name someone everyone knows as acting president. Bailey is sort of the comfort-food choice."

Sarah nodded. It made sense. "I'm sure Eloise can help him. According to my mother, she's been there almost the same amount of time as Lance was. She's cool under pressure, and I bet she not only knows everyone, but she knows where their skeletons are buried. Still, what about those who haven't had good experiences with Bailey-made decisions? I can easily think of a few: my mother, Emily, Marcus, and Cliff."

"The consensus is the few dissatisfied customers like your mother are in the minority and unlikely to make any kind of fuss. Instead, they'll look elsewhere for financing. The loss of a few accounts a year is expected."

Sarah knew Harlan was right. Rather than making a formal protest, her mother would simply move her accounts. "Is there a chance he could get the job permanently?"

Before Harlan answered, the office line ringing interrupted them. Sarah jumped up to run to her desk to grab her phone before the answering machine kicked in, but Harlan pointed at the extension on his desk. She grabbed his receiver. "Endicott and Associates. May I help you?"

Sarah listened to the voice on the other end of the call, thinking if callers ever wondered who the associates were. "Yes, sir. He's here. I'll put you through to him immediately."

She pushed the button to put the call on hold and held the receiver out to Harlan. "It's Chief Gerard."

CHAPTER NINETEEN

Sarah's uncertainty about whether to remain in Harlan's office while he took the call or leave, closing the door, was taken out of her hands when the second line rang. As she hurried to her desk before the answering machine intercepted the call, she hoped Chief Gerard's conversation with Harlan wasn't the harbinger of bad things for her mother.

"Endicott and Associates. May I help you?"

"Sarah, I need your help."

Hearing her sister's plea for help immediately conjured a memory of four months ago, but she couldn't imagine things had gone so wrong since they parted company at the Howellian. "What's going on?"

"I'm at the restaurant and things are worse than I imagined. There's hardly any staff here."

"Did they all quit with the chef?"

"No. They've been running short-staffed since the day they opened. From what I can gather, everyone has been doing double duty as line cooks, servers, and even dishwashers."

"You're going to have to take up the personnel

issues with Thomas. Sounds like he's been cutting costs by minimizing his staff. You can't work that way."

"And I don't intend to, but we have to get through Lance's funeral this week. It's scheduled for Friday afternoon at four."

"To avoid disrupting most of the workday."

"You got it. Grace is going to help me, and the folks who are here are all in, but there's no way I'll have enough people to staff the funeral reception."

"Maybe I didn't make myself clear enough. This is the time to negotiate with Thomas. If you hadn't jumped to say 'yes,' you had him where you could have gotten some concessions in terms of using his kitchen and personnel and sharing jobs with Southwind. Better late than never. You can couch it in terms of him not having egg on his face."

"I can't do that. I told him I'd handle this, and I will."

"How? Are you going to ask Marcus for help?"

"No. That's out of the question. The Wheaton city council won't meet until next Tuesday, so because I know Southwind won't be able to open at the earliest until next week, I called a few of its staff to help out."

"You don't think Marcus is going to be mad at you using Southwind's staff?"

"Not as long as Southwind isn't open. Remember, he's only paying a part of their usual wages, so he may be mad at me, but he'd never begrudge our dishwasher and a few members of the waitstaff a chance to make a little extra money, even if it is under the Howellian umbrella."

"Well, then let me ask you, how do you think you're going to get Thomas to pay for these people? After all, if he's been skimping on staff, why should this event be different?"

"Because he's getting a good fee for this reception and the extra dishwasher and waitstaff hours are add-on expenses he can pass on to Lance's family. Grace, as my sous chef, and the two people who already were on Thomas's payroll as designated line cooks will be doing what they were hired to do. That means they won't be adding to the ongoing Howellian payroll."

"And you need my help to . . ."

"I don't have enough servers. I was hoping you'd help me out like you did at the food expo. You'll get paid for your hours worked."

"Did you happen to forget I have a job and my hours call for me to work on Fridays? Besides, think back to the food expo. My talents as a server aren't much better than my efforts in a kitchen."

"Sarah, I know you work, but I can't imagine Harlan won't let you come to the funeral. By the time the service ends, no one will be going back to work. And, of all people, Harlan won't expect you to make up the time you attend the service. If you wear a white shirt and black pants or a black skirt, you can stow your purse and earn a few dollars."

"Surely you can find someone who isn't going to drop a tray or do anything else equally disastrous."

"Considering how much you hate anything to do with the food industry, I wouldn't be begging if I wasn't desperate. Please."

"Is that with sugar on it?" When Emily didn't pick up on their running joke, Sarah realized Emily was beyond finding any humor in this situation. "Sure, I'll do it, but only if you understand the risks and danger your guests may experience."

"Believe me, I'm desperate enough to take that chance."

After she hung up, Sarah realized neither of them had mentioned the refreshments for tomorrow night's YipYeow planning meeting. Considering how swept up she'd been in the moment of their discussion, Sarah understood why, at lunch, Emily latched onto the details of the Howellian job as Thomas explained them rather than negotiating a better deal. Emotions could really cloud reasoning. It made her appreciate Harlan's ability as a lawyer and a person who remained analytical even when emotions ran high.

She glanced at the base of her office phone. The button for the other line was still lit. She doubted there was anything good about this conversation between Harlan and Chief Gerard. It was too long. As she fretted, the light went out. Rather than waiting for Harlan to summon her or come out of his office, she went to his door and pushed it open. "Well? Was the call about my mother?"

Chapter Twenty

Harlan didn't answer. Instead, he walked around his desk until he stood in front of her. "Sarah, it isn't good. We'll figure it out, but Dwayne has your mother in his sights. He wants me to have her turn herself in."

She stepped backward and stumbled. He moved quickly to steady her but then turned away from her as her words flew. "That's ridiculous! She didn't do anything. Harlan, you've got to make him understand."

With sagging shoulders, he faced her again. "Sarah, I tried. That's why we were on the phone so long."

"Well, he's being unreasonable. You'll have to try again."

"You don't have to yell at me. I'm in the same corner as your mother and you. We're just going to have to cast more doubt on what he thinks is his evidence against Maybelle."

Sarah lowered her voice as she slid onto Harlan's leather couch. She leaned forward to where he still stood. "What evidence does the chief think he has against my mother?"

"Fingerprints."

"Fingerprints?"

"Hers are the only ones on the finial."

"That's impossible."

"Why?" Harlan sat on the couch next to her. He cocked his head toward her.

"It might not have the fingerprints of whoever bashed my fence because I think they used a bat or something like that, and Mom's fingerprints would have gotten on it when she picked it up on Main Street, but Cliff's should be on it, too. When he knocked everything off Mr. Knowlton's desk, the finial had to be one of the things that fell to the floor. He put the things that fell back in her purse or on the desk. Because he held it, his fingerprints should be on it."

"How can you be sure? Maybe it still was in her pocketbook or he overlooked it when he picked things up. Either way, Cliff's fingerprints wouldn't be on it."

Sarah shut her eyes and thought for a moment before opening them again. "I distinctly remember my mother taking it out of her purse and placing it on the desk. She did the same with her glasses, passbook, and telephone."

She bent her head and concentrated again.

Harlan didn't interrupt her thought process.

Sarah looked up and smiled. "Harlan, she never put the finial back in her purse."

"How can you be sure?"

"Because Maybelle took all those things out, and while she put the glasses back in her purse and used the bankbook and her phone to make points, she wasn't paying attention to the fence top. She left that sitting on his desk while she was sparring with Mr. Knowlton. It had to be one of the things Cliff knocked to the floor and picked up. If they're not, it proves someone wiped it clean after killing Mr. Knowlton and my mother handled it when she found him."

Harlan rubbed the back of his neck. "That's going to be hard to prove."

"Cliff should be able to confirm what I'm saying."

Harlan grimaced. "Which would mean he incriminates himself?"

Sarah slumped against the back of the couch. "I didn't think of that. Surely, Cliff will tell the truth."

"He won't lie, but, considering the heat of the moment when he burst into Lance's office, Cliff may not remember what he touched, what actually fell, or where he put anything he knocked off the desk. Wasn't he focused on Lance?"

Sarah nodded, remembering the force with which Cliff exploded into the office and the absolute hatred she'd felt in the look she'd seen Cliff and Lance exchange. She pushed it from her mind and concentrated on what might help her mother. "But what I saw and his memory aren't our only hope to cast doubt on the chief's theory. What about the security tapes?"

"Apparently, there's a problem with them."

"What?"

"I don't know. Dwayne indicated the lab still is working on them, but he wants to talk to her again. My feeling is he thinks he's close to having enough evidence to make a case against her. That's why I want to talk to your mother before he questions her again."

"Do you want me to call her to come into the office?"

"No. I told the chief she was in Birmingham and that, at best, it would be a few hours until she could get to Wheaton to meet with him. I need time to go over all of this with her, and I don't want to lie to Dwayne. Consequently, I'd rather go to Birmingham to talk to her and then, if she agrees, bring her back with me."

"Well, at least we should call her and put her on notice we're coming."

Harlan stopped her reaching for the phone. "On notice that I'm coming."

Sarah jerked her chin up and stared at Harlan, whose lips were pressed together. "I don't understand. Why aren't you letting me go, too? She's my mother."

"I'm aware of that. Dwayne's going to play your stories off each other. You've told me what you remember, but I need to know what your mother is going to say uncolored by your recollection. I'm sure you can find something to do here for the few hours until you close up." He pointed a finger at her. "And don't get any ideas about coming to Birmingham after work. Keep your cell by you. I'll let you know when we're on our way back to town. Now, let me give your mother a call."

CHAPTER TWENTY-ONE

After she was positive Harlan was gone and wouldn't be returning for something he'd forgotten, Sarah grabbed her purse. She made sure the answering machine was on, the lights off, and the door locked behind her. She'd promised Harlan not to come to Birmingham or to talk to her mother until after he did, but she couldn't sit and do nothing while her mother was being framed. Sarah didn't know how to get in touch with Cliff to see what he remembered, but there was one more person who might have been in and out of Mr. Knowlton's office or would know if anyone else had. Eloise.

Harlan and she hadn't discussed finding out what Eloise knew or what information she'd given Chief Gerard in her statement, but it made perfect sense to Sarah. Just like she knew more about Harlan's business and visitors than he realized, Eloise, as keeper of the gate for so many years, had to be familiar with where the bodies were buried in the bank. Sarah felt guilty shutting down Harlan's office early, but, with the bank lobby closing at five tonight, Sarah couldn't wait until she got off work. Hopefully she'd learn something that would help Harlan identify another suspect other than Maybelle.

At the bank, a young security guard she didn't recognize opened the door for her. She was disappointed not to see Alvin again but assumed he was at his regular day job. The other alternative, which she hoped wasn't the case, was that because the murder happened on his guard shift, the security service had replaced him.

Unlike how she customarily strolled through the lobby, enjoying the comfort its décor brought her, she didn't have time for that today. As she approached Eloise's desk, she stopped dead in her tracks. The blond teller from the other day was sitting there.

"May I help you?"

Sarah glanced at the nameplate sitting on the desk. Amanda Taylor. Even before she saw it didn't have Eloise's name on it, Sarah guessed from the woman's demeanor and how she picked up and played with a pen, this now was her desk.

Amanda Taylor smiled pleasantly at Sarah as she asked again. "May I help you, Mrs. Blair?"

Sarah slightly recoiled, surprised Amanda knew her name.

"I hope I didn't scare you. I recognize you from being in the bank the other day. I was working as a teller then."

"Um, I was looking for Eloise." Sarah peered around the lobby, but she didn't see Eloise. She pointed to the nameplate. "Congratulations on your promotion, Ms. Taylor. Is Eloise still with the bank?"

"Of course. She's a pillar here, but Mr. Bailey thought it would be easier for her not to be at this desk anymore. He's letting her use his old office until they decide exactly what she's going to be doing. May I help you with something?"

"No, thank you. I was walking by the bank and thought I'd pop in and say 'Hello' to her. My parents and I have known her forever. Is she in?"

Ms. Taylor gestured toward Mr. Bailey's former office. "I believe so. I didn't see her leave. If there's anything else I can help you with . . ."

"Thank you, but that's all I need today." Sarah smiled at Ms. Taylor. She kept the smile pasted on her face while she knocked and entered Bailey's former office. As she closed the door, Eloise turned away from the office's single hung window. The Eloise facing Sarah was the Eloise Sarah knew, welcoming expression, perfect makeup and hair, a St. John knit suit, and Chanel No. 5.

"Sarah, how nice to see you. Won't you sit down?" Eloise pointed to the two guest chairs facing the desk. "What can I help you with today?"

"Nothing. I came by to see how you are."

For a second, Sarah thought she saw a crack in Eloise's façade, but the instance was too fleeting to know if she'd imagined the kindly look slipping.

"How sweet of you." From where she stood by the window, Eloise gestured around the office with her hand. "As you can see, I'm still here."

Sarah joined her by the window. She was surprised it hadn't been updated like those near the front door, but she could see it was outfitted with alarm sensors and wiring. There wasn't much to be seen from the window except the next-door office building and a portion of the alley that was a drop closer to the city square than Lance's office.

Eloise peered out the window again, her profile all Sarah could clearly see. "Hard to believe the offices on this side once had the best view from the bank, isn't it?"

Even though she doubted Eloise was paying attention to her, Sarah nodded.

"When the bank was built, the main entrance and a hitching post for customers' horses faced the city square. The land on this side of the bank was undeveloped. From the windows on this side of the building, the view was rolling grassland, thick tree clusters, and the bluff in the distance. The trees and the bluff blocked seeing the river, but people knew it was there."

"With that kind of scenery outside my window, I'd have had trouble getting anything accomplished," Sarah said.

"I would have, too, but people did. The staff back then was minimal." She slipped past Sarah and sat in one of the guest chairs. She motioned for Sarah to take the matching one.

"Don't get me wrong, I always loved being able to see what was going on in the lobby and being close enough to keep up with Mr. Knowlton's customers and their needs, but an office with a window would have been nice."

Sarah took a better look at the well-coiffed woman who'd been with the bank as long as she could remember.

"Well, I finally get my window, at least temporarily, and you know what I've been thinking for the last hour?" Eloise didn't wait for an answer. "I've been thinking that building is so close to this one and casts such a shadow, this window would probably be more pleasant if it was covered with closed drapes."

"I guess Mr. Bailey didn't care about the view. As pale as he is, he probably preferred not worrying about sunlight streaming into his office."

"Probably. In all the years I've worked here, he had this office the longest and was the only one who never complained. Most people couldn't wait to get out of it."

"I can understand why." Sarah shuddered as a cloud passed, making the space feel even colder and darker. This time, Eloise did grimace.

"Mr. Knowlton always teased Mr. Bailey about secretly being a vampire because of his comfort with this office and the fact he enjoyed spending his daylight hours with his nose in his files."

"Surely that was a work ethic both Mr. Knowlton and you appreciated."

Eloise threw her a quizzical look. "You might say that, but enough of that. I can't say much about work ethic since you caught me daydreaming by the window. Guess I'll have plenty of time to daydream soon enough, though. The bank is officially giving me a buyout."

"Without a choice? When?"

"The end of the month."

"Why?"

"Mr. Bailey thinks it best for everyone." She snorted. "I guess I'm a little too old school. Computers and all are wonderful, but Lance preferred me to periodically reconcile some of our reports manually. When I explained Lance's procedure to Mr. Bailey, he told me in no uncertain terms that's not the way of the world anymore."

"What will you do?"

"I don't know yet. I'm sure something will come along. My hair may be gray, and I may be something of a dinosaur, but I'm not ready to go out to pasture." She bent toward Sarah. "Enough about me. Tell me, how is your mother?"

Sarah wasn't sure how much Harlan would want her to tell Eloise, but she felt comfortable in her presence, so she decided to be completely honest. "This has been and is a difficult time for her. Not only was finding Mr. Knowlton a shock, but now it seems she is the prime suspect."

"What! Why?"

Sarah decided not to mention the fingerprints quite yet. "Because she found Mr. Knowlton. Chief Gerard seems to think her being the only one seen, in a locked room, with the victim automatically makes her the guilty party."

"Poppycock. Chief Gerard is barking up the wrong tree. Your mother wouldn't hurt a fly. Besides, there were plenty of other people in and out of the office all day."

"That's what I thought, too. Can you specifically remember who might have gone into Lance's office after my mother and I came out? Surely there were other people in and out before my mother found him."

Eloise rested her hand under her chin. "Well, while your mother and you talked in the lobby and you were on your phone for a few minutes, Alvin stuck his head in and Amanda Taylor, Bailey, and I were all in and out a few times. Between getting Lance ready for the

council meeting and finalizing everything so he could
sign off on your sister's loan application before the
meeting, there was lots of coming and going."

"Mr. Knowlton had time to review the file and approve the application before he was killed?"

Eloise smiled and shook her head. "Don't be ridiculous. Mr. Knowlton didn't need to go over the details.
If your mother guaranteed the loan, that was good
enough for him. He was going to find out later why
Bailey denied it, but right after the two of you left his
office, he buzzed my desk and told me to get the
paperwork ready for his signature. Mr. Knowlton
planned to sign it before he left for the meeting, but
he apparently never got to it before I heard your
mother's gut-wrenching shriek." Eloise turned her
face toward the window. "The form is still sitting on
Mr. Bailey's desk waiting for his signature."

Sarah didn't want to upset her further, but she
needed to know who else might have gone in or out
of the president's office. Gently, she asked again.

Eloise still faced the window. "I wasn't watching his
door for the entire time the two of you talked because
I went to the storage room to get another package of
copier paper for my desk copier. I can't say for sure
if anyone else went in or out while I was gone, but
there definitely were others who went in after your
appointment."

"Who?"

"Mr. Howell may have gone in. He was standing at
the teller counter while you were on the phone, but I
don't know if he simply made a counter transaction
or stopped and said 'Hello' to Mr. Knowlton, like he
usually did."

"Thomas got to the city council meeting before me, but I never saw him here at the bank."

"Well, he was here for a few minutes. He waved at me as I returned to my desk. It makes sense he got to the meeting before you because I think he left the bank while you were on the phone with your back to us."

"You saw me on the phone?"

Eloise smiled. "Sarah, part of my job was to see everything in the lobby. If I remember correctly, you didn't leave for at least five more minutes after you finished your phone call and then your mother came over and visited with me for a while."

Sarah acknowledged Eloise was right. "But you said some folks definitely went in. Who were they?"

"I don't know. As I told Chief Gerard, I heard voices that didn't belong to Lance coming from his office. Whoever I heard may have gone in through the lobby or the alley during the time I wasn't sitting at my desk."

"Surely the security cameras recorded anyone coming and going from the lobby or the alley while you were away from your desk."

Eloise bent her head closer to Sarah's. "From what I understand, there may be a problem with some of the security camera tapes, but I'm sure I heard more than one person's voice between the time your mother and you came out of Mr. Knowlton's office and your mother screamed."

"What happened after my mother screamed?"

"Those next few minutes were confusing. We all reacted to her bloodcurdling shriek because it didn't stop. I ran toward Mr. Knowlton's office and opened the door. Mr. Bailey and Alvin were behind me."

"Mr. Bailey? I thought he was at city hall."

"He was back and forth running things over there for Mr. Knowlton, beginning when your mother and you were in Lance's office." She pointed to a stack of folders sitting atop her bookcase. "He was here in his office, about to take those folders to city hall, when we heard your mother scream."

Sarah apologized for interrupting and encouraged Eloise to continue her tale.

"As I was saying, Alvin had more ground to cover getting across the lobby than I did. Mr. Bailey came from this office."

"It must have been horrible seeing Mr. Knowlton and my mother."

Eloise nodded. "It was. He was so still. Your mother just stood there, behind him, screaming he was dead. Mr. Bailey and Alvin confirmed he was gone while I led your mother out to the chairs where you found us. While Alvin called for the police and Mr. Bailey ran over to city hall to tell everyone what happened, I stayed with your mother and kept anyone else from going into Mr. Knowlton's office."

Comparing the sequence as Eloise described it to the other versions she'd heard, a few things didn't make sense to Sarah. "I understand you also made coffee."

"Not then. We always keep that small table set up with coffee and water for our customers. While your mother and you were in the office with Mr. Knowlton, Amanda straightened up the table while I made a fresh pot of coffee. It's one of those machines where you change out the coffee filter and pour a pot of water into the reserve chamber."

"Was the extra water already there?"

"No, I had to go to our kitchenette to get it. That's how Cliff Rogers was able to get into Mr. Knowlton's office while you were in there. I had gone for water and was about to pour it into the coffee machine when I saw Cliff near my desk. Amanda said she never saw him slip behind her, but when Alvin and I realized where Cliff was headed, we both tried to stop him. Unfortunately, he was enough steps ahead of us that neither of us could catch him before he got into Mr. Knowlton's office.

Eloise took both of Sarah's hands and gazed into her eyes. "Sarah Blair, don't you worry. I've known your mother for a lifetime. She's not a murderer. We've all told Chief Gerard how Mr. Knowlton always had people coming and going through that door, especially on council days. I also told him I heard Mr. Knowlton talking with people, but I don't know who, after I went to get the copier paper. Eventually, he's going to have to look beyond your mother."

CHAPTER TWENTY-TWO

Outside the bank, Sarah checked her watch. Exactly time for both the bank and Harlan's office to close. No wonder Eloise had wrapped up their conversation. But what a conversation. There was so much she wanted to share with Harlan before her mother and he met with Chief Gerard, but she needed to get the time line straight in her mind to see what other questions it might prompt.

Sarah made her way to one of the benches in the square and pulled a pen and paper from her purse.

Cliff and Jacob go to see Lance. (Why was Jacob there?)

Maybelle and I arrive at the bank but must wait in the lobby because Cliff and Jacob are in Lance's office. I overhear Cliff threaten Lance and then see Cliff and Lance leave through the lobby of the bank.

Maybelle and I are ushered into Lance's office. Maybelle gets into it with Lance. Lance calls Bailey to bring the Southwind file in. He sends Bailey out of his office, through the lobby, to get ready for the council meeting. Lance and Maybelle continue their discussion.

Eloise goes to make coffee. Amanda is helping clean up the coffee table.

Cliff barges into Lance's office with Eloise and Alvin at his heels. Cliff knocks over Maybelle's purse and the things on the desk. Lance ushers Eloise and Alvin out through the lobby and then sends Cliff out the same way.

Lance agrees to review the Southwind file before the meeting. He shows Maybelle and me out via his door to the lobby.

Maybelle and I talk and I call Emily.

During this period, Eloise goes in and out of Lance's office and observes Amanda, Alvin, and Bailey do the same. At some point, she leaves her desk to get a ream of copier paper. She also reports seeing Thomas Howell at the teller desk and hearing voices, other than Lance's, coming from his office. Whose are they? How did they go into the office?

I go to the council meeting.

Either before or after I leave the bank, Bailey returns and goes into his own office. How many trips did he make to city hall?

Maybelle visits with Eloise then goes around the bank building and enters from the alley, through Lance's private office door. Maybelle says it was ajar. She finds him dead and screams.

Eloise, Alvin, and Bailey all run into the office. Alvin calls the police; Bailey goes to inform the city council, and Eloise takes Maybelle to a chair.

Reviewing her list, Sarah realized she especially needed to make Harlan aware of the unknown voices Eloise overheard and that more people went in and out of the office than originally thought. Surely those points would cast substantial doubt on her mother being the only one to use the alley to enter the supposedly locked room. They might also add credibility to her mother's assertion the door was open.

She hit Harlan's number on her speed dial, but her call went to voice mail. Sarah thought Eloise's details important enough to leave Harlan a quick summary. She only hoped when he finally called back he'd be so excited about what she'd learned he wouldn't think about what time she must have left the office to see Eloise.

Sarah thought about going to the police station to try to intercept Harlan but thought better of the idea. Her family's relationship with Dwayne Gerard left a lot to be desired. No sense being the one to come in and challenge his investigative integrity. Better to share the information with Harlan and let him use it in a subdued, but effective, legal manner rather than pinning the chief into a corner. There was no telling how he might react if he felt his chance of being named to the permanent position was jeopardized.

She stretched her neck, not realizing how tight her muscles were. There wasn't anything else she could do for her mother until she heard from Harlan. That left her needing to get ready for tomorrow's YipYeow organizational meeting. She still had to come up with an agenda, refreshments, and a way to keep all the different factions focused on their unified goal of raising money for the animal shelter rather than their private agendas.

There was no question compromise would be key to tomorrow's meeting, but she believed it could be achieved if everyone remembered what they were doing was for the good of the animals. Hopefully, any differences of opinion raised would be as easily resolved as when there was unanimous acceptance of Anne Hightower's suggestion at the city council meeting to name the event YipYeow Day. Her logical argument was that like restaurants were named things like Foodbar because they sold food and liquor or Dessert Bites because they specialized in bite-sized desserts, YipYeow uniquely represented the sound of the dogs and cats the shelter helped and many of the animals that would be paraded.

Sarah swallowed and hit her sister's name on her phone. She needed to know if she should stop at the grocery on her way home for a brownie mix or the ingredients for a chocolate velvet pie if Emily wasn't going to come through with her promised treats tied to cats and dogs. Plus, Sarah wanted to share the information she'd learned from Eloise.

Emily answered her phone without giving Sarah a chance to say "hello" or to explain why she was calling. "Sarah, I'm tied up right now, but stop worrying, you'll get the treats I promised. You already picked up cold drinks, coffee, and tea, right?"

"Yes, but you said something about having catnip tea, too?"

"I was going to send you a recipe, but when I thought more about it, I decided it wouldn't be a good thing to serve. Some people consider catnip tea something taken only for medicinal reasons. We don't want anything to distract from planning the event."

Sarah was relieved not to have to worry about making a special kind of tea. She began walking toward home while they continued talking. "When are you going to bring the snacks? I want to make sure I'm home or if you come earlier than I get off work, you leave me the instructions for heating and serving."

"You don't have to do anything except be home at least an hour before everyone comes. Marcus already has the sweet potato puffs with directions how to heat them. If he doesn't handle that himself, he'll tell you what to do. He's making dog- and cat-shaped cake and cookie treats. He will already have plattered them for you. Don't worry, Marcus will get you through tomorrow night."

"Marcus?"

"I reminded him you made Southwind a key sponsor of YipYeow Day because it was making human and dog treats for the event but suggested he could get even more exposure if he prepared refreshments for tomorrow night and invited the volunteers to the pub, which I'm sure will be open by then, to a post-event to celebrate the success of the day. He loved the idea, so he and Jacob are making the sweets tonight at Jacob's place while Grace and I already made more than enough of the sweet potato puffs. You're covered, but do me a favor."

"Anything. You've saved me from serving store-bought or, worse, going into my kitchen and creating a disaster. What do you want, oh, savior?"

"Massage his ego a bit tomorrow—give Marcus a shout-out or something."

"Won't you be at the meeting to do that?"

"Sorry, I'd hoped to get away in time for the meeting, but Grace and I are up to our necks getting ready for Friday's post-funeral reception and trying to generally get things under control here. It's a worse mess than we anticipated. We think we can pull it off, but it's going to be a long couple of days. The main thing is my favorite cook of convenience doesn't have to worry about the YipYeow meeting. Marcus has your back."

"And I am most grateful. I know you and everyone else can't understand how you can love everything about food preparation and kitchens while I tremble and break out in a cold sweat when I think about turning on the stove."

"Let's analyze that some other time. Gotta go. Love you."

"Love you, too." Sarah wasn't sure Emily heard her response before hanging up. Not a big deal, but if they'd learned anything the past few months, it was how much they couldn't and shouldn't take loving each other for granted.

Relieved she didn't have to whip up anything for the meeting, Sarah continued walking. As she turned onto Main Street, she intentionally stayed on Mr. Rogers's side of the street in case she spotted Fluffy. Approaching Mr. Rogers's house, she still hadn't caught a glimpse of the dog or any other living soul. At his house, she stopped and called the dog's name. She wasn't sure if her name really was Fluffy or if that was what Mr. Rogers had, for some reason, christened the pup.

Not getting an answer, Sarah abandoned the sidewalk and walked up his walkway. There wasn't any sign of the dog in the part of the yard she could see. In fact, the house looked deserted. No light shone

through his front windows. She wasn't surprised. Now
that his wife was gone, the house always looked dark
and abandoned. The aloneness of one person wandering in the space of a house like Mr. Rogers's was
one of the reasons she had no desire to live in the big
house on her own property. The more intimate carriage house and having RahRah for company suited
her far better.

Maybe Mr. Rogers's urgent need to coax Fluffy into
his house and the safety of the shelter was tied to the
changes in his own life. His nephews arguing about
his home and independence had to be frightening
and underscore some element of loneliness. Sarah
promised herself to reach out to him more. As for
Fluffy, she certainly hoped Mr. Rogers was able to
coax the pup back up on his porch for food and water.
Whether human or animal, there was nothing worse
than being scared.

CHAPTER TWENTY-THREE

The next day, between Harlan's full calendar of clients and an unusually high number of motions and pleadings needing to be typed and filed, should have whizzed by until it was time for the YipYeow organizational meeting. Instead, sweating out whether Harlan could convince Chief Gerard that arresting Maybelle was premature and would reflect badly on him if he was wrong made the day drag. When Harlan finally succeeded in getting the chief to stall for a few more days, Sarah was relieved, but it still didn't remove her nervous anticipation about the meeting.

Now she stood between her dining and living rooms sweating the final thirty minutes before her guests arrived. Marcus was whistling in the kitchen, where he was heating the sweet potato puffs. Considering Emily was out of pocket, stuck at the Howellian, his happy tune was a relief to Sarah. Even better were the goodies he'd brought. Beautiful trays of cat- and dog-shaped cookies and animal-topped petits fours.

She'd set up a beer, wine, soda, and water bar at the far end of the dining room and moved every chair she

owned into the living room. There wasn't anything
else she could think to do.

RahRah brushed against her leg. She picked him
up and surveyed the rooms once more. "RahRah,
that's it. Everything's set up for tonight except putting
you in my bedroom. Believe me, you'd rather be in
there than with some of the people who will be here
tonight."

Placing him in her bedroom, she took it as a good
sign when he burrowed into the towel she lay on the
end of her bed. She hated locking him up during
the meeting, but she knew at least one person coming
would make a fuss if he ran free. Jane, her ex-husband's
bimbo, who almost always was a thorn in Emily's or
her side, was probably going to be opinionated enough
tonight without giving her something else to complain about. Considering Jane's past interaction with
RahRah, they were both better off being separated by
the bedroom door.

Sarah didn't want to add to the tension between
herself and Jane and Anne. The two of them offered
to chair YipYeow Day, which was fine with Sarah, but
the mayor insisted on Sarah, ostensibly because the
fund-raiser was her idea, and she had an ongoing involvement with the shelter. The real reason, which
everyone knew, was that unlike Anne, Sarah had no
intention of running against him in the next mayoral
election.

Although Anne and Jane didn't make Sarah as nervous as the idea of cooking, she was leery of planning
anything with either of them. Perhaps she was para-
noid, but she felt they always came to whatever table
she sat at with hidden agendas. Maybe tonight would

be different, but she doubted it the same way she didn't believe a zebra could change its stripes.

Any further negative thoughts were knocked out of her mind by the chiming doorbell. She flung the front door open and found herself standing toe to toe with Jane. So much for the evening not starting off with a bang. "Hi, Jane. Come in."

Jane didn't budge from the doorway. "Where's that cat of yours?"

"Locked in my bedroom while this meeting is going on."

Sarah thought Jane muttered something like, "Good," as she entered the house, but Sarah was too busy welcoming the next people coming up the walk toward the snacks to continue their conversation.

Once Sarah was sure everyone had a proper opportunity to ooh and ahh in Marcus's presence about his beautiful desserts, she shooed people into the living room. The chairs in there easily filled and, while several people stood, the remainder of the overflow squeezed themselves into places on the floor.

Sarah walked to the front of the room, where the shelter's new executive director, Phyllis Peters, stood by the fireplace.

"I can't believe how many people are here tonight, Sarah. I don't know how the shelter or I can thank you for this."

"Thanks aren't needed. Let's hope the fund-raiser is as successful as the turnout for organizing it."

"Agreed. Oh, there are the Williamses. They adopted the cutest Maltese last week. I better go say hi to them and a few of our other special patrons."

While Phyllis went to make nice, Sarah took a

moment to survey the crowd before calling the meeting to order. There were many people she didn't know, but she recognized quite a few besides Jane and Anne. Eloise and Mr. Rogers had grabbed her over-stuffed fireside chairs. Jacob waved at her from a place on the floor, near Mr. Rogers's feet, where he sat with Cliff. Across the room from them, she was surprised to see Mr. Bailey and Thomas Howell seated with a few of the mall shop owners and two ministers. Harlan leaned on a wall at the very back of the room near some of her neighbors and the youngish-looking coroner, Dr. Smith. She wondered if he was here because he liked animals or if he was their official police presence in Chief Gerard's absence.

Sarah swallowed and cleared her throat. Realizing she'd stuck her hands into her pockets, she pulled them out, so she wouldn't be slouching forward. Still wanting to hold on to something to steady her nerves, she compromised by locking her thumbs into the belt loops of her jeans.

"Thank you all for coming tonight and for being so supportive of the Wheaton Animal Shelter. The mayor is sorry he couldn't be with us tonight, but I'd like to introduce you to Phyllis Peters, the new executive director of the shelter."

Phyllis stepped forward and echoed Sarah's welcoming remarks and the gratitude the shelter had for everything being done on its behalf. Before she gave the floor back to Sarah, she invited everyone to feel free to call her to find out about fostering and adoption opportunities.

"Thank you, Phyllis. I hope your phone rings off the hook tomorrow, but tonight we're here to talk about YipYeow Day, which we hope will become an annual fund-raising event. The plan, as originally proposed, is to have an animal parade in a few months. Participation will require submission of an entry form and fee. All fees will be one hundred percent donations to the shelter. The parade itself will go around the block the shelter is located on and then people can come inside where there will be a showcase of adoptable animals set up."

A hand went up, but Sarah ignored it. "As I said, that was our original plan, but it changed during the city council meeting when the council, whose vice president, Anne Hightower, is here tonight, voted that if we hold the function when there is a gap in the city parks' calendar, a week from this Saturday, they will close four streets for two hours, provide police and sanitation services for the event, and give us free use of the park pavilion area for the afternoon. This will allow us to raise more funds from vendors and sponsors. More importantly, we'll have more room to showcase adoptable animals from the shelter."

When the room burst into applause, Sarah stopped speaking. She continued when the applause died. "Of course, Wheaton, the mayor, and the city council will be identified in our literature and signage as sponsors, but I'm glad to announce that since that council meeting, Wheaton Tractor and Southwind Restaurants, Inc., which, by the way, through Chef Marcus, provided your treats for tonight, also signed on as named sponsors. In addition, before his death, council president Lance Knowlton informed me his bank would be a cash sponsor."

This time the young man who'd raised his hand before shouted out his question. "For how much?"

Sarah quickly glanced in Mr. Bailey's direction before concentrating on the full group again. "Although Mr. Knowlton mentioned a very generous sum, our sponsor committee needs to confirm that amount with the bank."

"That won't be necessary." Mr. Bailey was on his feet. "We believe the more corporate sponsors obtained for YipYeow Day, the more successful this fund-raiser will be. Because of that, we would like to make a seed contribution of a thousand dollars."

"How wonderful," Sarah said, disappointed the bank wasn't coming in at the original five thousand dollars Lance had mentioned.

Bailey held up his hands to quiet the politely applauding group. "But that's not all we want to do. The bank will match up to an additional five thousand dollars of contributions made to the shelter in memory of our beloved Lance Knowlton."

Sarah was thrilled. In the end, the bank would be donating even more than Lance promised. Before she could properly thank the bank and Bailey, Harlan interrupted her. "I'll meet the thousand seed contribution and my law firm, Endicott and Associates, also will match up to five thousand dollars in donations. This event is important to our animals, so I hope you'll accept the bank's and my challenge."

"I can't believe this! Thank you!"

Harlan blushed. "Considering the importance of this project, I think we should create a committee dedicated to seeking corporate contributions. We can target Wheaton businesses and perhaps reach out to some of the larger Birmingham businesses."

Anne Hightower objected. "We've never sought designated business contributions for the shelter. Designated gifts from businesses may reduce their donations elsewhere."

"But Ms. Hightower," someone Sarah didn't recognize said, "some businesses won't give to the same thing year in, year out, so we should get in their cycles now."

"Well, I, for one, feel uncomfortable soliciting from businesses."

Jacob jumped to his feet. "I can understand that. I don't think anyone who is or might be running for office should do business solicitations. It might be considered a conflict with their campaigns. Because I don't have that problem, I'll be glad to chair the business solicitation committee and make some of the bigger asks myself."

Sarah, observing the giant grin he bestowed upon his sister and her "if looks could kill" glaring response, struggled not to laugh.

"But there may be confusion because of our shared name," Anne said.

"Believe me, dear sister, we may both be Hightowers, but no one will ever confuse us."

Before the war between the siblings escalated, Sarah intervened. "This is wonderful. The success of YipYeow Day is guaranteed with this kind of start. Which brings me to why we're here tonight." She held up a poster that depicted the closed streets, parade route, and pavilion setup. "In order to make this work, we need to form several committees, including sponsorship, vendors, and publicity. Are there other thoughts and ideas you'd like to share?"

Hands flew up, and Sarah recognized them in turn. Bailey offered to handle the treasury aspects of the event, including setting up a no-fee checking account for YipYeow Day. The woman who, with her husband, owned the copy shop said they'd print all tickets and signs for free. Cliff offered to build a raised platform for the speaker and to showcase the animals needing a home.

Although Sarah was tempted to ignore Jane's raised hand or to recognize her as "Bimbo," she called on her by her given name.

"I'll be glad to set up a food table. I'm sure I can come up with some pet-related recipes."

"That sounds lovely," Anne interrupted, "but you better coordinate with Chef Marcus. He's going to have a Southwind food table of human and animal treats."

Sarah did a double take. Anne, who was Emily and Marcus's chief nemesis at council meetings, was now standing up for Marcus and his plans for an official food table at the event. Perhaps this was a sign that the rest of the permits would come through by a week from Saturday so Marcus could officially open the Southwind Pub and hold the reception as planned. She certainly hoped Anne's change of heart and treatment of Marcus, like he was her new best friend, meant that.

"This is all wonderful," Sarah said. "Before we break for refreshments, is there anything else anyone wants to say?"

One of the two ministers sitting across the room

raised his hand. When Sarah recognized him, he stood. "I'm Pastor Paul Dobbins from the Little Brown Church on West Jefferson Street. On behalf of LBC, I think I have another way which might help raise more revenue for both the city and the shelter."

All eyes, including Sarah's, turned toward Pastor Dobbins. She couldn't imagine how the YipYeow parade would financially benefit the city, considering the manpower and services it was donating.

"As part of my community outreach work, I'd be glad to host a nondenominational Blessing of the Beasts service at LBC. That kind of service was a big hit in the parish I was in before my recent assignment to LBC."

"How does it work?" Anne Hightower asked.

"Very simply. Everyone brings their pets to the church or wherever we decide to hold the service. After I present some general but applicable biblical and literature readings and remarks, I say a blessing over all the animals the community wants blessed. It doesn't matter if it is a dog, cat, hamster, bunny, or rat—all are God's children. The only problem is that the weekend YipYeow Day is scheduled, I can only do it on Sunday morning."

Anne Hightower stood. "That wouldn't be a problem."

Sarah opened her mouth, but it was a few seconds before she could stammer out any words. "Actually, it might be. When Mr. Knowlton and the mayor discussed what we wanted to do before we brought the final proposal to the council meeting, they found the pavilion and walkways were only available on that Saturday. Wedding and reunion parties have completely booked the Sundays and other Saturdays for the next few months. The mayor also indicated the city's offer was contingent on having the event on Saturday to avoid paying a Sunday overtime premium."

"That settles that," Anne said. "but I don't think we should pass on Pastor Dobbins's generous offer. We can hold the Blessing of the Beasts at LBC on Sunday, charging a token additional fee to those registering for YipYeow Day and making it free to those who adopt an animal on Saturday."

"But security—"

"Not a problem. LBC is a small church, so I don't see a problem obtaining a few private security guards for the Sunday service. In fact, I'll commit Hightower Realty to underwriting a primary sponsorship covering whatever the security detail cost is."

"That's very generous of you. I hate to play devil's advocate, but—"

"But you will, Sarah."

Sarah shrugged. "I can't help it. We need to realize it will mean more planning and committee work to have what amounts to two events, even if we advertise them as one."

Next to her, Sarah heard a rustling as Eloise rose from her chair. "I think Sarah is making some good points we need to consider. After all, this is our first time doing this and our resources are limited. Looking around this room, except for a few people who couldn't come tonight, we're it when it comes to worker bees. We'll be stretched thin trying to do everything for two days, especially if we market this and pull in people from Birmingham and other neighboring communities. I think we should hold the Blessing of the Beasts as something we add next year if this year's YipYeow Day is a success."

"Eloise and Sarah, I appreciate your opinions, but there are definite advantages to a two-day event." Anne held up her fingers so everyone in the room could count with her.

"First, if we attract people who spend the night, our hotels, restaurants, and city will reap the benefit of the money they spend on meals, lodging, and miscellaneous things. Second, the potential of overnight visitors using hotel rooms means we can employ the resources of the Convention Bureau for things like registration, name tags, and even some giveaways on both days. This means those of you in this room won't have to do the mundane things associated with an event. Personally, I don't see how we can lose."

Anne turned to address the greatest part of the audience. "What do you think?"

One of Sarah's neighbors yelled, "I think we should do it. I know I'd bring my dog to both."

"What about the rest of you?" Anne said. "Let's have a show of hands who think we should make this a two-day festival?"

When only Sarah, Eloise, and two others didn't raise their hands, Anne declared the motion passed but hastened to add that, of course, it wasn't a real motion, simply the volunteers' overwhelming opinion. At that, Jane raised her hand. Sarah and Anne simultaneously called on her.

"I know the Convention Bureau will ease the burden on our volunteers, but I think Sarah is right when she said planning our first YipYeow event as a two-day festival is too much for one person."

Sarah couldn't believe her ears. Was Jane siding with her?

"Rather than overburdening Sarah, considering she has a real job, too, I think we should leave her in charge of only the Saturday event. I'll gladly volunteer to work with Pastor Dobbins to arrange and publicize the Sunday Blessing of the Beasts. Would that be okay with you, Pastor?" Jane batted her eyes at him.

"Most definitely. And if all of you wouldn't object, I'd love to get my wife, Yvonne, who couldn't be here tonight, to work with us. This kind of event and its overnight aspect is her specialty. Full disclosure, for those of you who don't know, she recently accepted a job as the assistant director of the Wheaton Convention Bureau. I'm sure, with Yvonne's guidance, as Ms. Hightower explained it far better than I can, this is exactly the type of thing the Convention Bureau exists to help with."

Sarah felt sick to her stomach as Anne demurely accepted Pastor Dobbins's praise by glancing at the floor.

After a few seconds, Anne raised her head and again assumed control of the meeting. "Well, folks, sounds like we have a plan. Before we go any further, let's give Sarah a big hand for pulling this together." After the clapping concluded, she continued, "Now, it's up to all of us. I know, whether it's marketing, ticket sales, or some other task we need you to help with, you'll be willing to do whatever it takes to make YipYeow Day, or should I say Weekend, a success. I think Sarah said the committee sign-up sheets are in the dining room right next to those delicious Southwind desserts."

"One moment, please."

The voice belonged to Thomas Howell. With every eye on him, including Sarah's, he walked to the front of the room and positioned himself behind his uncle's chair, his hands resting on its high back. "I know those desserts are calling, but before you take advantage of them, I have another idea I'd like to share with all of you."

Sarah stared at him. She had no idea what he was going to propose. A quick glance at Anne's and Jane's blank faces told her they didn't, either.

CHAPTER TWENTY-FOUR

"For those of you who don't know me, I'm Thomas Howell, the owner of Birmingham's Howellian Hotel and George Rogers's nephew." He placed one hand on his uncle's shoulder.

Sarah couldn't clearly see Mr. Rogers's face, but she bet it wasn't a happy one.

"Having spent a lot of quality time in Wheaton, its charities and people mean a lot to me. My work demands I live in Birmingham, but because of the time I spent here with my late mother, aunt, and, of course, my dear uncle, I've always thought of Wheaton as being my Alabama home. I'm very familiar with what a worthy cause and agency the Wheaton Animal Shelter is, but I'm preaching to the choir telling that to you. You volunteers are the glue that's going to make this project work."

Sarah wasn't sure what he was going to say next, but she didn't feel she could cut him off.

Palm up, he raised the hand not on his uncle's shoulder and paused, giving the audience more time to focus on his next words. "I'm going to sign up to help with one of the Saturday committees, but I have an idea for something else I can do to benefit the shelter."

Sarah didn't know if she should be excited or apprehensive. "Oh?"

"I always believe in saying 'thank you' for the hard work people do." He waved his raised hand to encompass the room. "In a very short period, you, your families, and your friends will give a lot of time and energy behind the scenes and at the YipYeow events. I'd like to say thank you by my throwing, with no slight to the hotel's dog photo exhibit, but because of my mother's love for cats, a nod to our cat exhibit, Catapalooza Night at the Howellian ballroom the Saturday night of the event. Catapalooza will be both a formal community fund-raiser geared at those who love animals in Birmingham and serve as a special thank-you to all of you."

This time, Anne responded before Sarah could. "That's awfully generous, but another one of our sponsors, Southwind, whose restaurant will be open by then, already is hosting a volunteer reception that night. Besides, I expect we'll be getting volunteers signing up to help as late as YipYeow weekend."

"I didn't realize Southwind was hosting an event that night." Thomas ran the hand he'd offered the audience through his hair. "But that's okay. Marcus, where are you?"

As Thomas peered around the room, Sarah saw Marcus's hand go up. She hoped this didn't erupt into a nasty confrontation.

"Marcus," Thomas said. "Your new restaurant is a pub concept, isn't it?"

When Marcus acknowledged he was correct, Thomas continued. "That's perfect. Southwind can host a more casual reception while we make Catapalooza Night at the Howellian a true black-tie-optional fund-raising event with a silent and live auction. We can use both receptions as carrots to entice people to sign up to help sooner than later. I don't know what Marcus is going to charge, but the shelter can advertise the Howellian evening at fifty dollars for members of the volunteer committees and one guest, but seventy-five dollars per person in advance for non-volunteers and a hundred at the door."

Marcus was now on his feet. "The Southwind reception will be free to all volunteers."

"That's wonderful, Marcus. You'll have the local event anyone can come to, and my hotel will help the shelter by reaching an additional donor base. We can market Catapalooza also to animal patrons who live in Birmingham." Continuing to hold onto his uncle, Thomas gestured like a showman while taking a partial mock bow. "Of course, all proceeds of Catapalooza, after expenses, will go directly to the Wheaton Animal Shelter."

"It's a very nice idea," Sarah said, "but I think it goes back to what Eloise said earlier this evening. Our volunteer pool is limited. I don't see how we possibly can man two days of the festival and handle an event in Birmingham, too."

"Oh, the volunteers won't have to do anything for this reception, other than coming and being honored. My team will take care of everything, including decorations, food, and a few auction items. I'll even donate two paintings from our gallery to give high rollers something to bid on. Turnout should be good because so many people from Wheaton haven't had a chance to experience the hotel, plus Birmingham has a strong base of animal lovers who can be counted on to take part in a shelter-related fund-raiser."

Before any further objections could be raised, Thomas announced Catapalooza was a done deal for the Saturday of the event. He urged everyone to hurry into the dining room to sign up for a committee and grab a treat before they were gone.

Most of the people followed his directive, but some, like Sarah, stayed behind in the living room. She looked around for Marcus, but he wasn't in either the dining room or living room. Able to see the front door from where she stood, she observed Anne and Jane slip out without bothering to sign a volunteer list. Apparently, their mission was accomplished. How they took over her meeting irked her, but not as much as the fact she relinquished control without making enough of an effort to get it back.

"Don't be mad because things didn't quite go the way you planned."

Sarah jumped. She hadn't realized Eloise was next to her. "Thomas and Anne have both had a lot of practice handling rooms like this."

"That's why I appreciated you trying to support my position."

"It was nothing. I knew how Lance envisioned this festival. He may have been a political animal, but his heart was in the right place when it came to Wheaton and its people." Her voice cracked. She quickly turned her face away from Sarah.

It was the first time Sarah had heard Eloise use her

boss's first name. She reached out to give the older woman a hug but stopped when Eloise pivoted back toward her, her executive assistant face back in place. It was Eloise who squeezed Sarah's arm.

"Before I go, I want you to know, when he talked about your plan for raising funds for the animal shelter, he told me you were the real thing, too. That's why the mayor and he were glad, despite having to twist your arm a bit, when you accepted the chairmanship of YipYeow Day."

"Thank you. Knowing that means a lot." Sarah broke off in mid-thought as Thomas, munching on one of Marcus's cat cookies, joined them. She frowned, unable to dwell on how ironic it was he was here while her sister was stuck working at his hotel in Birmingham. Emily wouldn't be thrilled to learn she was hosting a black-tie-optional party against what was probably the first event at her own restaurant.

"I was surprised to see you here tonight, Thomas."

"You heard how I feel about Wheaton. I didn't want to miss the organizational meeting."

"It was kind of you to offer to host a reception, but do you really think it's wise to have two competing events for the same organization on the same evening?"

"It's my pleasure to host this because the shelter is something I truly believe in. And don't worry. Having the two functions the same evening isn't going to be a problem. Between you and me, we're going to draw two very different crowds. Catapalooza will have more of a spending crowd coming with a fundraising mentality while Marcus will host the true volunteer celebrators."

"I gathered from what you said, by your team, you were talking about Emily and her staff. Perhaps you should check with her whether they can handle another Saturday-night event before we schedule this reception?" Observing him grasp his cookie so tightly crumbs dropped on her floor, she involuntarily took a step closer to Eloise.

"Sarah, Emily is employed by me. I think you have a misconception of how things work at the hotel." He glanced at his watch. "It's getting late. I better hit the road. With attending the funeral, followed by the hotel hosting the meal for those mourning Lance, it's going to be a long day."

"Probably not as long as Emily and Grace's today and tomorrow."

He put his hat on and tapped its brim with two fingers from his now-unclenched hand. "Touché. Tell you what. I'll let you know the details of the volunteer appreciation evening after I talk to Emily. Maybe you'll join me for dinner at the hotel again after this event is over?"

"We'll see." Sarah stood frozen after he walked away. Watching him leave, she seriously questioned if she still wanted to take up cooking for him.

Eloise interrupted her internalizing anger. "Maddening, isn't he? His motivation is good, but he's used to getting it done exactly as he wants."

"You sound like you're talking from the voice of experience."

"I am. Remember, I've been around him and his kind a lot longer than you. He's a true entrepreneur. They always have an angle—a piece of the action they hope benefits them. You've got to be on your toes because if you get mad, you won't get even when you must. And, if that's the case, you also won't protect those you care about if it ever becomes necessary."

Sarah shuddered. She couldn't help noticing the deep lines caused by Eloise's taut facial muscles. "You make everything sound so logical and simple. I don't know why I can't keep my emotions out of anything I do."

Eloise relaxed. "That's what makes you who you are, as well as the perfect person to lead this fund-raiser. I better be going or you'll still have me here for breakfast, and I understand you're not much for whipping up things in the kitchen."

They both laughed.

"Don't forget to call on me. I may seem demure, but I'm a pretty good organizer and taskmaster. Also, even if Bailey is handling the treasury, you ought to have a finance committee to watch over his shoulder."

Sarah was startled by Eloise's suggestion YipYeow Day should keep an eye on the acting bank president's handling of the event's proceeds. She examined her face for a telltale sign of distrust versus simply thinking a finance committee was a good business practice, but Eloise's expression was again impervious. "Are you trying to warn me about something?"

"If there was something to tell you, I would. I'm simply suggesting what I would do in this situation. This is a big undertaking. Too much for one person to watch every aspect of it. Lance always believed in a system of checks and balances."

This time, Sarah didn't hesitate. She gave the older

woman a hug. "It's getting dark. Are you parked in the driveway or on Main Street?"

"Neither. I walked."

Sarah pointed to where Harlan stood by the open front door waving good-bye to Mr. Rogers. "Why don't I get Harlan to drive you home?"

"That won't be necessary. I like an evening walk, and Main Street is perfectly safe. If there's one of Marcus's to-die-for cookies left, I'll snatch it and be on my way."

Sarah, still chuckling at Eloise's blunt comments, picked up a kitchen chair to return it to the kitchen.

"Here, let me help you with that." Bailey took the chair from her. "Where does it go?"

"In the kitchen. Let me grab another one."

With his help, she quickly had all the chairs back where they went. "Thank you."

"No problem. I want to talk to you about how we'll handle the money for YipYeow Day. As I offered, I'll open an account with the shelter's name on it tomorrow with the bank's first thousand dollars. We can set up a box to receive donations at our branch, and I'll work with Phyllis for how we'll handle registrations, day-of-the-event adoption fees, and any other pass-through or matching money, like Harlan's."

"Sounds good. Considering all the different aspects of the weekend, I'll be glad to assign a volunteer finance committee to work with you."

"Thanks, but that won't be necessary. I'll draft Amanda Taylor, from the bank, to help. She's taking on new responsibilities and will be eager to work with us on this." He precluded Sarah from arguing with him by noting he couldn't permit a non-bank employee to see internal bank records associated with the new account or to even receive the statement from him if they weren't on the account.

"With Catapalooza, things will be a little trickier, but I'll get with Thomas on that. You don't have to worry about any of the financial details. I'll prepare a balance sheet and profit and loss statement reflecting everything for Phyllis and you to review. If it's okay with the two of you, because our lead time is so short, I'll just do one final accounting instead of providing periodic reports?"

What he said made sense. The time was so short, she couldn't argue for a formal finance committee; instead, to appease Eloise's objection, she'd make sure the volunteer coordinator always had two people manning wherever money might change hands, like the registration desk. "I don't think anyone will object to that. I know I won't. Having the financials off my back will leave me time for more fund-raising and logistical concerns. Thank you."

"My pleasure. I enjoy Wheaton, and this is a good way for me to use my skills to help with a worthwhile project. Need to run, but I'll be in touch."

After walking Bailey to the door, she stayed there with Harlan in the hope the last stragglers would get the hint it was time to leave. Her presence worked. She was just about to close the door on the wafting voices of her final guests drifting down her driveway when screeching tires followed by a scream pierced the night.

Stepping outside, Sarah saw bright lights flicked on

as a car sped down Main Street. As her eyes adjusted to the dark, she realized the few people still in her driveway were running toward a woman who stood, facing the street, in the shadows near where Sarah's fence had been vandalized. Sarah glanced at Harlan and they, too, ran. The screaming woman was Eloise.

CHAPTER TWENTY-FIVE

Petrified at what she would find, Sarah ran to where a shaking Eloise stood facing Main Street. A group of stragglers from the meeting were trying to comfort Eloise. Sarah pushed her way through them. Eloise didn't respond when Sarah said her name. Putting a hand on Eloise's shoulder, Sarah more loudly repeated her name. Still not getting any response, Sarah placed herself in front of Eloise's face. Only then did Sarah realize Eloise's eyes were wide open and fixed on something in front of Mr. Rogers's house. Sarah followed her gaze, but others, who'd already crossed the street, blocked her view.

After assuring herself Eloise was safe and in good hands, Sarah ventured across Main Street. She stepped carefully. The squashed remains of a flashlight and a cane were strewn across the asphalt. Frightened by the splintered cane's remnants, Sarah hustled through the semicircle of bystanders.

Her neighbor, Mr. Rogers, sat on the curb, the knee of his pants ripped. She surmised his hands were also cut or scraped because of the dark stains left wherever he touched the matted hair of the scrawny dog in his lap, who stretched to lick his face.

Sarah was relieved to see the boyish Dr. Smith seated on the curb, checking Mr. Rogers out. Finished, he rose. While he took a moment to pat the dog, Alvin joined Dr. Smith on the curb. Alvin pulled a notebook from the shirt pocket of his uniform as Dr. Smith held his hands up to hush the crowd of onlookers.

"Mr. Rogers is fine. He's got a few scrapes that I'll stay and clean up, but no need for anyone to worry. Did anyone see what happened?"

There were murmurs about a car speeding away, but the mumbled consensus seemed to be that by the time anyone reached the end of the driveway, Mr. Rogers was sprawled across the curb and sidewalk, the dog nudging him.

"Did anyone see the car or anything else?" Alvin asked.

No one volunteered any further information.

"If you'll wait just a moment, I'd like to get your names, please." He bent closer to where Mr. Rogers still sat. "Mr. Rogers, do you know what happened to you?"

"Of course. I didn't hit my head."

Everyone laughed. This was the Mr. Rogers they all knew.

"When I left Sarah's, I bumped into Eloise and we talked for a few minutes. We said good night and I flicked my flashlight on and was crossing the street when I glimpsed Fluffy here dash from the back of my house toward the front bushes. I stopped midway across the street and shone my flashlight toward the bushes. I was going to sneak up and try coaxing her out of hiding when suddenly I heard the crunch of a car's tires coming toward me. I sprinted for the sidewalk but tripped, dropping my light and cane. Luckily, I fell forward, breaking my fall with my hands and knee. The car screeched away and Fluffy's nose nudged my side."

"Did you see the car or who was driving it?"

"No. I fell forward. By the time I turned, it was gone."

"Well, it doesn't sound like there's anything to keep you folks here. If you'll all line up, please, I'll get your names. If anyone thinks of anything in the next few days, call the station and ask for Officer Robinson. Thank you for your patience. In the meantime, Dr. Smith will take Mr. Rogers up to his house and clean his scrapes."

"Why don't you bring Mr. Rogers back to my place? I've probably got everything you need, and it might be a good idea to take a quick look at Eloise." Sarah pointed to where Eloise and the other group of onlookers were on the other side of the street. "It was her screaming that alerted us something was wrong."

Mr. Rogers gazed at the dog in his arms, rather than looking where Sarah pointed. "Fluffy?"

"Bring her along, Mr. Rogers. We'll see if we can get her cleaned up, too."

Dr. Smith helped Mr. Rogers to his feet. Together, with Sarah, they started their parade up Sarah's driveway, picking up Eloise on their way.

Back at the house, Sarah hurried to round up alcohol, Neosporin, latex gloves, and bandages, taking only a moment to suggest to Marcus he see if anyone wanted anything to drink.

Passing her bedroom, she thought about letting RahRah out but decided the interaction between RahRah and Fluffy was too much of an unknown. The last thing she wanted was to add more confusion and tension to the evening.

By the time she returned with the medical supplies, Marcus had served everyone who wanted one a drink. Sarah was glad to see color had returned to Eloise's face. She wondered if her slightly flushed cheeks were attributable to the scotch on the rocks or simply calming down. Either way, she thought Eloise looked a hundred percent better.

Dr. Smith pulled his gloves off, expertly rolling the used gauze and bandage wrappers from his cleanup job into one. "Eloise, you were still on the sidewalk?"

"Yes. When George stopped midway across the street and called out something about Fluffy, I stood there a minute to watch what he was doing."

"Did you see the car that almost hit him?"

Eloise shook her head. "Like I told Alvin, when he arrived after you were already across the street with George, I was watching George. Even if I saw the car in broad daylight tomorrow, I wouldn't be able to recognize it. Cars never have been my thing."

A small yip from Fluffy drew everyone's attention back to George. "George, what are you going to do with that dog?"

"Take her home, give her a bath, and put both of us to bed. To paraphrase *Gone with the Wind*, I'll think about the vet and the shelter tomorrow. Now, if you'll excuse me, I thank you all for your help, but I've had enough of this fun."

Already half out of his chair with Fluffy in tow, Mr. Rogers was stopped by Dr. Smith grabbing his arm. "My car is outside. Let me run you home. You've crossed the street one too many times for tonight."

Before Mr. Rogers could squinch his face into a full-out pout, Eloise interrupted. "Are you going in the direction of the strip center, Dr. Smith?"

"Yes."

"Would you mind giving me a ride, too? I think I've had enough street crossing for tonight, too."

"My pleasure. Let's go, everyone." With thanks for the drinks and the quick hospital setup, the three departed, leaving only Harlan and Marcus, who Sarah asked to please stay a little longer.

Harlan made himself comfortable in one of the overstuffed fireside chairs, while Marcus cleared the drink glasses. Taking advantage of Marcus's cleaning up, Sarah released RahRah from his term of imprisonment.

She brought the cat back into the living room just as Marcus plopped into the chair Mr. Rogers had sat in earlier. "All done except for putting up your soda and bar. Other than my trays, the vultures didn't leave much."

"I can't thank you enough. Be assured, empty trays wouldn't have been the case if I cooked or baked. Speaking of drinks, can I get either of you something else?" When both declined her offer, Sarah sat cross-legged on the floor in front of them. RahRah rubbed his head against her. She picked him up and cuddled him. "I guess he's forgiven me for locking him up. I still can't believe someone tried to kill Mr. Rogers tonight."

"We don't know that for sure," Marcus said.

She lay RahRah in her lap. "Yes, we do. Harlan and I saw the driver turn his lights on after he sped past Mr. Rogers. Normal drivers don't do that. What do you think, Harlan?"

"This time, I'm inclined to agree with you. Most drivers, and we don't know if it was a man or a woman, who forgot to turn their lights on and saw an older person fall, would have stopped instead of gunning the motor."

"Maybe the person got scared?"

Harlan leaned back in his chair. "Maybe, but I'm skeptical because there's been so much going on between him and his nephews and with the different economic development factions."

"And don't forget, his fence and mine were vandalized. It might have been a warning, instead of a prank."

"But you're on opposite sides of the street and opposite sides of the redistricting question," Marcus said.

"Never mind. I didn't look at it from that perspective. At least he's okay and the best thing is, after all he's done to get that dog to come to him, Fluffy came through for him when she thought Mr. Rogers might be hurt."

Harlan laughed. "I think Fluffy is going to be your neighbor for quite some time. Hope RahRah and she get along."

Sarah glanced at the cat in her lap. "As long as Fluffy understands her place, RahRah and she will do fine together. RahRah can get along with anyone except Jane. Speaking of Anne and Jane, Harlan, what happened tonight?"

"You got played."

"That I know. Once I realized Jane and Anne were on the same side, I knew I'd lost control, but Pastor Dobbins?"

"He was the only honest one."

Sarah put her hand on RahRah's back. "What makes you characterize him as honest?"

"He admitted up front his wife is the new assistant director of the Wheaton Convention Bureau and he's trying to help her out by holding the event the next day."

"I don't see how her work with the Chamber fits into what happened here tonight."

"You just made the classic mistake. The Wheaton Chamber of Commerce and the Wheaton Convention Bureau are two different entities. The Chamber works to bring recognition to the event itself, while the Convention Bureau supports the event in ways that bring outside people and money into the city. If people book rooms for an overnight stay for a reunion, meeting, or event like YipYeow Days, the Convention Bureau hopes good word of mouth will result in more conventions and events coming to Wheaton. By having YipYeow take place over two days, there's a good chance some people will stay overnight, which translates to rooms booked and a positive early outcome for Yvonne Dobbins, the minister's wife."

"Great, my little shelter fund-raiser has become a

win for the minister, his wife, and Anne Hightower, but how does Jane fit into this?"

Marcus drummed his fingers on his chair's arm. "I can answer that. The word on the street is now that Emily and I bought out Jane's interest in Southwind, she hasn't been able to find another job, so she wants to open her own restaurant."

"I've seen all the hoops Emily and you are going through. Can Jane do that?"

"With help from behind the scenes. Her bigger problem is she needs a location, more capital, and city concessions before she can open her doors."

Sarah took her hand away from RahRah's back and crossed her arms in front of her. "So, Jane's going about it the way she does everything—kissing up and trickery rather than leadership and hard work. Can't other people see it?"

Harlan leaned back and let out a low whistle. "Did you really ask that question?"

"I know I shouldn't get so mad, but it's not like Jane playing up to whoever might be her benefactor is new."

"Don't we all know it," Marcus said. "But this time she may have lucked into the mother lode."

"The Hightowers?" Harlan's words hung in the air.

"On the money."

RahRah jumped out from under Sarah's petting hand. In response to his rejection, Sarah straightened out her legs. "I hear what you two are saying, but there's a link missing for me. I'm convinced, even though Jane can be devious, tonight's takeover had Anne's fingerprints all over it."

Harlan agreed with her. "So, what are you going to do about it?"

"Nothing I can do about what's been planned, but I can make sure I do my best controlling the actual YipYeow Day. I'll need your help, Marcus, to make sure nothing more goes awry with your food sponsorship."

"The only thing that could go wrong is if we can't get the pub open in the next week. Harlan, do you think Anne can or will stop us?"

"No. You heard her tonight. She plugged you as a sponsor and even mentioned you should be open in the next week. Her beef isn't with your restaurant re-opening in the strip center. In fact, she wants those jobs back in Wheaton so she can claim them when she runs for mayor. Her issue is with turning Main Street into a food and entertainment district. The big house is where she'll focus on throwing up roadblocks."

"How does Thomas Howell come into this? After Emily and I had lunch with him the other day, I saw him at a table with Jacob and Anne. They all looked quite chummy."

Marcus shook his head. "I don't like the sound of that any more than I like your sister taking over his food operations. Emily sees the best in people, but there isn't a good bone in Howling Hotel Tom. If he's in cahoots with Anne, it can't bode well for us."

Sarah nodded. She only hoped he was talking about the restaurant operations, but she had a feeling his words included his relationship with Emily.

"Now you see why Emily and I want to recruit someone impartial to be considered for the empty council seat."

Harlan chuckled. "Impartial or who represents your views?"

"Harlan, you know better than anyone what havoc will occur if the Hightowers can operate without any checks and balances. If they control that seat, there won't be a chance for economic development in downtown Wheaton for years. They'll let the town dry up and rot unless there's a way for them to trim their own corner off any deal."

"That's a little strong, don't you think, Marcus?"

"No, I don't. Without Lance, the council is split four to four. Not only do we need someone who supports economic development, but we also need someone who makes decisions for the good of Wheaton. Harlan, why don't you throw your name in? We might not agree with all your decisions or votes, but we know you'd be fair and impartial."

"And I'd probably have a heart attack within six months. I'm a lawyer, not a politician. Tried it once and quickly learned I'm much better dealing with people like the Hightowers from behind the scenes."

"It just isn't fair. You know, they say money talks and something else walks. Well, we sure saw that tonight." Sarah kicked her foot against the floor.

A startled RahRah ran across the room and hid under the couch.

"Sorry, RahRah. I should have opened my mouth and objected more."

Harlan laughed again. "You really didn't have a choice. This was a room of animal lovers. Who in the group wasn't going to want their pet blessed? Be honest, if you hadn't been afraid of the extra responsibility of planning the Blessing of the Beasts, wouldn't the idea of having RahRah blessed have sounded good to you?"

Shooting a quick look at RahRah, whose head peeked out from under the couch, Sarah couldn't help but smile. "You got me on that one, but I still hate being played."

CHAPTER TWENTY-SIX

At seven A.M., thirty minutes before her normal wake-up time, Sarah's doorbell rang. Still groggy, she grabbed her robe and cinched it closed on her way to the door. "I'm coming!"

Through the windowpane, she saw Cliff turn to leave.

"Wait!"

He kept walking until she opened the door and called his name.

He came back up the steps. "Good morning. Hope I didn't wake you."

"I'd be lying if I said no."

Cliff laughed but covered his mouth with his right hand, changing it into a cough.

Sarah ignored his obvious attempt at politeness. She was more interested in his bruised knuckles. "My manners must still be asleep. Won't you come in?"

"Thank you. I'm sorry for waking you. I forget normal people don't start their days as early as those of us in construction who start working before the sun is at its hottest."

"I hadn't thought about construction workers keeping a similar schedule to farmers, but I guess it's the same premise—up and out when it's light but before the heat of the day. But you didn't ring my bell at this hour to educate me on the hours construction workers work."

"No. I came by to fix my uncle's fence. He told me what happened after I left last night. As you can guess, he never called my brother or me, so I'm glad you were there for him."

"I'm not the one to thank. Dr. Smith, from the police department, patched him up. How is your uncle this morning?"

"Back to his normal spitfire self and completely taken by his new puppy. He's bathed, brushed, and cut away whatever was matted or tangled and plans to have her at the vet when the office opens. Although he said he will put her up for adoption through the shelter, I'm sort of hoping he decides to keep her. I haven't seen him this engaged since my aunt died."

"I'm glad to hear he's okay, but as much as I care about your uncle, I know you didn't wake me simply to report on his physical and emotional well-being." Or, she thought, to tell me how desperate your brother might be to send him to a retirement home. "Let's sit down and you can tell me what I can do for you."

She backed up in the entryway to let him pass to the living room. As she did, Sarah caught sight of herself in the hallway mirror. Her robe was opening near the neck. She grasped it, forcing the two ends closer together.

Cliff cleared his throat and ran his bruised fingers

through his surfer's hair. "Before I go to the store and match the materials I need to repair his fence, my uncle pointed out where you've got sharp jagged rods sticking up. He thought, because you hadn't gotten it repaired yet, you might like me to fix yours at the same time. If some kid playing on it hurts themselves, his parents could sue you, saying it was an attractive nuisance."

He was right. Talking about one of his cases, Harlan had once explained the concept of attractive nuisance. He'd said it was something dangerous that could lure someone in, like a pool without a fence. She remembered the owner could be held liable if someone was injured. With the weekend coming up, it would be a good idea to get her fence fixed.

"Um, my mother was going to have someone fix it, but, with the confusion of this week, I think it slipped her mind. How much would you charge to do the job?"

"Only the cost of materials."

"I couldn't. I know there's labor involved."

"Consider my labor a swap for the way you helped my uncle out and how, as he tells me, you keep an eye out for him."

"It's more the reverse."

"Is this the famous RahRah?" He reached down and patted RahRah, who was rubbing himself against Cliff's leg.

"It is. Did your uncle tell you about him?"

"No, Jane did. She told me what a terror he was when I repaired the mess he made here the day she moved him in. He doesn't seem so bad to me."

Sarah raised her chin and tightened her arms,

holding her robe closer to her. "Jane tends to exaggerate and have a problem with animals."

Cliff glanced at Sarah, while he continued petting RahRah.

She thought about refusing his offer, but that would only be spiting herself. Besides, Jane wasn't his only customer. Her sister and Marcus obviously also respected his workmanship. "I'd be appreciative if you fixed my fence, too, but are you going to be able to do it today?"

Sarah pointed to his hand. "Your hand looks badly bruised. Is it broken?"

Cliff flexed his hand and slipped it into his pocket. "Nothing broken. It's sore, but I can work with it."

"Was it a work-related accident?"

"No." Instead of meeting her gaze, he stared at his feet. When he finally looked up, he had the look of a little boy caught with his hand in the cookie jar. "I feel like a fool admitting this, but I hurt it when I punched Lance after we had words."

"When did you punch Lance?"

"When he still wouldn't talk to me about why the bank called my mortgage."

Sarah wrinkled her brow in confusion. Unless he threw the punch before he came out of Lance's office with Jacob, she wasn't sure when he'd hit him. Cliff was upset but not physical in her presence. "Because of Emily and Marcus having their loan rejected, I can commiserate with you having your loan called. I'm sure it messed up whatever job it was related to. Speaking of finances, do you need some money in advance to buy the finials and whatever else you'll need to do my job?"

"No. I'll lay it out and you can pay me when I finish. And by the way, the bank refusing my loan didn't interfere with any of my jobs. This was for a personal project."

Remembering what Jacob had said about the loan being for a cabin he was building for himself, Sarah pressed him for more information. "Were you building something for yourself?"

She held her hands up. "You don't have to answer that. Sometimes I get a bit nosy."

"No, it's okay. I'm building a small cabin on the bluff, just outside the city limits."

"The bluff overlooking the water?"

"Yeah."

"I knew it was bought because of the 'No Trespassing' signs. Before they went up, on bad days, I used to ride my bike out there, just to sit and think. It's such a peaceful place."

"You're so right about that. Feel free to come back anytime you need that kind of peace. Ignore the signs. I know the owner intimately."

Both laughed.

"I might just take you up on that. It always was one of my favorite places."

"Well," Cliff hesitated. He slipped his hands into his pockets and glanced at her sideways without moving his head. "If you'd like to see my work in progress, I'd be glad to show you. Maybe tomorrow? Or, do you work on Saturday?"

"I don't work on Saturdays, but with YipYeow Day only eight days away, I think I better hold off visiting until after it's over. Did you have to stop working on the cabin when the bank called your loan?"

Cliff shook his head. "I juggled enough things to finish the exterior, but there still are a lot of interior finishing touches needed. It still doesn't make any sense to me why Lance called the loan. All I was trying to do was refinance to take advantage of the lower interest rates."

He took his hands out of his pockets, bent his bruised hand a few times, and then supported it with his opposite hand. "Maybe I didn't handle myself well, but there wasn't any reason for Lance to pull the rug out from under me. My cash flow and savings are good. Why, I even recently bought a new boat with no problem whatsoever."

"It sounds like instead of calling your loan, they rejected your request for a new loan. I think refinancing is always handled as a new loan, so instead of Lance, it probably was Bailey who denied your loan." Sarah parroted Lance's words to her mother about credit issues, types of loans, and other things that might have resulted in Bailey's denial.

"Neither Lance nor Bailey ever said anything about problems with any of those things. If they had, it might have made more sense, or at least I could have explained or clarified whatever mix-up occurred. All Lance told me when I went back to see him was he was busy getting ready for the council meeting and there was nothing more to discuss for now. He basically dismissed me like I was five. That's when I acted like I was and punched him."

Sarah stared at Cliff, a light dawning for her as she realized Cliff must have visited Lance for a third time. Watching him rub his hand, just like he did on the way into the city council meeting, she felt uneasy.

"Cliff, did you go back to see Lance after you were in his office with my mother and me?"

"Yeah, one of my more brilliant moves."

Thinking over this bit of information, it dawned on her that Eloise hadn't mentioned seeing him a third time. Sarah tried to reconcile what Cliff was saying with what Eloise told her. Maybe he'd come when Eloise was getting the paper or perhaps he was one of the mystery voices. She made sure she could see his eyes clearly before she posed her next question. "Cliff, how did you get into his office the third time?"

"From the alley. I figured if I went through the lobby, I'd never get to see him."

"Was the door open?"

"No, I knocked, smiled, waved at the security camera, and waited until he let me in."

"Did anyone see you in his office?"

Cliff raised a brow in confusion. "How could they? I don't know if anyone other than Lance saw the camera feed into his office."

"Why did you go through the alley? In fact, why did Lance let anyone in from the alley?"

He shrugged. "It was no big deal. That was the way Uncle George always went to see him. I guess it was convenient if you were coming from this part of town or the renovated square, but I never thought about why we went that way."

"I'm surprised the bank permitted people to come through the alley entrance. I would think it would have been off limits to the public."

"Between you and me, I think Lance liked having a bit of flexibility. Sometimes his watchdog guarded his schedule so tightly she didn't give him the freedom he wanted."

It took Sarah a minute to put two and two together and figure out Eloise was the watchdog. "I thought Lance and Eloise had a good relationship."

"Don't get me wrong. Lance and all of us loved Eloise, but she ran interference for him with the tenacity of a tiger. That's why Lance didn't stop folks like my uncle from doing an end run around Eloise by using the alley entrance. In some ways, I think it was a cat-and-mouse game for Lance because normally he'd give himself away by calling her to bring something he needed into his office."

"Did he call her in this time?"

Cliff thought for a moment. "He tried just before I punched him, but she didn't answer."

"Do you remember about when that was?"

"Not exactly, but it was before you saw me at the council meeting."

"Cliff, this could be important. How long were you there?"

"I don't know. When I got there, Lance opened the door and immediately lit into me. Told me I needed to grow up if I ever wanted to be a successful businessman. I tried to get a word in edgewise about my mortgage, but, like I told you, he cut me off and told me to leave because he needed to finish doing something before the council meeting. He said he'd look into it later and tried to call Eloise, but she didn't answer."

"Did you go?"

"I should have. Instead, I tried again to make him listen to me. He refused and dismissed me with some crack about if I was ever going to amount to anything,

I might do well to model my business dealings after Thomas. Between that comment and being dismissed, I saw red and hit him. I immediately regretted it, but it was too late. He ordered me out of his office, sat down at his desk, and acted as if I didn't exist."

"What happened then?"

"I muttered an apology, but he ignored me and busied himself with his paperwork. There wasn't anything else to do, so I left his office and went to the council meeting."

"And you're sure no one saw you?"

Cliff ran his hand through his hair again. "Eloise or someone else may have come in after I left, but not while I was there. I felt like such a jerk, I didn't hang around or go through the lobby. I went out the same door I came in."

"The alley door? Did you close it behind you?"

"I can't remember if it snapped shut or I pulled it shut. I feel sure it was closed, but I can't swear to it."

CHAPTER TWENTY-SEVEN

Although she hoped Cliff hadn't killed Lance, Sarah was excited she'd identified at least one more suspect Harlan could point out to Chief Gerard. She couldn't imagine how the chief would be able to deny the fact that one person, and maybe more, other than her mother, was in Lance's office before his murder. And, in this case, the suspect admitted physically attacking Lance.

Still, while Cliff left to pick up what he needed to fix the fences, she said a silent prayer the chief, if he worked at it, would uncover more suspects. She knew her mother wasn't the murderer and she didn't want Cliff to be, either. Despite his loose-cannon style, he, like his brother, had several redeeming qualities. Still, being realistic, one of those who'd told her Cliff was a good guy was now dead.

She needed to get ready for work, but her mind kept returning to her exchange with Cliff. If neither he nor her mother were guilty, who was? Eloise? She claimed to have heard different voices in the office, but was she telling the truth? For the person who knew everything, she couldn't pinpoint who they

were, whether Lance was one of the speakers, or even
how many people she'd heard at any given time. What
if, instead of going to the storage room, she'd gone
into the office, killed Lance, and circled back through
the alley, accidentally leaving the door unlocked? But
why? If Lance had Eloise reconciling balances, could
she have helped herself to some money and hidden
it? Maybe keeping things tidy on the outside was why
Bailey, now serving as the acting president, had replaced her with Amanda.

And what did Sarah really know about Amanda?
She didn't even know how long she'd been a teller
and what her qualifications were for being moved
into Eloise's job. Maybe Eloise was like those often-
overlooked employees who killed the boss when a
sweet young thing took over his attention. Or perhaps
Amanda had seen a chance to move up if Lance was
out of the way.

Then again, Eloise could have been gone longer
than she thought, giving Bailey, Amanda, Thomas, or
even Alvin the chance to pop into Lance's office and
commit the deadly deed. For that matter, Eloise could
have done it if she was away from her desk for less
time than she admitted. The more Sarah thought
about it, the more she realized she was relying on
Eloise's statements. She'd been letting her feelings
about Eloise keep her from being a suspect.

Using YipYeow Day and its finances as a cover,
Sarah decided she needed to make another visit to
the bank. It might also be a good idea to go see
Thomas again.

If she could think of this many possible scenarios,
she couldn't understand why Chief Gerard wasn't

looking into any of them. She'd have to discuss them with Harlan and see if he could light a fire under the chief.

Thinking about lighting a fire brought Sarah's attention back to being one of Emily's servers at the reception after the funeral. She glanced toward her closet. Considering the short time between today's two events, she needed to wear something other than her usual little black dress. She pulled a sweater, muted skirt, and a pair of black slacks from her closet and examined them. Her mind made up, she hung the skirt back. As graceful as she was as a server, pants and flats were a better choice than a skirt and heels.

She turned the slacks and sweater around in the light, checking there were no spots from an earlier wearing. Satisfied, she started to dress but, worried about messing up her outfit, she decided to take care of RahRah first.

RahRah had contentedly rubbed against Cliff's leg while Sarah and Cliff talked in the doorway, but once the door closed, he'd raised his head and strutted into the kitchen. She didn't even have to look to know he went to his personal spot, where the warm sunlight streamed into the kitchen. Sure enough, she found him in the kitchen, stretched across the cool linoleum as far as he physically could.

"You are a creature of habit."

Other than twitching his little black nose, RahRah didn't budge while she filled his water bowl and opened a can of his favorite wet food. Usually, he showed some reaction to being fed wet food instead of the dry stuff, but not today. His lack of movement came across as loud and clear as a printed "Do Not Disturb" sign.

"Not hungry or having a bit of an attitude? It doesn't matter. I'm going to work. Remember, though, I'll be a little late tonight, but your food and water are here."

Chapter Twenty-eight

Harlan's car was in his rear lot when she pulled into her parking spot. She let herself in through the back door and immediately went to his private office. He was standing on top of his desk, screwing in a light-bulb. "Is this where I'm supposed to ask how many lawyers it takes to change a lightbulb?"

"Very funny. One of the bulbs burned out yesterday and we were out of this wattage in the storeroom, so I stopped at the hardware store on my way in this morning."

He finished the job, lowered himself off his desk, and sat down to work. He put on his readers and picked up the top folder from the center of his desk. When she didn't leave, he looked over his readers at her. "Shouldn't you be out front at your desk?"

From his clipped speech and immediate return of his attention to the still-closed folder, she wondered if Harlan was exhibiting a bit of attitude. "Actually, I have some news I want to share with you."

Although he didn't wave her toward his guest chairs or the couch, as was his norm, she dropped her purse in one chair and sat in the other one facing his desk. She told him what she'd been thinking.

His flat expression surprised her.

"Isn't this something you can use?"

"I'm sure by now, Chief Gerard already knows or will figure out Cliff came back a third time. Remember, Chief Gerard has Eloise's statement that she talked to Lance a few times and heard multiple voices in his office when she got back to her desk. He's going to consider this confirmation of what she related about overhearing voices in the office."

"Can't you cast doubt on her statement or prompt him to investigate further by arguing perhaps Cliff, in his moment of anger, did more than punch Lance? You could suggest he picked up the finial and, in a fit of rage, hit Lance over the head with it instead of punching him. After all, Cliff admitted that when he left, Lance was seated at his desk. That puts Cliff in the right position physically to have struck Lance from behind."

"Why would you want me to cast blame on Cliff? Isn't it bad enough Dwayne has your mother in his sights? Now you want him to go after someone who wants to date you?"

"What?"

"I ran into Cliff at the hardware store. He was picking up things to fix your fence and asked if you're seeing anyone."

Heat rushed up Sarah's neck. It wasn't the guy fixing her fence's business to be discussing her social life with her boss. If she didn't know better, she'd think, from his tone, that Harlan was jealous. She stared at him and thought back to their conversation on the square. He'd helped her so much since Bill divorced her, but even the other day, she hadn't imagined he cared for her in any way but as a friend. Until this moment, she hadn't thought of any possibility for them to be more than friends. She quickly decided, at least for now, she wasn't going to, either.

"Harlan, what's gotten into you? I shouldn't dignify your crazy thoughts, but I'm not dating Cliff."

"He seemed to think you're going out to the bluff soon to see his cabin."

"I told Cliff I missed visiting the bluff since it sold. For years, that's where I went when I needed to clear my head. No one ever stopped me. I don't even think the prior owners ever stepped foot on the bluff. The last time I went there, sometime last year, must have been after Cliff bought the land because there were 'No Trespassing' signs posted everywhere."

"As if that would keep you out."

Sarah ignored his snide remark. "Cliff invited me to come out and enjoy the bluff whenever I want. I told him I'd take him up on that. I've missed going there. That's when he offered to show me his cabin, but I declined because I'm swamped with YipYeow Day. What's important here isn't whether I'm ever going out to the bluff again, it's all the things I've found out that might help prove my mother isn't a murderer."

Harlan didn't say anything for a moment. He ran his hand through his thinning hair. "Sarah, you've come up with a lot of different possibilities. No matter how we paint it, Dwayne's not going to believe or waste time considering, even for a moment, Cliff murdered Lance. Cliff is an open book to Chief Gerard."

"I don't understand."

"Dwayne has known Cliff since Dwayne was a beat cop. He's aware of Cliff's past."

"Oh? Did they have some run-ins in the past?"

"Nothing major. Excessive partying when Cliff tried college and malicious mischief and a hot temper during the few months he stayed with his uncle after he washed out of Alabama. Dwayne is also aware that once Cliff became involved in the building industry, he straightened up. And the chief knows his uncle was proud enough of the change in Cliff to back him when he started his construction company. By the way, Cliff paid back that loan with interest."

"Does that mean Cliff is one hundred percent the good nephew? Or is Mr. Rogers now afraid of him, too?" Before he could answer, she supplied the words for him. "I know, Cliff is a good guy, but I gather Thomas isn't?"

"Let's just say he's a different animal from the same mother."

Sarah's antenna went up. "Harlan, Em's working for Thomas. Is there something she should know? I don't care about attorney-client privilege. You've got to tell me."

"Nothing to tell right now except warn her to keep her eyes and ears open."

"With the mission Emily's on, that's going to be harder than you think. Eloise saw Thomas in the bank lobby when Mom and I were there. I never saw him, but maybe Thomas left through the front door then snuck back in through the alley or originally came in through the alley and left through the lobby. He could have been one of the voices Eloise heard."

"Anything's possible, but that's up to Chief Gerard to find out. It's the chief's call how far he investigates."

She stood and paced around his office. "I can't accept that. This is my mother we're talking about. If Chief Gerard isn't going to do his job thoroughly, I'm going to have to dig a little deeper."

"How many times do you have to be told to leave it to the professionals?"

Sarah snorted. "Little good that did last time."

"Maybe not, but in this instance, if Chief Gerard doesn't investigate every possible suspect, he's giving me reasonable doubt to play with in a jury's mind if he insists on trying to make a case against your mother."

"What?" Sarah felt a sudden wave of coldness surge throughout her. This was real. Harlan was thinking ahead to trial strategy. "Harlan, are you trying to tell me my mother is definitely going to be arrested and put on trial for murder?"

He shook his head. "That's not what I'm saying. I don't know what's going to happen, but as your mother's lawyer, I need to be prepared for any possibility."

Silently thinking about what all of this might mean for her mother, she left his office. Back at her desk, an email message from the mayor's aide was waiting. Because he hadn't been able to attend, the mayor wanted a full report on the accomplishments of Sarah's committee since the meeting. Sarah drafted a pithy comment about how the city didn't even act in less than twenty-four hours after any of its meetings. Cooling off, she deleted it. Instead, she called Pastor Dobbins to see if he could give her more information about the Blessing of the Beasts.

By the end of their call, she felt relieved. Sunday

shouldn't be a problem. Pastor Dobbins not only had done this type of blessing many times, but he had a script ready to go. Better yet, the LBC Ladies' Auxiliary, excited their church was hosting the YipYeow Days Blessing of the Beasts, insisted on preparing refreshments for after the service. He'd chuckled when he told her they already were designing a menu of sweets, finger sandwiches, and drinks.

Equally important in Sarah's mind, Pastor Dobbins's wife, as he'd expected, was on board with the Convention Bureau helping with signage, registration for both days, and name tags. Her only concern was she wanted to highlight the Southwind Pub party rather than the Howellian fund-raiser because she hoped it would entice people to spend the evening in Wheaton. Almost apologetically, the pastor hoped that would be okay. Sarah reassured him that emphasizing the event at the reopened Southwind Pub was better than okay.

Satisfied she had enough information to share, Sarah typed a reply to the mayor's aide, stressing everything already accomplished and what was in the planning stage based upon last night's meeting. When she hit send, she felt pretty good about her reply. Better than she felt about the funeral it was time to attend.

CHAPTER TWENTY-NINE

The crowd at the funeral was even more than Sarah expected. It was standing room only in the town's largest church. The church's décor reminded her of the interior of the bank, probably because they were built around the same time. Polished paneled walls, a high-set altar, and beautiful stained-glass windows gave her a sensation of awe.

Many people, including her mother, were already seated in the sanctuary when Sarah joined the line of people paying their respects to the family and the deceased. The line moved at a good clip but then suddenly slowed. Wondering if the inching line would delay the beginning of the service, she glanced ahead to ascertain what the problem was.

It was Jane holding up the line as she grasped the hands of Lance's widow and kept talking to her. Sarah couldn't hear what she was saying, but she interpreted the expression on Jane's face as earnest, while Lance's widow simply appeared bewildered. As she watched, the minister placed his hand on Jane's arm and helped move her along.

Sarah was relieved as the line picked up speed until

she heard Jane, who somehow was now standing beside her, say, "I'm surprised your mother had the guts to be here today."

"Excuse me?"

"You heard me. I'm surprised, after what we all know your mother did to poor Lance, that she dared to show her face at his funeral. She should already have been locked up and the key thrown away."

Not wanting to make a scene, Sarah turned her face away from Jane and moved forward with the line. Jane didn't follow. Sarah quickly reached Mrs. Knowlton and paid her respects, before leaving the altar to sit with her mother. She wondered how many other snide remarks were being made in the sanctuary. Judging by her mother's ramrod-stiff posture, Jane's comment wasn't the only one.

Covering her mother's hand with hers, Sarah looked around the church. The other pews and even the balcony were now full. Lance Knowlton may not have pleased everyone in town, but they'd all turned out to say good-bye to him.

Differences between family members also seemed to have been forgotten today. Jacob sat with his father and sister in the second row. Mr. Rogers and his nephews were a few rows behind them. Eloise joined them, rather than sitting on the other side of the church with Mr. Bailey, Amanda, and a small group of people Sarah recognized as working at the bank crowded into one pew.

When the line finally dwindled, the minister stepped forward and signaled the family to take their seats on the side of the altar. He appeared to be about to begin the service when Sarah spotted Chief Gerard, as she was sure most of the other funeral goers did, slowly walk up to the front to pay his respects to the family. He bent over the short railing separating the family from the actual altar area and spoke for a few moments to Lance's widow. Finished, he turned and came back up the center aisle, passing the row where Sarah and her mother sat. Sarah waited a few seconds and then craned her neck to see where he went. He was two rows behind them.

In all the mystery books she'd read, the police came to the victim's funeral to observe the mourners because they knew the murderer would be present. The killer came, being cool about his presence, to enjoy his handiwork. Sarah hoped the chief's seat choice wasn't telegraphing his thoughts about Lance's murder. She peered around the sanctuary again, figuring if the police behaved like fictional characters, the murderer had to be somewhere in the room.

No one jumped out at her.

CHAPTER THIRTY

Sarah hurried downstairs to the fellowship hall during the final hymn. Using flowers, colored table-cloths, and food, Emily and Grace had transformed the fellowship hall from its usual utilitarian look. Even Sarah, who rarely noticed that kind of thing, was aware it was lovely. The only thing that bothered her were the pretty napkins placed strategically on the serving tables with the Howellian insignia. In Sarah's gut, she knew they should read Southwind.

She walked up to a serving table where Grace was arranging different types of pickup desserts for the funeral reception. For a moment, with Emily out of sight, this felt like a déjà vu moment. It had been Grace who helped Sarah keep things going during the food expo when Emily was taken to the police sta-tion. Sarah originally had been nervous working with Grace, but her initial misgivings had rapidly disap-peared. Despite her appearance and youth, Grace was one hundred percent wiser in the kitchen than Sarah. Her knife skills and following of restaurant protocol were impressive.

"Hi, Grace! Looks like you have everything under control, but is there anything I can do to help?"

Grace jumped, almost dropping the tray. "You scared me. I didn't hear you come up behind me."

"Sorry." Sarah repeated her offer to help.

"It would be great if you could finish transferring these desserts from our serving tray to the silver platter while I get the coffee urns ready." Grace handed Sarah the tray she'd barely held on to. "Just keep repeating the pattern I started."

"Will do. Where's Emily?"

"In the kitchen."

Sarah placed the tray in a clear space on the table. "I'll just pop in to say 'hi' to her before I finish this."

"I wouldn't do that."

"Why not?"

"Marcus and she have been exchanging words for about the last ten minutes. Better to stay out here and finish with the desserts."

"Aye, aye." Sarah gave Grace a mock salute while staring at the closed door to the kitchen. Getting into the middle of a disagreement between her sister and Marcus was the last thing she wanted to do. Instead, Sarah kept her head down and concentrated on carefully lining up the mini-desserts. She recognized the carrot cake and red velvet cupcakes, but she wasn't sure what the yellowish one in green paper with a dab of icing and a few nuts on top was.

Sarah looked around to see if Grace was busy. Not only was she doing something, but her back was to Sarah. Perfect. Sarah popped one of the unknown mini-cupcakes into her mouth. The delightful taste of banana nut bread filled her mouth. It was delicious, but Sarah made herself not eat another one. They were for the reception guests.

As she put the last cupcake on the silver platter, the kitchen door opened. Marcus came out. He walked to where Sarah was, but he wasn't looking at her. His gaze was on the x-shaped serving tables. Without saying anything to Grace or her, he turned and left the fellowship hall. Sarah watched him go until she heard Emily come up beside her.

"He's not happy with me," Emily said.

"He'll get over it."

"I hope so."

Any further discussion was cut off by the arrival of the first group of funeral guests. Sarah doubted any of this group was the murderer, but from the way they attacked the serving tables, she thought they all qualified as vultures.

By the time the first onslaught of mourners went through the line, Grace and Sarah were busily changing out the trays of finger sandwiches, desserts, and other goodies with refills Emily prepared in the kitchen. From the comments she overheard, Sarah knew the reception was a success, and it was being laid directly at the feet of Thomas Howell and the Howellian.

She could tell, from the way he was holding court in the middle of the room. Thomas knew it, too. Observing his smile, glad-handing, and physical demeanor would have been enough for her to gather an impression, but it was confirmed when he signaled her over as if she was a taxicab he was hailing.

"This is Sarah Blair," he announced to anyone in earshot. "Sarah's sister, Emily, is my Howellian executive chef." He waved his hand toward the serving tables. "Everything you see here is just a taste of our hotel menu. We pride ourselves on serving the best, whether at the hotel restaurant or in your home."

He lowered his voice so only Sarah could hear him. "Speaking of serving, would you please get me a tonic water with a twist of lime?"

Sarah nodded and went to the bar for his drink. When she returned with it, he took it without breaking stride on advertising the Howellian to take the time to thank her. Disgusted, she went to the serving table and joined Emily in consolidating some of the trays. The crowd had thinned to the point they wouldn't be putting out any additional food.

She looked around the room to see who was left and was surprised to see Marcus had returned and was engaged in a discussion with Anne Hightower and George Rogers. Curious, she picked up a small tray of desserts, walked over to them, and stood silently waiting for a break in their conversation to offer them the goodies.

Up close, she could tell from his red cheeks that Marcus was exasperated but trying to hold it in.

"I appreciate that you feel all the permits and other minor technicalities for the pub should be resolved in the next few days, but when will the council hear the issue of my other restaurant? I know it was on last week's agenda, so why delay addressing it?"

Anne patted her hair. "I know it's important to you, Marcus, but the council has so much pressing business, including appointing a replacement to serve out Lance's term, that I don't see how it will come up for a vote for quite some time."

"But why?"

"Well, there's been a request for a feasibility study. If that's the case, you can't imagine how much work will have to go into studying it for compliance and the environmental impact on Wheaton of what you're proposing. If I were you, I'd put my energy into the pub and your catering business."

Mr. Rogers leaned on his new cane. "Looks like instead of spinning your wheels about a restaurant in the big house, you'd be far better off concentrating on that pub and your catering right away." He gestured with his free arm encompassing the room. "After today's shindig, I'd be worried about the Howellian cutting into your business."

"But this food is Southwind style. In fact, it's been made by Emily, my co-owner."

Mr. Rogers put his hand on Marcus's shoulder. "Son, I know you're not a fool. Look around here, this reception and my nephew running his mouth over there are what people are going to remember. Take what you can get for now and get your name back out there."

Sarah was afraid of what might come out of Marcus's mouth next. So far, he hadn't said anything that could be used against him, but she knew how he could blow his stack. She stuck her tray of desserts into their little discussion circle. "Would anyone like a dessert treat? There's mini red velvet, banana nut, and carrot cake."

Mr. Rogers took a mini red velvet off the tray. He popped it into his mouth. "Delicious."

Sarah handed him a napkin.

"Thank you." Mr. Rogers inspected her tray and

selected a carrot cake this time. She could tell from the smile on his face that he enjoyed this cupcake, too.

"Which one did you like best?"

"It was a tie." He reached for a banana nut treat. "I guess I'll just have to try all three to see if any of them are losers."

After he took his third treat, Sarah offered the tray to everyone again. This time Mr. Rogers declined, as did Marcus.

Anne glanced at her watch and declared, "Look at the time. I really must get going. Hopefully, I'll see all of you at Tuesday's council meeting. Thanks to your YipYeow meeting, I think we've identified some good candidates for appointment to Lance's slot."

Watching Anne's retreating back, Sarah held her tray out again toward Marcus and Mr. Rogers as she tried to think who in the room Anne might consider a good candidate.

CHAPTER THIRTY-ONE

Saturday morning was beautiful. The kind of day warm enough to go coatless, cold enough not to have to worry about becoming overheated. As Sarah went through her morning routine of brushing her teeth and dressing, she kept up a running chatter with RahRah, who comfortably snuggled into his already warm spot on Sarah's blanket.

"RahRah, do you think I should give Cliff a present? He wouldn't take money, except for the materials, for fixing my fence."

RahRah purred.

"I have a nice bottle of wine chilling in the refrigerator, but I don't want to be suggestive. I also could, on my way to the shelter, bring him a few of Emily's breakfast loaves. Aren't you going to tell me what to do?"

Although RahRah twitched his tail, he didn't give her a definitive answer. She pleaded again, and this time he jumped off the bed and sauntered to the kitchen. She followed. He stood in front of the refrigerator and nudged the freezer side with his nose.

Sarah opened the refrigerator door of her side by

side and reached for the wine but stopped when
RahRah placed his paw on the inner doorframe. "Are
you trying to tell me something?"

RahRah stepped back and again rubbed his head
against the freezer door.

"Sorry. I misunderstood you. Apparently, you think
the wine will give the wrong impression here, too."
She took three small loaves out of the freezer and put
them on the table. From her "don't throw away anything you might someday need" closet, she pulled a
gift bag and tissue paper still in perfect condition for
recycling. After examining the tag and realizing it was
addressed to her, she pulled it off before she dropped
the banana, spinach, and chocolate-chip loaves into the
bag's bottom and carefully arranged the colorful tissue
paper. Sarah held the bag up to show RahRah. "Perfect, don't you think?"

She laughed as he left the kitchen and started for
parts of the house unknown. She quickly retrieved him.

With RahRah fed and tucked away in the kitchen,
the breads on the front seat beside her, and the windows down, she was on her way to the bluff. She took
a deep breath of the clear air and savored the moment.

At the turnoff for the bluff, she realized a graded dirt
road had replaced the rutted access way people previously used. She was glad to see the road's path veered
away from the edge of the bluff. In the distance, Sarah
saw a log cabin set back far enough to allow a view of
the bluff, but out of range of spoiling the area jutting
out over the water. When Cliff talked about building
on the bluff, she'd feared his construction would have
destroyed her favorite scenic hangout spot. It hadn't,

because he obviously took great pains to adapt the placement of his home to the land's natural beauty.

Slowing to take in the view as the road curved, she smiled. Maybe she was more like RahRah than she thought. RahRah's great joy was sunning himself in his spot in the kitchen. Until last year, her sanity moments came when she stretched out in the sun on the bluff.

Knowing she couldn't stay in the turn of the road forever, she gave the car some gas and drove up to Cliff's log cabin. It wasn't large, but, from the few amenities, including the wraparound porch, she could tell this cabin, like its positioning, was a labor of love.

As she parked, Cliff walked down the steps to her car. He was quite a bit more kempt than the day she first saw him in the bank. His hair was combed, beard trimmed, and his washed-out blue jeans and red-plaid flannel shirt fit her original Paul Bunyan with surfer-coloring impression of him.

She was surprised to see a book in his hand. From her conversations with Harlan and Jacob, she had the impression the outdoors and construction suited Cliff but reading and writing were things he avoided.

She glanced at the cloudless blue sky as she reached across the seat for the present she'd brought. "I'm on my way to town, but I wanted to thank you again for fixing my fence."

She handed Cliff the wrapped loaves of breakfast bread.

"Thank you. You shouldn't have."

"But I wanted to."

Pleasantries exchanged, they awkwardly stared at each other.

Sarah broke the ice first. "What are you reading?"

"A book."

She laughed and pointed at the book in his hand. "That much I figured out. Which one is it?"

Cliff blushed. "*Tom Sawyer*. I wasn't much of a reader in my younger days. Now, up here, I sit on my porch and read for hours. I'm trying to catch up on the classics I missed along the way."

He held the book so she could see its spine. She recognized the decorative leaf motif surrounding the book's title. "Emily and I had a series of books with that same styling when we were children. I think they were weekly giveaways or only a dollar or so at the grocery when we were kids. They're still sitting on a shelf at my mom's house."

"Our mothers must have shopped at the same supermarket, because that's where these came from, too. They were boxed up after she passed and left at Uncle George's house. We've been helping him go through some of his stuff recently. When Tom and I opened this box of books, he didn't want them, but I couldn't bring myself to give them away until I read them."

When he stopped speaking as if lost in his thoughts, Sarah jumped into the silent gap. "If your mom was like mine, I bet she read them to you before you could read them for yourself."

"She did, but enough of that. Do you have time to see the cabin or take a short spin on the river?"

Sarah consulted her dashboard clock and did some quick mental calculations. "I'm on dog-walking duty at the shelter in an hour, so I really only have time for the Cook's tour."

"Great."

He opened the car door for her. Once she was out, he slammed it shut and led her up the steps to his porch. Two rockers, a swing hung by chains, and a table graced the porch. The interesting thing to her was the different textures in the hewn-wood pieces. She wasn't familiar with any store that sold rockers or swings finished in this manner. "Did you make these?"

"Yes. Bit by bit. I have a shop set up in a shed out back, plus I had access to a makeshift workshop while we were working on the hotel. At night, I took out my frustrations by building furniture for the cabin."

"Did you make things other than the rockers and swing?"

"A few things."

"Like what?"

"My dining table with its benches and a frame with built-in shelving for my bed."

"That sounds interesting. I can't wait to see your bedroom." Now, it was Sarah's turn to be embarrassed. "I didn't mean that the way it came out."

"Are you sure?" Cliff smiled.

Sarah face was flaming hot, and she was probably blushing like her mother and sister often did, but she had to admit he was worth blushing about. She turned away from him and focused her gaze on the end of the bluff. The view from his porch, and probably from the picture window cut into the front of his house, was magnificent. He'd positioned the two to allow one to take in the land rolling down toward the water perfectly. From where she stood on the porch, she could see that even the curve in the road was planned to make sure the view wasn't intruded upon. Without thinking, she blurted out her hope no one ever built a house between his porch and the bluff.

"They won't while I own the property. To me, the bluff is sacred. It's why I bought this land."

"I understand. For years, I thought of this as my secret place. I found it exploring on my bike when I was a kid. Until you bought it, there were never people up here." She paused and reflected a moment before sharing a little more of herself with him. "This is where I came when I wanted to think or simply get away."

"Feel free to use it anytime you want. I'm rarely home, and the bluff is always there."

"Thank you. There might come a time when I take you up on your offer."

The smile vanished from his face, replaced by a look of concern that she appreciated. "Something going on?"

"No. Thanks for asking, though."

Cliff turned his head toward the bluff. "Sometimes, even when things are going well, it's nice to have a safe spot. I think that's why I bought this land immediately. There was something calming and restorative about this view and the water."

Sarah nodded in agreement.

"When I'm here, if I'm not woodworking or reading, the water is my getaway. I've already been out once today and left the boat tied at the dock to go out again. Tell you what, my cabin will keep. You told me your time today is limited because of needing to be at the shelter, so why don't we take a short spin. It's beautiful today. What do you say?"

She glanced through the window into his cabin and back at the water. There was no question it was beautiful. "I'm game. Lead the way."

He immediately took off toward the point of the bluff. As they neared the area where she normally perched and looked out at the water, she saw a path cleared on the wooded side of the bluff. Railroad ties and gravel created natural-looking steps and landings. She followed Cliff down the path to a boathouse and dock. Its strategic placement in the trees blocked it from being seen from the top of the bluff.

She couldn't believe the view from where they stood on a wide dock, complete with chairs and a propane-powered grill, connected to a dock with two slips. Being more level with the water emphasized the power of the current and its speed as it flowed. She shifted her gaze from the water and trees to Cliff's water toys.

A pontoon boat was tied off in one slip while she could see a motor boat had been winched up and secured above the other. A flat-bottom boat was pulled high onto the shore next to a small shed. Cliff went directly to the shed and opened it. From where she stood, she could see extra life jackets, tubes, and water-skiing toys neatly hanging on one wall. There was a Jet Ski parked in the far corner. While she wasn't sure if the Jet Ski was operational, there was no question the boats were.

Cliff handed her a life jacket. "When I was out earlier, the water was like glass."

Sarah settled into her seat on the pontoon boat while Cliff cast off. He started the motor and carefully guided the boat out of the slip. As he eased it out, she couldn't help but notice how the lines of his face and the angle of his shoulders relaxed. She hadn't realized how much tension he carried. She glanced back as his boathouse became smaller in the distance and then looked up toward the bluff. From the water, his house wasn't visible. Considering his toys, the property, and his house, Sarah wondered if he was overextended or if Lance and Bailey made a mistake denying his refinancing application.

Sarah leaned back, enjoying her cushioned seat. Although she'd been out on this river often in motorboats, this was her first time cruising on a pontoon. It definitely was a smoother ride and she liked the idea of room in the center of the boat for passengers to move around. Sarah took in the scenery, but her focus was on her skipper.

Cliff sat in the captain's chair, with a cap perched on his head. Whistling softly, he pushed forward on the throttle and drove the pontoon boat into open water. While the boat picked up speed, he concentrated on the river and his instruments, seemingly oblivious to her staring at him. Sarah couldn't believe this was the same person who had menacingly threatened Thomas Howell. Reconciling his volatile and good sides was difficult, but there was no question today's Cliff was the good guy everyone talked about.

A bird squawking overhead caught her attention. As she looked up, Cliff slowed the boat and pointed to a high tree near the shoreline. "Can you see the nest near the top? I think she's got some babies up there. For a while, the male bird brought food to her, but the last few days, she's ventured from the nest."

Sarah followed the line of his gaze and finger. For

a moment, all she saw were the leaves of the tree, but a faint movement caught her attention. She strained her eyes and caught the mother bird perched on the edge of the nest. The bird bent forward, her beak aimed into the nest. Sarah wished she had binoculars. "Cliff, how did you spot the nest? I can barely see it."

"The past few weeks when I cruised the river, whenever I got near this area, the birds screeched and screamed. I didn't know why. Finally, I brought a pair of field glasses out with me, idled the boat, and watched and waited. Eventually, the birds got used to me because they hushed and went back to building their nest. I check on them whenever I come in this direction."

Sarah kept her eyes trained on the birds and the nest. "I'm jealous of you."

"Why?"

"For finding the time to enjoy things like this. I always seem to be running from one thing to another or putting out some type of crisis." She glanced at her wristwatch. "Oh, my. I didn't realize how long we've been out here. I've got to get back or I'm going to be late."

CHAPTER THIRTY-TWO

Sarah ran into the animal shelter, almost knocking Phyllis Peters down.

"Whoa! Where's the fire, Sarah?"

"I'm sorry. Are you okay?"

Seeing the grin on Phyllis's face, Sarah knew she'd done no damage. She apologized again. "Normally, I'm very punctual, but I lost track of time and then I ran into traffic."

"Sarah, it's not a big deal. You're only fifteen minutes late. Harlan has already started walking and playing with the dogs."

Even as she said, "That's great," Sarah inwardly groaned that on the one day she went to the lake and was late, Harlan was on time. Usually, she was the one who arrived first and spent the afternoon teasing him about how he could be on time for everything Monday through Friday, but never on Saturday. "I guess I better join him."

"Wait a moment. I want to talk to you about YipYeow Day."

"Is there a problem?" The last thing Sarah needed was to have to deal with another headache.

"None that I know of. I thought it would be a good idea to review the schedule of events. I want to make sure we have the animals in place and everything ready for the different speakers."

Sarah ran through the planned day, including who was assigned to do what. When she finished to Phyllis's satisfaction, she realized another fifteen minutes had elapsed. "I really need to go help Harlan. He's going to be wondering where I am."

Without giving Phyllis time to come up with another question, she fled in the direction of the animal runs used for big dogs near the rear of the shelter. As she expected, Harlan was walking two of the larger dogs.

He relinquished one of the leashes to her. "I didn't think you were going to make it today, so I doubled up to make sure no dog missed a walk. I guess you got tied up with YipYeow stuff."

Deciding a fib was better than giving him more to be annoyed about, she crossed her fingers. "I actually was here, a few minutes late because of traffic, but Phyllis stopped me to review the plans for YipYeow Day. She felt certain you could handle things while she and I talked."

"I did."

"See, she was right about you." Sarah hoped her teasing would wipe the look of displeasure off his face, but it didn't. "Harlan, is something wrong?"

"Yes. Remember what I told you about how I thought Dwayne would react even if we handed him Cliff as a suspect on a silver platter?"

Sarah nodded, afraid to speak.

"Well, it went as well as I expected."

"You said you weren't going to talk to him about Cliff."

"No. I specifically remember what I said. I told you 'no matter how we paint it, Dwayne's not going to believe, even for a moment, Cliff murdered Lance,' but that I could use it to raise reasonable doubt if we went to trial."

"I'm confused."

"I decided to try your idea of prompting Dwayne to look at other suspects, but, as I feared, he's got blinders on about Cliff. He said he's investigated some of the other possibilities I raised but he still believes your mother is the best suspect. And, well, he's gone so far as to talk to the city prosecutor. They're going to bring their case against her before the grand jury when it meets in ten days to see if they can get an indictment."

"But what kind of a case can the prosecutor present? Everyplace I look, there's a hole."

"He doesn't need to prove her guilt. Only enough for the grand jury to decide if criminal charges should be brought. The prosecutor will show your mother was alone with him in his office, she deliberately didn't use the public lobby entrance, and the only fingerprints found on the murder weapon are hers. He's got the elements covered. I'm sorry."

"Don't be sorry yet, Harlan. We still have a few more days to prove her innocence." This time he didn't tell her to leave it to the professionals.

CHAPTER THIRTY-THREE

Throughout the rest of the weekend and Monday, try as she might, Sarah couldn't think of a way to get her mother off the hook. She racked her brain and tried out her ideas on Harlan about everyone who might have had an opportunity to kill Lance. Although they both agreed Amanda and Bailey had opportunity, financial motives, and got promotions out of Lance's death, they also were faced with the fact that both ran into Lance's office from the lobby after Maybelle screamed.

Harlan questioned the veracity of Eloise's time line and unconfirmed reporting of the voices she heard, noting that she had opportunity when she allegedly went for the copier paper, but Sarah pointed out that they knew she'd heard at least Cliff's voice and that Eloise, too, responded to the scream from within the lobby. In the end, they were no further along in coming up with a new suspect than they were on Saturday. All they had concluded was that there were time periods everyone could have been outside the bank long enough to have gone in and out of

Lance's office through the alley before returning to the interior of the bank.

Consequently, this morning, Sarah couldn't concentrate on work. Her ringing desk phone made her think of the dinging bell signaling a round break for a boxer during a fight. "Endicott and Associates."

"One of these days, you have to explain to me who the associates are."

It amused Sarah that sometimes her sister's mind worked in the same way as hers, but it wasn't enough to make her crack a smile today. "Emily, what's up?"

"Can't a person simply call to tell her sister what a wonderful day it is?"

"She could, if her name wasn't Emily Johnson, who hasn't made that kind of telephone call even once in the almost thirty years she'd been on earth. I repeat, to what do I owe the pleasure of this call?"

"Good news."

"About Mom?"

"I only wish. More about us. Mr. Bailey called first thing this morning to apologize for the error and tell me he signed the paperwork approving our loan application."

"Did he mention why he had a change of heart during his apology?"

"He said something about Mom's guarantee not being associated with the paperwork when he reviewed it but that Mr. Knowlton, before his death, recognized it was missing and made a note on the file. Once Mr. Bailey found the note, he immediately had his assistant locate the documents and he corrected his error. I blocked out the rest of what he said about how he hoped this was the beginning of a long and satisfactory relationship between Southwind and the bank. Whatever really happened doesn't matter. We've got the financing."

"Congratulations." Sarah didn't mention what Eloise had told her about Lance having the new paperwork drafted prior to last week's meeting. "Marcus must be happy."

"He's over the moon. Not only did the loan come through, but Cliff finished the venting, the stove arrived and was installed, and because Cliff was able to catch the building inspector, who happened to be in the building today, everything was signed off. Isn't it wonderful, Sarah? We'll be able to open the pub in time for soft openings before this weekend's YipYeow events and then we can plan a grand opening."

"That's wonderful." Sarah thought about the Saturday-night reception Marcus planned for the YipYeow volunteers. Now it could go off without a hitch. That was, unless you considered the fact that one half of the Southwind ownership team would be preparing the food at the Howellian.

"What did Marcus say about you not being there for the Saturday-night reception?"

There was a pause before Emily responded. "He's not thrilled, but he's come around to realizing my six months of work will make us far more solvent. Besides, we'll start soft openings at Southwind tomorrow and I'll be in and out for those first services. Sarah, I called because I need to ask another favor of you."

"What?"

"Because Southwind is opening and having its reception on Saturday night, I can't use Marcus's staff, except for Grace, at the Howellian. I called in all my chits, and I pretty much covered my kitchen-staff needs, but I'm short a few servers. I know you're going to be out in the sun most of the day with the YipYeow parade and the pet adoptions, but would you please help me out Saturday night?"

Sarah didn't have to think twice. Of course she would be there for Emily. It seemed ironic to Sarah that her cool, collected sister needed her help twice within two weeks. Considering, since childhood, Emily was the careful planner while Sarah stretched out on the couch watching *Perry Mason* reruns, their role reversal felt strange to her.

"What do you need me to do and how do you want me to dress?"

"Typical passing of hors d'oeuvres, replenishing serving tables, clearing away cups and plates people put down, and other duties as assigned. As for your other question, black pants and either a comfortable T-shirt or thin blouse works. Thomas provides a white jacket with the Howellian insignia for each server."

Sarah bit her tongue to avoid making a crack about the jacket. "You can count on me to be there. You might want to tell Thomas he'll need to have an extra jacket for me."

"Why?"

"I'm not sure I can keep it white all night."

Sarah was still chuckling at the thought of the different things she could accidentally spill on the server's jacket when Harlan came out of his office. "Guess what, Harlan?" She didn't wait for her boss to venture a guess. "Emily called. Their loan was approved. That takes care of any financial issues involved with the pub and the house, if you get it rezoned at today's meeting."

"That's what I came to talk to you about. Hopefully,

the rezoning issue is going to be pulled from this week's agenda and not addressed until next week."

"Why? Is it that feasibility study Anne was telling Marcus about?"

"Yes, but a study hasn't been ordered yet. It's still only a request at this point. That's why I want the topic pulled from this week's agenda. There's a chance we can get enough votes for an up-and-down vote next week rather than the issue being stopped indefinitely for a study."

"Why would a study take so long?"

"Because they'll include environmental impact and a million other things to be considered."

"Do you think delaying for a vote will really be to our advantage?"

"It's our best shot. The council is split four to four on rezoning. We won't know which way it will go until we know who fills Lance's seat."

"Have they scheduled an election?"

"Filling his slot isn't done by public election. The council appoints someone to fill out the remainder of his term. That person will have to run again in the next general election."

"What's the delay appointing someone? Can't they do it today?"

"Coulda, woulda, shoulda, but the council is split."

"I know, you said, four to four."

"They're even more splintered on a possible replacement for Lance. Behind the scenes, Anne hasn't stated her preference, but two council members are advocating Jane."

"Jane? Why?"

"They think she would have been Bill's choice. They're hoping because of her desire to start a new business, she'll vote for an entertainment district."

"What about the other councilmen?"

"Two are advancing their own candidates, and now there is a new dark horse being backed by three members of the council."

"Who is it?"

"Bailey. This faction thinks he will give them the same edge Lance did—a joining of the council and the bank at the hip. They claim Lance's dual role made things go smoother when the city was looking for financing or needed answers on bond issues and other money-related situations unique to Wheaton."

"I'm surprised Anne isn't backing Bailey. My understanding is she is an investor in the bank. Surely she'd be able to influence him. I would think he'd provide her with more value than Jane or anyone else."

Harlan threw his hands up in a gesture of futility. "I'd have thought that way, too, but who's to know what goes on in Anne's brain? Maybe she's afraid she can't control him as much as she wants? Perhaps she believes there should be an arm's-length relationship between the bank and the city council? Or she may think he'll sell out for rezoning because new businesses mean more deals for the bank? Who knows?"

"Whatever it is, you can bet she'll cast her vote for whatever way benefits the Hightowers."

"That's a little snide, but I don't disagree with you. Anyway, let's hope I can get our motion withdrawn or tabled for today's meeting."

Chapter Thirty-four

On Saturday, with four hours to go until YipYeow Day officially began, Sarah paced the park pavilion. There wasn't a cloud in the sky. She checked the forecast on her phone—no hint of rain in the forecast until midweek. That was a relief!

Volunteers were prepping the area around the speakers' stage Cliff had built. To the right of the stage, in the open area where he'd constructed a raised platform, lined-up cages already sat in anticipation of when the adoptable animals arrived from the shelter. On the other side of the stage, vendors and volunteers mingled arranging tablecloths, goods, and signs for prizes and services. Food would be put out closer to the event.

Everything was going too smoothly.

Sarah anticipated the proverbial other shoe dropping at any moment. Her nerves were on edge because the week had gone too well. Harlan obtained a one-week reprieve before the rezoning question or the feasibility study was considered. No new council member was appointed, but Harlan was hopeful a compromise candidate, on the side of the white hats, would be appointed soon.

The week had also gone well because Marcus, with limited help from Emily, but plenty from Jacob, held three successful Southwind Pub soft opening nights. Almost as good, nothing blew up at the office, and her mother was still a free woman, at least until the grand jury met next week. More important, she'd personally collected and turned over to Bailey YipYeow corporate sponsorship checks in the amount of fourteen thousand dollars.

The fourteen thousand dollars included Harlan's five-thousand-dollar matching contribution, but the rest were smaller contributions from most of the downtown merchants and two anonymous givers. She felt like she should pump her fist in the air or take a little bow for having met her secret goal before the first animal strutted forward in the parade. By her calculations, her fourteen thousand dollars, plus the bank's seed money and its five thousand matching funds, equaled the twenty thousand dollars she'd dreamed of raising. Anything made from registrations, parade-related contributions, adoptions, and tonight's Howellian Catapalooza affair was gravy.

Speaking of money, Sarah observed Eloise rolling an overloaded cart and the largest lockbox she had ever seen toward the registration table. Sarah recognized the brown boxes on the cart as being the ones the T-shirts donated for those who registered came in, but it was the lockbox that amused her. Eloise wasn't kidding around. Sarah wondered how anyone could lift it.

Even if the box was lighter than it looked, it wasn't

the only thing that impressed Sarah. This was the first time she'd seen Eloise out of her bank uniform. Her jeans, sneaks, and what Sarah swore was a L.L.Bean–type button-down blue oxford cloth shirt looked good on her.

She waved, trying to catch Eloise's eye. "Eloise!"

Eloise waved back. They met up at the registration table.

"Do you need some help?"

Eloise picked up one of the boxes and put it on the ground behind the table. The weight of the box had been keeping a sign from blowing away while Eloise pushed the cart across the pavilion area. Eloise handed the sign and a roll of masking tape to Sarah. "Why don't you hang this on the table for me and then put a small sign on the fishbowl."

Sarah saw the fishbowl sitting on the cart and placed it on the table. She hung the big sign off the table and taped the "small donations requested" message on the fishbowl. "I didn't realize you were manning the registration table today."

From where Eloise was placing another box within easy reach of the registration chairs, she tilted her head back and met Sarah's gaze. "There may not be a finance committee, but I thought we should have more than one person handling money today. That way, there's confirmation of what we take in in cash from registrations and the sale of extra T-shirts."

Sarah remembered Eloise mentioning something about needing a finance committee overseeing the treasurer, but she hadn't thought much about it after her discussion with Bailey. "Eloise, are you implying something about Mr. Bailey?"

"Not necessarily. It's just my nature to have checks and balances on money. I get nervous if there isn't a way to reconcile things. Just like we can follow the corporate money, it's important we are clear on the funds raised today from individuals and those raised tonight at Catapalooza. Perhaps you should have someone checking up on me, too."

She smiled, but it was tight-lipped.

That was when Sarah remembered the bank gave Eloise a buyout after she proposed hand reconciling some of the accounts at the bank. She tried to think of a graceful way to press Eloise to explain her misgivings in more detail, but before she could, Bailey joined them. He was carrying a small lockbox.

Although it was the weekend and was going to be a warm day, Bailey was dressed in a suit and tie. "Good morning, ladies. You're both here early."

"So are you," Sarah said.

"Well, I wanted to make sure everything was set up for registration." He held up the lockbox. "I was told someone was bringing the T-shirts, but I thought we should have some cash on hand to make change as people register. I got some from the bank to start us off today."

Sarah felt like a third wheel when he stared straight at Eloise. "Don't worry, I notated taking one hundred dollars from the YipYeow account to use for petty cash change. I'll make another bookkeeping entry when I return the hundred dollars to the account."

Reading into what she observed as Bailey and Eloise's respective body language, Sarah got the distinct feeling they had the same misgivings about each other. Unsure whom to side with, Sarah felt more confused than ever.

"I got money, too." Eloise pointed to her lockbox.

"Was that from your own account? If so, let's not use it. It will be a lot cleaner trail if we don't mix your personal funds with the YipYeow monies. Why don't you go put your lockbox back in your car, so we don't have any chance of commingling the funds?"

Bailey looked at his watch. "I promised to meet up with a few of the vendors to collect donations from them an hour before the parade. That still gives us a little over two hours until then. Amanda should be here in thirty minutes. I think it's important we try to keep two people at the desk at all times, but instead of you sitting out here in the sun all day, why don't we work out a schedule once she gets here so we can all have some time off?"

Although his offer seemed genuinely nice, Sarah had the distinct feeling it wasn't one Eloise could refuse. Eloise apparently agreed because she didn't protest.

Not needing to do anything else at the registration desk, Sarah took one more look around the pavilion for anything out of place. There wasn't. Everyone had everything under control. Satisfied, and needing a little time of her own before the festivities began, she headed home to get RahRah ready for the parade and his job as grand marshal. It tickled her every time she thought of him in that role. To her, the idea of a cat serving as the grand marshal was ludicrous.

Sarah had included the suggestion of RahRah as a way of keeping the spotlight on the animals as a joke in one of the incessant emails with the mayor's assistant. The assistant shared what she, too, thought was a good laugh with the mayor. Rather than being amused, the mayor loved the idea. After all, he considered RahRah to be something of a town hero, as well as a property taxpayer. Consequently, the mayor decreed it only fitting RahRah and Sarah ride with him in the lead car.

Because Sarah hadn't planned on any cars leading the parade, she thought the mayor's assistant's return email was in jest. But it wasn't. When Sarah finally wrapped her head around the idea, she hated to admit it was kind of exciting.

Now, walking home, she thought again about how many weird adventures RahRah's coming into her life created. She hoped the two of them avoided anything unpleasant today, especially when getting him ready for the parade. In preparation, she'd brought up the topic during a few of their one-sided discussions. So far, he hadn't exhibited any signs of being thrilled about the prospect of being in the parade, let alone serving as the grand marshal. Perhaps she could win him over, or at least generate some excitement, when she changed his collar from his everyday red leather one to either his rhinestone sparkler or his Fourth of July red, white, and blue extravaganza. Being honest with herself, neither would probably make much of a difference.

Turning onto Main Street, she saw Mr. Rogers coming toward her. He had his cane in one hand and held a leash attached to the cutest ball of white fur in the other.

"Is that Fluffy?"

"Sure is. She's a love, she is." He bent down and

patted the little dog, who sat quietly next to him. "Cleaned up nicely, don't you think?"

"I would never have known it's the same dog. I had no idea how adorable she was under all that grime and matted fur."

"Most people wouldn't."

"It must have been quite a job to groom her."

"Not really. She was good as gold. Most dogs would have fussed, but she sat quietly like she knew I was helping her."

Sarah bent and extended her hand, palm down, so Fluffy could smell it. Once she was sure Fluffy was comfortable, she reached forward and gently rubbed her head.

"Maybe she knew, after what happened the other night, that the helping was reciprocal."

"Possibly. She's pretty bright. Knows all her commands and even a few tricks."

"If she's that trained, I wonder how she got separated from her owner? Whoever it was, obviously invested a lot of time in her."

"I can't imagine. I put up a few signs on the next blocks and checked with the shelter, but there haven't been any inquiries for a sweetie like her."

"Are you going to keep her?"

"For now. She's been through so much that, rather than upsetting her again, Phyllis and I decided to let her stay at my place while we look for her rightful owner. It might be easier on her than taking her down to the shelter. Phyllis promised to let me know if anyone asks for a dog matching her description." He bent and rubbed Fluffy behind her ears. "Fluffy's such a little lady. I'm secretly hoping we don't find her owner."

CHAPTER THIRTY-FIVE

Preparing RahRah for the parade was easier than Sarah anticipated. He didn't hide or squirm when she announced it was time to get ready for YipYeow Day. In fact, he was quite patient with her fumbling fingers while she changed his red collar for the sparkling one. She was glad because she wanted to be early to give everything a final once-over.

Once RahRah was dolled up for the parade, it was Sarah's turn. Normally, she preferred to blend into the background, in something dark and slenderizing, but when would she have the chance to ride in the grand marshal lead car again? Because she wanted to sparkle as much as RahRah, but knew her time might be tight between the YipYeow activities and running to Birmingham, she opted for black pants, a black shell, and, despite the heat, her silver sequined jacket. It radiated elegance. The jacket also tended to shed, so she waited to the last moment to put it on lest RahRah accidentally ingested a fallen sequin.

Ready, she put him in his carrier. Although Sarah feared he might balk at the plastic box, he went in purring. Maybe her discussions with him about being the grand marshal had made an impression.

Outside, she debated whether to take her car or walk but decided because she had to bring RahRah home, it wasn't worth hassling with traffic and parking. On Main Street, she heard a car behind her slow down. Instinctively, even though it was daylight, she stepped farther away from the street. Hearing her name, she glanced to her left and saw the front window of the car, which was gliding even to her pace, was rolled down. Sarah relaxed. The driver was her mother. "Mom, what are you doing here?"

"Maybelle, honey. I'm here to support you."

"But you don't like animals. You complain you're allergic to them." A horn honked behind them.

"I took an allergy pill. Get in. I'm holding up traffic."

Without another word, Sarah followed her mother's directive by squeezing RahRah's carrier and herself into the front seat.

"Put on your seat belt."

"Yes, ma'am." Sarah juggled the carrier against the dashboard while she manipulated the shoulder harness into its locked position. Only then did her mother proceed. "Thanks for coming today."

She wasn't sure if her mother grunted or not. "Where's the best place to park?"

"Probably at my house." She laughed at the look her mother shot in her direction. "But, at this point, I'd turn right at the next corner and see if you can get into the city lot on the left. It's the one closest to the pavilion area where the parade ends and all the festivities will take place."

"Did you say right or left?"

"Turn right. The lot is on your left."

It was all Sarah could do not to laugh at the determined look on her mother's face. She busied herself peering into RahRah's carrier rather than facing her mother. "You're early."

"I wanted to miss the traffic and make sure I got a parking spot. Besides, I called Eloise this morning and we agreed to meet for coffee at Buffalo Betty's when she's on her break from the registration table."

Sarah was surprised. She didn't remember hearing her mother ever mention doing things with Eloise. "I didn't know the two of you were friends."

When her mother kept her eyes glued on the road and didn't answer, it dawned on Sarah her mother wasn't leaving it to the professionals, either. "You're meeting her to pick her brain, aren't you? Harlan told you what she told me, didn't he?"

Her mother nodded as she pulled into the parking lot. "He did. Things are still a bit confusing to me from that day, so I thought I'd compare what I remember with what she says."

"Do you want me to come with you?"

"No. Leave this one to me. You go handle the animal parade."

Maybelle leaned over and gave Sarah a kiss before each set off on their own mission.

Because of where her mother parked, Sarah decided to check out the pavilion area before reporting to the parade starting point. She was glad to see the setup committee had finished covering each table and had decorated the speaker's platform with adorable animal-inspired cutouts. Several vendors were busy putting signage, handouts, samples, and takeaways out at their tables. Looking around, Sarah made a mental note to come back later to pick up some of the freebies for RahRah.

She waved at Phyllis and three or four people she recognized as shelter volunteers getting the animal cages for the adoptable animals ready with water. She hoped that when they brought the animals over in another half hour or so, they'd be swamped with offers of potential adoptive homes. Although she was glad to put her efforts into raising money for the shelter, her real joy came when an animal found a forever home.

Sarah was about to see if they needed more help when she spotted the Southwind catering van parked next to a SUV on the far side of the pavilion. She made her way in that direction. Nearing the vehicles, she heard voices coming from behind them that she immediately recognized as belonging to Jane and Marcus, but she couldn't decide if they were arguing or not.

Rather than announcing herself, she stopped to listen for a moment from her side of the vehicles, where they couldn't see RahRah and her. They weren't shouting, but they were disagreeing with each other about their table placement. Each was claiming they were entitled to two tables.

Confused, Sarah looked back at the pavilion area, where their tables were set up. She saw the problem immediately. The tables were placed at a ninety-degree angle, framing where the cemented portion of the park pavilion ended. One arm of the angle had two tables, while the other had only one. Having carefully drawn the schematic diagrams to mark how this area would be shared by the vendors, adoptable animals, and food booths, she knew both Jane and Marcus were supposed to have two tables. Either someone had goofed delivering or setting up tables or their fourth table had walked.

Sarah called out to Jane and Marcus while she glanced around the pavilion, hoping to see someone from the setup committee. Marcus and Jane immediately came around the vehicles, talking over each other as they pointed the problem out to her. Unfortunately, there didn't seem to be a member of the committee in the vicinity.

To buy herself more time, she hushed them. "One at a time. I can't understand you."

Jane pushed herself into Sarah's personal space and gestured to where the tables were. "I'm supposed to have two tables. I can't possibly prep and serve my food on one. If I'm going to give Southwind a run for its money in the future, people need to taste my food right today."

Marcus echoed Jane's comments, but for himself.

"I understand. You both should have two tables. Let me see what I can do. I'll be right back."

Leaving them to bicker or make small talk, she peered around the pavilion area, but she didn't see a member of the setup committee. That was when she had an idea. She looked to see if Mr. Bailey, from the bank, was still at the registration table. Not only was he there, but Amanda was sitting with him behind the table. Perfect.

Bailey stood as she approached the table. "Long time no see."

Sarah smiled at him and Amanda. "Mr. Bailey, I've

got a favor to ask. We have a little problem in the food area." She explained about being shorted a table and asked if it would be possible to take one of their registration tables.

"Of course. I wish all problems were that easy to resolve." He turned to Amanda and asked if she would be okay sitting there alone for a minute."

Amanda flashed him a big grin. "Of course, Mr. Bailey."

"Great. Sarah, you said Marcus is over there. Why don't we get him to give me a hand with the table?"

Thrilled, Sarah went to tell Marcus and Jane her resolution to their problem. A grateful Marcus immediately locked his van and followed Bailey back to the registration area.

The minute they left, Jane went to her SUV and returned with a bag, which she dumped on the side that already had two clothed tables. Sarah didn't offer to help. Instead, she just stood there, holding RahRah, who was being remarkably calm in his carrier. "From what you said, I gather you're planning to open a new restaurant?"

After dropping a second armload on a table, Jane finally responded to Sarah. "Hopefully. By the way, this is a food-preparation area. You need to get that cat out of here. Now."

Amazed by Jane's tone and abruptness, and surprised not to get a thank-you, Sarah turned and walked toward the parade starting point. She wondered if steam was coming out of her ears.

Chapter Thirty-six

Sarah refused to permit Jane to ruin this day for RahRah and her. From what she could see as she walked toward the parade starting point, everything else was going smoothly. There still was plenty of time until the parade, but people and their animals were already lining up at the parade's starting line. Sarah waved at a few people she recognized but didn't stop to chat. Instead, she made her way to where she assumed the grand marshal car would be parked.

To her surprise, rather than the convertible she expected waiting for RahRah and her to sit atop while they waved to the crowd, she saw the mayor standing next to a traditional hay wagon attached to a tractor. Her heart sank. Unlike her dress pants and sequins, the mayor was wearing dénim overalls over the YipYeow T-shirt and a straw hat. She wasn't sure what it was, but something dangled from his mouth.

Apparently, his idea of Wheaton's grand marshal vehicle differed from those she'd grown up watching lead the Macy's Thanksgiving Day parade. Sarah swallowed hard. "There's no going back now," she whispered in the direction of RahRah's carrier. Pasting a smile on her face, she joined the mayor. She was relieved to see him remove a piece of straw from his mouth. From the distance, she'd feared it was a corn-cob pipe.

He gestured toward the wagon. It wasn't quite what she expected of a hay wagon, either. When she thought of hay rides she'd been on, she remembered sinking into mounds of loose hay. This time, the bales were deliberately positioned in tiers with plenty of room left for sitting or standing. A cloth or sheet covered the second highest tier, which backed up to the top layer creating a makeshift bench. Sarah assumed that was where the mayor, RahRah, and she would sit, the cloth protecting them from any prickly strands of straw.

Her assumption was confirmed by the mayor, his eyes focused on the highest tiers. "Isn't this perfect?"

Remembering what her mother instilled in her about lying, Sarah couldn't bring herself to voice a response. Instead, she simply nodded.

The mayor beamed. "We might as well get in position. We're leading the parade. There's a small ladder on the other side of the wagon. Let me go first so you can hand RahRah to me. That way you'll have both hands free on the ladder."

Sarah followed him around to the other side of the wagon, where a young man she didn't know stood. She was relieved to see, rather than being a real ladder, four narrow portable steps were pushed flush against the truck. The mayor easily scampered up them and reached down for RahRah's carrier. Sarah was glad he did. Even when the young man moved behind her like a safety monitor, she felt a little shaky because the steps lacked a guardrail.

After she mounted the wagon and took RahRah back from the mayor, the young man picked up the steps and handed them to the mayor. He stowed them in a corner behind a bale of hay while Sarah settled herself on her part of the covered seating area. She placed RahRah's carrier near her feet, opened it, and took him out. He squirmed to free himself from her grasp, but she held him firmly. She quickly realized, though, that if he kept this up, the short distance was still going to be a long parade.

"Settle down, RahRah. You need to behave like a grand marshal or you're going to force me to put you back in your carrier. If I do, you're going to miss out on a lot of fun."

Sarah reached into her pocket for a tidbit treat. The shelter vet, who Sarah adored, strongly encouraged restricting a cat's diet to meat, fish, chicken, and vegetables. Normally, Sarah followed the vet's instructions to a T, but, just as she believed every now and then humans should be given a treat, she felt cats deserved them occasionally, too. Because of her philosophy, she always kept a small jar of store-bought treats in her kitchen.

In order not to feel too guilty, Sarah religiously took the large premade treats she bought and broke them into smaller pieces. That way, when it was appropriate, she fed RahRah only a nibble. These bite-sized treats perfectly satisfied RahRah. Today was no exception. He snatched the treat from her fingers and gobbled it down before settling comfortably in her arms, purring softly.

Sarah glanced in the direction where people were lining up. The street had filled with owners and pets. Many, including quite a few cats, were leashed; other animals stood by their owners waiting for a command. For the first time in the past few days, she relaxed. YipYeow Day showed all the promise of being a success.

A voice yelled, "Hold on tight! We're off."

The hay wagon lunged forward. Surprised, Sarah clutched RahRah more tightly as he slipped down the crook of her arm. She nestled him closer to her body, while she whipped her head backward to see who was driving. Apparently, while she fed RahRah his treat, the person who helped with the steps had slipped into the driver's seat.

She glanced at the mayor. He was in his element, busily playing up to the crowd by waving and blowing kisses. Seeing he wasn't the least bit alarmed they were moving, she opted to aid RahRah in doing the queen wave with his paw as they passed a group of young children. Their smiles made the silliness of the moment well worth it. How many would one day recount the first time they saw the town's animals parade by and remember being waved at by a cat?

Although their driver inched them along, so they didn't get too far ahead of the walkers, the hay wagon quickly reached the pavilion parking area. Cutting the motor, the driver came around the side. While the mayor handed the steps to the young man, Sarah, assuring RahRah it would only be for a few minutes, put him back in his carrier. She handed the carrier to the driver and scampered down the stairs ahead of the mayor.

As pets and owners finished the parade route, the pavilion area quickly filled. Some checked out what the vendors were giving away, while others waited in line for Marcus's or Jane's food. Sarah wondered how Jane felt about the many animals in the food area. She bet it was killing Jane, but she didn't dare complain about their presence.

In the adjacent grassy park area, dogs and humans chased Frisbees and balls. The best thing, Sarah thought as she once again freed RahRah from his carrier, was the number of people clustered around the adoptable pets.

Whistling feedback from the speaker's microphone made her realize the mayor was ready to give his opening remarks. She turned to listen but saw her mother, Mr. Rogers, and Fluffy near the food tables. Tuning the mayor out, Sarah worked her way over to them.

The lines in front of Marcus's and Jane's tables reminded Sarah of how the Southwind booth at the food expo was four months ago. Marcus had at least three people in his line for every one waiting for Jane's food. She watched the two chefs in action for a moment. Jane seemed scattered while Marcus efficiently and expertly engaged the crowd while he prepared and filled their orders. She hoped the preference people showed for his food would translate into business at the pub.

Observing Marcus juggling all aspects of the Southwind booth, Sarah felt an inner pang she couldn't identify. One part was admiration for how he handled things while the other was absolute annoyance with her sister and Thomas Howell. She couldn't help but compare today with how Emily and Marcus usually functioned so well together.

Normally, the contrast between her sister's blonde cheerleader size and his massive clog-wearing balloon-clad body amused her, but today she felt something lacking as she watched him work without Emily. It particularly irked her that tonight, while Marcus hosted the no-cost volunteer reception at the Southwind Pub, Emily would be building a good reputation with the beautiful people of Wheaton and Birmingham at a restaurant Sarah now considered to be a serious Southwind rival.

When Marcus saw her, he waved but continued working. If she hadn't had RahRah with her, she would have donned a Southwind jacket and helped with anything he felt safe having her do. That probably wouldn't be much, considering the last time Marcus gruntingly approved a kitchen task for her, she hadn't even been able to take out the garbage without stumbling over a corpse.

Like the rest of her family and friends, Sarah didn't understand how Marcus and Emily could be so proficient in the kitchen, while she was liable to be scorched if she got anywhere near the vicinity of the "k" room. Even though her mother would have let her shadow her in the kitchen like Emily did, Sarah preferred watching *Perry Mason* reruns.

Emily ended up able to do almost anything in a kitchen, while Sarah could empty the dishwasher during the first commercial, set the table at the show's midpoint, acknowledge her father's arrival from work during the third commercial break, and come upstairs for dinner when the credits rolled.

Unable to help Marcus, she joined her mother and the others. Maybelle was nibbling from a plate of the pickup items Marcus was serving. Sarah put the cat carrier on the ground and shifted RahRah so she held him with one arm. "Those look good."

Maybelle held her plate where Sarah could get a better look at the assortment of appetizers gracing it. "Sausage and cheese balls, quesadilla triangles, spanakopita, and pizza pinwheels."

Sarah took one of the cheese balls from her mother's plate and popped it into her mouth. The tangy taste was delightful. "These are delicious."

Before she could snatch another, her mother pulled her plate away from Sarah's reach. "Get your own."

Mr. Rogers laughed. Fluffy, who lay next to him, raised her head and wagged her tail. He bent and patted her head. "See how good she is? I told her to lay down and stay and, even though I can tell she'd like to get in on the action, she's obeying the command."

"Much better than this one." Sarah, now using two hands, struggled to keep her twitching cat contained. "I don't know if it's the smell of food or all the other animals, but I'm not sure how much longer he's going to let me hold him."

"You should get a leash for him, like I have for Fluffy."

"I might just do that. I always thought leashes were silly for cats, but looking around at the ones a few people are using today and trying to hold this squirmer, I've changed my mind."

"You'll know for next year," Maybelle said.

Sarah jerked her head up. "What about next year?"

"Honey, look around this pavilion area and the

park. You've got a success here. George, don't you agree this is the first of many YipYeow Days?"

"Most definitely. And once you've successfully led something like this, everyone will want you to be in charge again."

Sarah's groan was drowned out by the town square's clock chiming. Once it ended, so her mother and Mr. Rogers could hear her, she continued the conversation where they left off. "Mr. Rogers, that's not what I needed to hear right now."

When Maybelle agreed with Mr. Rogers, Sarah groaned again. This time they both heard her and laughed.

"You wait and see," Maybelle said.

"I will, but right now, I think I'd better put RahRah in his carrier and get him home."

Maybelle looked confused. "Don't you need to wait for YipYeow Day to end? This place isn't going to clear out for at least another hour or so. People are having too much fun."

"You heard the clock. Today's YipYeow activities officially end in thirty minutes. Even if people stay in the park, Marcus and Jane will handle closing the food tables while Phyllis oversees the adoption area until people stop taking animals home. Because I'm going to Birmingham to help Emily, and we weren't sure when the adoptable animal area would close, Phyllis and I divided the YipYeow responsibilities. We both planned and fund-raised, and while I made sure the setup committee did its job, Phyllis agreed to oversee the festival's conclusion. Between Phyllis and the volunteers, I'm sure everything will get done without me."

"I promised George and Fluffy a ride home. If you want to give me a moment to finish this plate, I'll give you a lift, too."

"That's okay, Mom. With the crowd the way it is now, it will be faster walking. If the three of you wait awhile, I'm sure it will thin out."

CHAPTER THIRTY-SEVEN

Sarah dropped her sequined jacket on her bed and hurried to get RahRah settled before she fought the traffic to Birmingham. Even with rushing, she barely arrived in time for the server orientation Emily held an hour before guests arrived.

Although tonight's meal was a buffet, Emily explained it was important for servers to understand the makeup of each dish. They had to be ready for any questions that arose in the dining room because Grace and she would be busy with preparation and expediting refills from the kitchen. Sarah marveled at how cool and calm her sister was while educating the servers and dealing with the details of the kitchen.

After describing the contents of each dish, Emily put samples of them on the bar for the servers to taste. Sarah slipped the three-by-five index card she'd made cheat-sheet notes on into her pocket before sampling everything. There were three main dishes. One was a succulent chicken breast in a simple sauce, the second a breaded tilapia, and the third, which was the vegetarian choice, a deconstructed eggplant lasagna. The side dishes included two salad choices, two vegetables, two starches, orange or yeast rolls, and an assortment of mini-desserts. Water, tea, coffee, and a special Howellian Catnip drink were the only beverages for the evening.

From the little bit Emily and Marcus had taught Sarah when she'd helped serve or poked around behind the scenes at the original Southwind and during their discussions about having a pub concept versus a fine-dining establishment, she knew tonight's buffet, while plentiful, had significant profit built into it. The chicken and tilapia options were two of the cheapest items a restaurant could put on their menu. Still, like Marcus's food at YipYeow Day, everything was delicious.

Marcus planned to serve buffet style at the Southwind Pub tonight. She wondered if his menu would be similar to Emily's to contrast with the pickup type food he offered this afternoon. Nice as everything would be at the Howellian tonight, Sarah wished Emily and she were at Southwind Pub.

When Emily finished their formal group orientation, she sent everyone except Sarah back to double-check their individually assigned stations one last time. Guests would bring plates back to their tables from the buffet lines, but clean water glasses and table settings had to be waiting for them. Extra napkins, silverware, and trays on which to place dirty dishes for the busboys were in easy reach but out of the sight line of the guests as much as possible.

"Sarah, you're going to be my floater tonight."

"I don't understand."

"You'll work your way around the dining room helping out where needed. In the beginning, you'll serve appetizers and pre-poured drinks, but as the night goes on, you'll restock the prep stations as needed and make sure the busboys remove any stacked dirty dishes they miss. Most importantly, your job is to communicate the status of the buffet line table to Grace and me. For example, if everyone attacks one of the salads, we need to know to bring out a replacement. The same holds true with the hot dishes because, especially early in the evening, one of us will expedite refills while the other one will be popping things in and out of the ovens and microwaves. When the crowd wanes, that's important for you to tell us, too. We don't want to heat and waste food. If we keep our service on target, our bottom line will be more profitable."

"It sounds like you could end up with extra pans of different things."

"That's the idea. I want tonight to look plentiful, but anything we don't serve, we'll refrigerate until we incorporate it into tomorrow's menu."

Sarah shuddered at the thought of pans of leftovers being recycled. She hated leftovers. "Is that a common restaurant practice?"

"Definitely. No restaurant can afford not to work this way. The same principle holds true with effectively using every part of an animal."

"I hadn't thought of it from that perspective."

"Thankfully, most people don't. Next time you're in a restaurant, listen closely to that day's specials. We may have served fresh shrimp and grits on Monday, but on Tuesday, we blend the shrimp with a tomato base and spices and serve a completely different dish. By the same token, if I buy whole chickens, I'll make dishes incorporating half a chicken broiled or baked, but I'll also make other menu offerings using the breasts, thighs, wings, livers, and even the bones."

"I think you're turning me off to restaurant dining."

"Nonsense. Believe me, what I can do with the fat I skim off a chicken will make, and has made, your head spin with delight. Besides, you're not exactly the one to go all righteous on me. You'll do anything to avoid being in the kitchen. Think how much prepared frozen stuff you've scarfed down at fast-food restaurants."

Sarah couldn't deny what her sister said.

"I've got to get back to the kitchen to help Grace. Would you please clean this tasting area up before the guests start arriving?"

"Sure."

Sarah stacked the dirty forks, serving platters, and plates she and the other servers had used and carried them into the kitchen. After asking Emily, she put them in an area near the commercial line dishwasher. She grabbed a rag and returned to the main dining room. Leaning over the bar to wipe it clean from the tasting, she felt a presence behind her. She whipped around, her rag in front of her, and almost ended up wiping Thomas clean. "You scared me."

"Sorry. I didn't mean to. Did I miss the tasting?" He pointed to the bar area she had just finished wiping.

"Yes. And it was delicious."

"I wouldn't expect anything less from Emily. Her skills in a kitchen amaze me."

"Me, too. I'm so easily flustered in a kitchen, but she makes everything seem easy—that is, until I try it."

"I know what you mean."

Sarah was surprised to hear Thomas talk about

trying his hand in the kitchen. He impressed her as someone who had others prepare his meals and do anything else he needed so his manicured hands would always be protected. Perhaps he was talking about making something simple on his cook's day off. "Are you a cook of convenience, too?"

"A cook of convenience?"

She was amused by his confused expression. "That's what Emily's dubbed me. I specialize in taking shortcuts and using prepared things, like premade piecrusts, instead of making everything from scratch. She thinks being a cook of convenience is sinful."

Now it was his turn to be entertained by what she'd said. "I can't imagine anything you could possibly do that would irk Saint Emily."

His use of the word "saint" bothered Sarah. She stared at him, unable to ascertain if he was joking or there was a newly developed tension between Emily and him.

"Seriously, give me an example," he pleaded.

She thought for a moment. "Do you remember the spinach pie my sister made from scratch at the food expo?"

He nodded. "It was delicious. That was one of the things that made me interested in your sister cooking at the Howellian."

"Well, I make a spinach pie, too. The big difference is she uses real spinach while I mix Stouffer's spinach soufflé with packaged shredded cheddar cheese and other prepared ingredients. If I do say so myself, the end result of my recipe isn't bad."

"I'm sure it's not, but I admire both your sister's cooking and her flair for food presentation. Whether she's making one dish or one hundred dishes, her food always comes out without losing its aesthetically pleasing look. That's not an easy task. Most chefs, like me, can prepare one perfect dish at a time. It takes a special chef to make two hundred plates with the same consistent high-quality look. No matter how hard I've tried, I've never mastered high-end mass production. With the events we've had this past week, Emily has given me a crash course."

She jerked her head up with more than a quizzical look on her face before she could control herself. Perhaps Marcus's fears about Thomas's motivation for hiring Emily were justified. "I'm sorry. I didn't know you were a chef."

Thomas mimicked being a witness swearing on a Bible. "Guilty as charged, but not at the same level as your sister or Marcus."

Sarah waited, hoping he would tell her more about this new wrinkle in his background.

"Uncle George wasn't too pleased with either Cliff or me when it came to our academic prowess. We both bounced around a bit during our first year of college. The difference was Cliff hung in there until he flunked out while I withdrew three weeks into my first semester, came home, licked my wounds, and signed up for junior college classes for the next term. I took just enough of the same cooking courses Grace has been taking at the junior college to get the basics under my belt. At that point, I realized restaurant and hotel management, rather than cooking, was my calling. The next year, I was accepted at a four-year school from which I earned dual bachelor's degrees in business and hotel/restaurant management."

"I had no idea."

"Most folks don't. Instead of listing my degrees, I usually say I'm the hotel's highest-paid janitor. I balance customer satisfaction against keeping my eye on the bottom line, but on an everyday basis, I deal with everything from the wine served to the cleanliness of the beds and silverware. The buck stops with me. Speaking of which, I better change my hat from thinking about the kitchen to making our special guests feel welcome."

CHAPTER THIRTY-EIGHT

During the time she'd been talking to Thomas, the massive ballroom had begun to fill up. Caught with the rag still in her hand, she hurried to hide it behind the bar and pick up the tray of special Howellian Catnip drinks the bartender readied for her. She recognized many of the guests she offered a glass to from the society pages as Birmingham business leaders and philanthropists, but she was surprised at how many of the "beautiful" Wheaton people who'd attended YipYeow Day were here mingling tonight, too. If they were here, it meant the rank-and-file volunteers were the ones, she hoped, filling the Southwind Pub.

She doubted Marcus would be disappointed with a salt-of-the-earth turnout for more than the first few minutes. Although the Wheaton group gracing the Howellian, if rezoning went through, would eventually be regulars at Southwind's fine-dining restaurant, it was the everyday neighborhood folks who were going to make or break the pub.

"Excuse me, waitress. Would you bring that tray of drinks over here, please?"

For a moment, Sarah didn't realize she was the

one being spoken to. She'd gotten so lost in checking out the crowd, she'd forgotten to do her job. "Of course, Anne."

Sarah hastened to offer a Howellian Catnip and napkin to Anne Hightower. As Anne handed her glass to the gentleman she was talking to and took another, Sarah realized from the glacial stare Anne gave her that Sarah had committed a second error as a server by using Anne's Christian name instead of referring to her as Ms. Hightower. "Is there anything else I can get you, Ms. Hightower?"

"No, thank you."

Sarah perceived a light of recognition in Anne's eyes. "Sarah? What are you doing here?"

"Emily asked me to help out as a server." Sarah flashed a smile as she tried to retreat from Anne and the gentleman she was speaking with, but Anne put her hand on Sarah's arm.

"Sarah, I'd like you to meet Linc Adams. Linc is a lawyer and political guru here in Birmingham. Linc, this is Sarah Blair. Normally, she works for Harlan Endicott, but today she was the mastermind behind our very successful first annual Wheaton YipYeow Day."

Linc extended his hand, but between Anne still grasping her arm and her balancing the tray with its remaining glasses, she couldn't take it. He dangled his hand in midair for a moment before returning it to his side. "Blair? Any relation to Bill Blair?"

"He was my ex-husband."

"I'm sorry about your loss. He was a fine guy. We had a number of business dealings together."

Thinking having business dealings with the rat wasn't much of a reference, Sarah muttered a thank-you.

Anne pointed out Sarah was Bill's ex, not his widow. Linc said something mollifying his previous statement, but Sarah wasn't listening. On the pretext of needing to serve the rest of the drinks on her tray, she extricated herself from Anne's grip and from hearing any more praise for Bill.

Spotting her mother, Cliff, and Mr. Rogers talking in the corner of the room, she went up to them and offered them the remaining two Howellian Catnips on her tray. Her mother grabbed one. Cliff passed, but Mr. Rogers took the last one.

"Cliff, I'll be glad to get you one of tonight's signature specials."

"No thanks. I don't drink."

"Would you like something else, a tea or soda?"

"I'll wait until we eat." He turned toward his uncle and Maybelle. "I see the buffet line is open. Would the two of you like to get some food and grab a table together?"

Maybelle drained her glass and handed it back to Sarah. "Would you get me another one of these, please? I'm not hungry. George, here, ruined my appetite."

"Now Maybelle, all I said was Southwind should stay where it is. Running the pub location will keep Emily and Marcus plenty busy. They should drop all this nonsense about changing our neighborhood."

"That's not all you said."

Considering Maybelle and Mr. Rogers had been on opposite sides of the rezoning issue for months,

Sarah didn't understand why they were fighting now, in the middle of the Howellian party. With a raised eyebrow questioning what was going on, she glanced at Cliff.

He shrugged. "I don't know exactly what they're fighting about tonight. They were going at each other like this when I walked up to them."

Sarah glanced at her mother and waited for an explanation.

"George accused me of being a fool with my money. Told me women don't understand the real world of finance and I should keep my pretty little nose out of business deals."

If Mr. Rogers had said anything close to that, Sarah knew her mother would consider them fighting words.

"It's one thing to disagree about rezoning Main Street, but it's another thing to attack me or my family personally. Sarah, are you going to get me another drink?"

"Yes, ma'am." Sarah went to the bar and exchanged her tray for a full one. She tried making a direct beeline back to her mother and Mr. Rogers but was stopped by people removing glasses from her tray. By the time she reached Maybelle and gave her the requested Howellian Catnip, Sarah wished she hadn't had one left on her tray. Her mother's belligerent tone, as Cliff vacillated between calming her mother and his uncle down, made Sarah realize this might not be her mother's second drink of the evening.

"I'm sure my uncle didn't mean it the way it sounded. He's always told me how much he admires you."

"But apparently not my business prowess."

Sarah couldn't decide if her mother's flushed face was from whatever was in the Howellian Catnip special or anger, but she had no question how agitated Mr. Rogers was simply by looking at the way his bow tie bobbed against his Adam's apple.

"Maybelle, that's not what I said. What I specifically said was that backing Emily and Marcus in changing the big house into a restaurant is like fool's gold. You're going to have to spend a fortune to bring that house up to code. I can't see you or anyone pouring money into that folly."

"If you remember, they said Alaska was a fool's folly. Personally, the only fool I see in this room tonight is you."

The lights blinking in the room interrupted any further discussion. Thomas Howell strolled to the center of the room, in front of the buffet line. He raised his Howellian Catnip in the air. "On behalf of the Howellian and the Wheaton Animal Shelter, welcome to Catapalooza. We can't thank you enough for being here tonight. Your generosity, as well as support of our silent auction, has made this the highest grossing fund-raiser the Wheaton Animal Shelter has ever had. On behalf of the animals you are helping, who cannot speak for themselves, I raise my glass to all of you for making a difference this afternoon and this evening."

The room burst into applause as Thomas, with a flourish, lifted his glass. When it died down, he pointed to Bailey, who stood at the far end of the buffet. "Come over here, Bryan."

Bailey shook his head and raised his hand in protest.

Thomas laughed. "For those of you who don't know, Bryan Bailey, who is too shy to come up here, is probably one of the most important people here tonight. Not only is he our friendly Wheaton banker, and a creative wonder at financing construction, including this gorgeous hotel, but he's been the chief fund-raising finance person for this YipYeow event. According to him, we've raised a tad over twenty thousand dollars for the Wheaton Animal Shelter—and that doesn't count what, thanks to you, we'll be adding to the total from tonight. Again, my thanks to Bryan Bailey and you."

When someone shouted out a thank-you to Thomas for hosting Catapalooza, Sarah wondered about the number Thomas had quoted. She didn't know what his reference to a tad more meant. Because Bailey and she already had over twenty thousand dollars in corporate sponsorship money before the day began, the adoption fees and donations in the fishbowl, registrations, and T-shirt proceeds, should have put the total for today a few thousand dollars over her original goal. She didn't know if Thomas was unsure of the exact total or if either Bailey, Amanda, or Eloise had shorted today's numbers. She would have to investigate the numbers tomorrow, but, for tonight, she needed to focus on her floater responsibilities and Thomas's smooth patter.

"It isn't often we can make a difference. That's why your money is appreciated. Please remember, tomorrow you're invited to bring your pets to the Blessing of the Beasts at the Little Brown Church. If you don't have a pet, feel free to stop by the shelter and adopt one before the service."

Everyone laughed.

"In the meantime, enjoy yourself this evening. Not only do we have food and drink available here in the grand ballroom, but the other parts of the hotel, including the jewelry shop and art gallery, are open for your viewing pleasure. Fifteen percent of anything you purchase in the hotel tonight will also be donated to the shelter." Thomas took a sip of his drink and walked from the center of the room to where Emily stood near Bailey. He handed his glass to Emily, put his arm around Bailey, and the two men left the room.

Sarah held out her empty tray toward Emily. "Would you like me to take that glass, ma'am?"

Emily placed it on the tray.

"What's with those two?"

"I don't know," Emily said. "I had no idea they were so chummy."

"I had no idea Thomas trained as a chef before he went into the business side of the hotel business."

"Neither did I until this afternoon. He had me showing him how to plate something and he used some terms that made me tease him about talking like a chef. That's when he told me he is."

"I'm surprised he didn't tell you before today."

Somehow, Emily looked smaller than ever to Sarah. "I think it slipped out. I don't think he ever planned to tell me. Sarah, I've been such an idiot!"

"How?"

"All week, Thomas has been asking me questions about what I'm doing and how Marcus and I do things at Southwind. He's been so nice, I thought he was simply being polite. You know, trying to put me at ease with my new boss."

"So, you answered, in detail, everything he asked?"

"Yes, but now, I think Marcus was right."

"What are you going to do about it? Will you quit?"

"I can't. I gave my word to work for six months or until he finds a new executive chef."

"Maybe you can argue he is the executive chef?"

"No. He may be a slimy fox, but he's no executive chef. Besides, if I don't stay, I won't get paid for the six months, which was the reason behind agreeing to do this job."

"But circumstances have changed. You'd be better off sharing fewer secrets and putting your energy and reputation into Southwind than staying here."

"I made a promise. Integrity means something to me, even if I'm not sure at times how much it does to other people. Here, give me that tray. We're done serving appetizers and drinks to the entire group. Most of the guests already have gone through the buffet line. It's time for you to float."

"Speaking of floating, when you're out of the kitchen, keep an eye on Mom. One of those more alcohol than food nights. What did you put into those Catnip drinks?"

"They're basically wine spritzers with a nip of wine and a dab of food coloring. Knowing Mom, she'd have to drink a tray of them before she might get tipsy. What did she have before she got here?"

"I have no idea, but she's in rare form."

"Great! Another thing to make this a perfect evening. At least it will be over soon."

"What makes you say that?"

"See how the room emptied out after Thomas spoke? Because we're not serving an open bar and the Howellian Catnips hardly have any alcohol, people ate, stayed for his remarks, and are either checking out the hotel or leaving to spend the evening doing something more fun."

Sarah glanced over Emily's shoulder. "Don't look now, but I think if you don't get out of here right now, your evening is only going to get worse."

CHAPTER THIRTY-NINE

Emily didn't even turn around to find out what disaster might be looming. She took off for the kitchen. Sarah, having spotted Anne and Thomas in heavy discussion walking in their direction debated whether to follow Emily's lead or make like a fly on the wall to overhear what the two were talking about. Because of Sarah's instinctive curiosity, the latter won out.

She sidled over to one of the large trays on a folding stand placed near the tables to be filled with dirty dishes. This tray was empty. She knew she couldn't simply stand there and eavesdrop. Happily, the table closest to Anne and Thomas was recently abandoned by its guests. Without rushing, she went to the table and, with her back to Thomas and Anne, slowly began stacking the dirty dishes and silverware. Meticulously, she scraped the food from each plate onto a master plate, instead of merely taking her stack to the big tray and having them dealt with in the kitchen.

At first, she thought Anne and Thomas were arguing but soon realized that wasn't the case. They were discussing the merits of rezoning and what the various properties could be used for other than restaurants. Sarah failed to hear every word, but it sounded like Anne might be softening. She was listening intently to Thomas describe how shops, an antique building, a bed-and-breakfast, and yuppie apartments could also fit into the existing buildings with limited remodeling.

It was all Sarah could do to keep her mouth shut as Thomas waxed eloquent, without mentioning any of the high-ticket items usually associated with remodeling old buildings. Things like replacing wiring, asbestos removal, bringing things up to code, or paying for permits were left unsaid. Anne seemed to be buying in, especially when he said he thought he had almost all the property in the bag. Sarah assumed he counted his uncle's house in the "we got you" column.

This time, when Anne spoke, her voice was lower. Unable to hear her clearly, Sarah moved closer, gathering the dishes from the other side of the table. She caught a glimpse of Anne's face. Rather than the relaxed but intent listener from moments earlier, the lines of Anne's face were tight. More like when she went in for the kill during a council meeting. Each word was clipped and enunciated.

"Thomas, my father always taught me not to count our chickens until they hatched. Too many developers have been left with egg on their faces because they owned all but one piece of land. You may sweet-talk well, but my family's position hasn't changed. We're fundamentally against what you're proposing. It isn't to our city's benefit to destroy what we have for the sake of making people like you rich. Bring me a plan with some merit and I'll listen. I pride myself on being open-minded but honest. My decisions reflect what I believe is in the best interest of the people of Wheaton."

"The people or the Hightowers?"

"That's not the way to make friends, Thomas. And you want friends. Bailey tells me you're fairly leveraged."

"I'm covering all my debt plus some."

"True, for now."

"Touché. Want another Catnip special?"

"Catnip?"

Thinking it best to move on, Sarah picked up her stacked plates but, rather than leave them in the dining room for someone else to bring to the kitchen, she decided to take them herself. Her back was to Anne and Thomas when she heard Thomas call for Emily. Sarah turned toward Anne and Thomas as Emily came out of the kitchen.

With one hand holding her chest, a flush-faced Anne pointed at Emily with the other. "Do you know what catnip does to someone with a heart condition? Thomas, I'm going to hold you and her responsible for trying to kill me."

CHAPTER FORTY

Sarah froze in place at Anne's words. She took a quick peek at her sister. Emily looked as stunned as Sarah felt. "Emily?" Sarah waited for her sister to say something.

Emily simply shook her head. Sarah wasn't sure if she was disagreeing with what Anne said or shaking her head in utter disbelief. She would have asked her if Thomas hadn't planted himself in front of Emily and Sarah.

"Emily, do we have a problem?"

When Emily again shook her head, Sarah was afraid her sister was in shock and not actually responding to the question being posed to her, but Emily, looking past him at Anne, found her voice. "Thomas, I don't know what Anne is talking about. I didn't use catnip in any recipe we served tonight."

"But," Anne said.

"You're right, catnip taken orally in small doses can cause problems for some people taking digitalis or lithium, but the Howellian Catnip didn't have catnip in it."

"I don't understand," Thomas said.

"It's very simple. Thomas, you dubbed tonight's event Catapalooza because of the hotel's cat exhibit and told me to tie the appearance of our food and décor to cats. Because of my limited budget, it was impossible to have an open bar. I decided to go with a signature drink much like a lot of brunches serve mimosas. The Howellian Catnip was a wine spritzer with more Sprite or 7-Up than wine. The name came from combining our cat motif with the nip of wine we put in it. There was absolutely nothing in terms of the drink or the ingredients used in any of our dishes that should have been a problem for Anne or any of our guests."

"That's well and good," Thomas said, "but people remember accusations, not back-page retractions."

Sarah couldn't disagree with Thomas. She remembered how things had been for Emily and her four months ago. Even now, if she got a cold stare in the grocery store, she knew, without any uncertainty, the other person was thinking she might be a murderer—no matter how erroneous the thought was.

Listening to Emily's even-toned but carefully controlled response, Sarah knew a similar thought must have crossed Emily's mind.

Sarah wasn't too happy when Thomas replied, "Well, we'll have to see what happens."

CHAPTER FORTY-ONE

Considering the tension of the day before, Sarah was relieved when the Blessing of the Beasts went off without a hitch. The sanctuary of the Little Brown Church was filled with humans and their animals. Looking around, Sarah saw all the city council members and almost everyone who'd been part of planning or executing yesterday's parade or the two receptions. Only Emily and Grace, who Sarah knew were prepping for another dinner at the hotel, were missing.

She did a double take when she spotted Thomas and Cliff standing next to each other. Thomas held an animal carrier on which she could clearly see lettering advertising his hotel. Knowing the hotel didn't permit real animals, she wondered if he was carrying a porcelain or clay cat as a publicity gimmick. If he was, it only complicated her feelings toward him, especially because he was here while her sister and Grace were stuck in Birmingham prepping food to make him look good.

If Thomas was engaged in a publicity ploy, she wondered if Cliff was in on it, too. She hoped not. Before she could fret much more, she sighted a bundle of green and yellow perched on Eloise's shoulder. Leave it to Eloise to bring a parrot to the Blessing of the Beasts. Apparently, because Eloise's hair was perfectly in place and there was nothing protecting the shoulder of her designer jacket, it was a trained parrot. Considering everything she knew about Eloise, that figured.

A few of the folks, like her mother and Anne Hightower, who Sarah noticed had regained her normal color and appearance of health, were obviously there simply as observers, cheerleaders, or mingling would-be candidates because they didn't have pets. Most people, though, came with at least one pet.

The variety of animals held up for the blessing was fantastic. Sarah expected and wasn't surprised to see cat owners, like herself with RahRah, and dog owners, including Mr. Rogers and Fluffy. Even the rabbit and gerbil owners didn't surprise her. The three iguanas and two snakes were a bit more difficult for Sarah to imagine bringing to a public service like this for a blessing.

The idea of snakes and iguanas gave her the willies. She bet she wasn't the only one eyeing the baby boa with trepidation. As their owners took them from the sanctuary to the fellowship hall, Sarah vowed to avoid them, despite their newly blessed state of being.

At the reception, she looked around for Pastor Dobbins. She wanted to congratulate him on his lovely service and the general success of the Blessing of the Beasts. He may have played her for the benefit of his wife and himself, but there was nothing to fault him on in terms of the blessing he delivered. The readings were short and well-chosen, the choir's songs interwoven beautifully, and Pastor Dobbins's blessing inclusive. His ability to involve everyone in something joyful resonated with Sarah, especially in light of the many Wheaton lives touched by sorrow during the past week.

Picking up a cookie, Sarah also was grateful for the abundant spread the ladies of the church auxiliary had made. She was going to have to write them a note commending them on having outdone themselves. Glancing around, Sarah saw many familiar faces devouring the home cooking of the ladies' auxiliary. The glad faces and chow-down-take-no-prisoners behavior made it clear that those attending were more than satisfied. She wished she could bottle the enthusiasm and excitement in the room.

When she noticed Harlan on the other side of the hall with Chief Gerard and the chief's bulldog, she laughed. The chief and his dog were the perfect illustration of the saying about pets and owners growing to look like each other. From their jowly faces to their round bellies, they looked more like twins than Emily and she did.

She hoped Harlan and the chief were sharing more than compliments about the food with each other. If Harlan could figure out how to get the chief off Maybelle's case, things would be perfect.

Speaking of perfect, Sarah looked around for Mr. Bailey. Not only did she want to clarify what Thomas had said about the financial success of YipYeow Day with him, she wondered how much more Catapalooza added to the bottom line. Thomas's repeated implication that the donated amount would be a net amount after expenses had her nervous.

Sarah didn't see Bailey, but she observed Mr. Rogers and Fluffy leave his nephews and make a bee-line straight toward her mother. Maybelle also must have seen him heading in her direction because she abruptly turned and began talking to the person nearest her. Even though the woman had the most beautiful chocolate Portuguese water dog puppy, Sarah was sure, knowing her mother's lack of affinity for animals, her mother's selection was random. Sarah was positive her assumption was correct when her mother tilted her head and glanced sideways in Mr. Rogers's direction.

Maybelle must have ascertained Mr. Rogers was only a few feet from her because she not only seemed more engrossed in her conversation but, completely out of character, she bent and petted the woman's dog. Watching all of this from a distance, Sarah wondered exactly how much interest her mother would fake for the Portuguese water dog simply because she was still furious with Mr. Rogers.

It didn't take long to find out. While Maybelle continued her oohs and aahs over the dog, Mr. Rogers closed the gap between them and tapped Maybelle on the shoulder. Sarah couldn't hear what he said, but there was no question about the adamant way her mother shook her head while she grabbed the arm of the woman she'd been talking to and focused her attention exclusively on her. Despite him still talking to her, Maybelle ushered her new friend closer to the fellowship hall stage, where Pastor Dobbins stood, guitar in hand.

Mr. Rogers didn't move. From her vantage point, Sarah perceived his shoulders droop as he continued to watch her mother's back. Only when Fluffy rubbed against his leg did he respond. He bent, as if sharing a thought with the dog. Their exchange finished, he led Fluffy toward the hallway between the sanctuary and the fellowship hall. Because the hallway, on this level, housed the bathrooms, water fountain, and a door leading to an outside area the church had designated for any necessary pet breaks, it had been well used after the Blessing of the Beasts. Uncertain if Mr. Rogers was leaving or simply taking Fluffy out, Sarah considered going after him but was distracted by Pastor Dobbins's first song.

She was surprised how good he was. In rapid succession, he demonstrated an enjoyable repertoire of pop, country, and Christian music. Over the years, she'd never thought of ministers as being fun. Most of the ones she'd heard preach had turned her off as they tried to scare their congregants straight with talk of fire and brimstone. Hearing Pastor Dobbins's songs and experiencing how he handled the Blessing of the Beasts, she made a mental note to try one of his Sunday services.

Before singing what Pastor Dobbins announced would be his last song, he again thanked the ladies' auxiliary and urged everyone to please eat another one or two desserts or he'd be forced to finish them. When the audience stopped laughing at his joke and he began his finale, Sarah saw her mother head toward the hallway Mr. Rogers had gone down a few minutes earlier. Sarah caught her mother's eye and drew a question mark in the air. Maybelle mouthed back, loud enough for a few people around her to hear and snicker. "Ladies' room."

Sarah hoped Mr. Rogers was still where her mother would run into him. Perhaps, if he had taken Fluffy to the animal spot to do her business and Maybelle saw him there, her mother would use the puppy's cuteness as an opening to clear the air. Then again, her mother wasn't one to easily kiss and make up.

At that thought, Sarah hurried into the hallway to catch her mother. Maybe, with a little divine daughter intervention, Mr. Rogers and her mother could be coaxed into burying the hatchet they'd thrown at the cocktail party somewhere other than in each other.

CHAPTER FORTY-TWO

Except for Sarah and RahRah in his carrier, the hallway was deserted. Considering how many people she'd seen coming and going before Pastor Dobbins's concert, she was surprised. She peeked through the glass window in the door to see if her mother, Mr. Rogers, and Fluffy were outside, but the pet area was empty.

"You look deep in thought."

Sarah tensed her entire body at the sound of her mother's voice. She hadn't heard her come up behind her in the hallway. "I was contemplating the feeling of emptiness in this hall. I thought I'd run into more people."

"The same thought crossed my mind a minute ago. I guess this hall must have an outside door or connect to a building exit."

"Guess so. We can either find it or go out the way we came in. The concert is over."

"I'm up for exploring, especially if it brings us out closer to my car. Let's see what we find."

Together they walked down the hallway, searching for a door, but their chosen path led back to the sanctuary. Her mother tapped her foot. "There has to be another way out. Probably from one of those little offshoot halls we passed. Let's look on our way back to the fellowship hall."

Sarah readily agreed.

Maybelle picked a hallway that was passable, except for boxes stacked four high against one wall. At one point a few had fallen, but Sarah could see around them. She let her mother lead the way until Maybelle admitted, "I don't think this is the way out, either. Sorry."

"That's okay. We'll just go out the way we know through the fellowship hall."

A yipping sound caught Sarah's ear. "Did you hear that?"

"What?"

Perhaps her ears were playing tricks. A moan and scratching noises from just ahead, where the boxes were knocked over, convinced her otherwise. This time Maybelle must have heard the noises, too. Without waiting for Sarah to join her, she rushed to the fallen boxes.

"Sarah! It's Fluffy. A box is on her leash . . . Oh, no. Quick, call an ambulance. It's George! Hurry! There's blood everywhere."

Sarah ran forward, already pulling her phone from her pocket. Taking in that Mr. Rogers wasn't conscious, but was breathing, she dialed 911. She left her mother to watch him while she ran back to the fellowship hall for more help and to see if Thomas and Cliff were still there. The first person she saw was Harlan. "Harlan, Mr. Rogers has been hurt. Have you seen his nephews?"

Harlan pointed across the room. "Where's George?"

"Down the hallway. Halfway to the sanctuary. Mother is with him."

Harlan didn't stop to ask questions before grabbing one of the town's nurses and hurrying to see if they could do anything before the paramedics arrived.

Seeing Mr. Rogers's nephews and Bailey about to exit the building, she waved to get their attention. "Wait! Your uncle's been injured," she yelled as Thomas pulled the door open. "Don't leave!"

The three men came back into the room. She pointed toward the hallway entrance she'd just used. "Your uncle's hurt. Mother is with him."

Cliff grabbed her flailing arms. "What?"

"We found your uncle and Fluffy near some boxes." She swallowed and took a deep breath. "I think some-one attacked him."

In the distance, she heard sirens. Cliff's eyes widened. He released her arms and ran into the cor-ridor, followed by Thomas and Bailey.

She started to follow, but Harlan, who had re-turned, stopped her by snagging a piece of her shirt. She tried to pull away to see if she could help with Mr. Rogers, but his grip was firm. Once she focused on him, he let go but signaled her to wait a moment. He pulled out his phone and placed a call. He quickly explained the situation to whoever was on the other end of the line. "That's right, Dwayne. Maybelle and her daughter, Sarah, discovered George Rogers. He's been roughed up badly. We've already called the paramedics. I can hear sirens, so I assume they're almost here."

He listened for a moment. "Don't worry. I'll keep

Maybelle and Sarah here and try to secure the place, but most people, like you, have left." He paused and met Sarah's gaze. "I don't think Mr. Rogers will still be here by the time you arrive. You don't seem to understand. He's in no shape to talk to anyone."

Sarah adamantly shook her head. How stupid was the chief? There was no question in her mind from the look of abject horror she'd seen on her mother's face and his shallow breathing that there probably wasn't a minute to spare getting Mr. Rogers to the hospital.

Harlan clicked his phone off. "What happened? How is Maybelle involved?"

She stared at him. Why was he asking her about her mother's involvement instead of letting her go help Mr. Rogers?

"Sarah, I need to know your mother's involvement before Chief Gerard gets here."

"Why?" Before he answered, she realized how this was going to look. Her mother already was a primary suspect and here was a second injury, hopefully not another death, in a hallway where it appeared she might have been alone except for Mr. Rogers and Fluffy.

"Near the end of Pastor Dobbins's performance, my mother signaled me she was going to go down the connector corridor to the ladies' room. I knew Mr. Rogers and Fluffy went that way a little earlier, and I hoped I could get Mother and him together to make peace with each other."

"They'd had a falling-out?"

"Last night."

"Did anyone else know about it besides you?"

"Cliff, for sure. And probably a lot more people at the Howellian party. Mom wasn't too subtle in her anger with Mr. Rogers." She debated whether to mention her mother's drinking. Knowing someone might, she opted to tell him. "Harlan, she'd probably had a few drinks too many last night."

From the way he tightened his lips, she knew he wasn't pleased with the information. "Did Maybelle know Mr. Rogers had gone down the hall before her?"

"I don't think so. He tried getting her to talk with him earlier, but she refused. By the time he left the room, she was standing closer to the stage, not looking in his direction."

"And you know this because?"

"Because I was standing in the back of the room, watching Pastor Dobbins's show, and couldn't help but notice what was going on around me. Anyway, when she signaled me she was going down the hall, I acknowledged it, as did several people because she mouthed her destination rather loudly. A moment or two later, I decided maybe, if Mr. Rogers went that way because he took Fluffy to the designated animal spot, I could grab them both and make them talk to each other. When I went into the hall, it was deserted. I looked out into the animal spot, and there wasn't anyone there, either."

"Where was your mother?"

"I don't really know. She came up behind me and startled me. That's when we decided to find an exit door. We ended up in the sanctuary, so we decided to look for a hallway on our way back to the fellowship hall. Instead of a door to the outside, we found Mr. Rogers and Fluffy."

"What happened then?"

"I called nine-one-one and came back to the fellowship hall to get help and find his nephews, but I ran into you first."

"And you left Maybelle alone with him?"

"Yes. Why not? When I ran from the room, she was bent over him." Now it was Sarah's turn to grab Harlan's arm. "How is Chief Gerard going to take that?"

"I don't know, but here he is, so we're going to find out."

Chapter Forty-three

For a third time, Sarah repeated to Chief Gerard exactly what she'd told Harlan. Periodically, he threw in a question about whether she was sure her mother joined her from behind or perhaps from down the side hall, but her answers remained consistent. She glanced across the fellowship hall to where her mother sat alone at a table. Fluffy lay curled against her mother's feet, next to RahRah in his carrier. Chief Gerard already had questioned Maybelle, but he refused to let her leave, even after she signed the statement she gave Officer Robinson.

Sarah could see how upset her mother was. Once again, there had been, as her mother told Chief Gerard, blood everywhere. When she bent down to help George, it was impossible not to get it on herself. At least, unlike last time, Mr. Rogers was alive, or Sarah hoped he was. He'd been taken to the hospital immediately, but Chief Gerard had prevented her mother and her from calling to check on him.

Finally, with a nudge from Harlan, Chief Gerard permitted them to go.

Maybelle jumped to her feet, causing Fluffy to move quickly to avoid being stepped on. "What about Fluffy?"

"I guess Alvin will have to take her to the shelter," said Chief Gerard.

"You can't do that. She saved George."

"Maybelle, I understand how you feel, but there's nobody to care for her. George can't, and those nephews of his are both at the hospital. The shelter will find a place for her."

"We can take her."

Sarah wasn't sure she'd heard correctly. Her mother, who swore she was allergic to every animal under the sun, was not only volunteering but insisting Fluffy come home with her?

As if she knew she was being talked about, Fluffy cuddled closer to Maybelle's legs. Sarah watched Chief Gerard look from the dog to Maybelle and back to Fluffy again. "Ah, Maybelle, I'm a dog man, too." He bent and gently picked up Fluffy.

Sarah tried not to laugh. She could swear Fluffy's chocolate eyes were focused on him as if she were romancing him to get her way.

He gently rubbed Fluffy's ears. "You've been through a lot today, girl. I'm not going to upset you any further." The chief handed Fluffy to Maybelle. "You can take her home until we sort this out."

Maybelle clutched Fluffy close to her and thanked the chief. Given the green light to leave, Maybelle led Harlan and Sarah from the fellowship hall. Once the group was out of the room, Maybelle sneezed. She thrust Fluffy at Sarah, who was already carrying

RahRah. "I couldn't let him take her to the shelter, but you're going to have to take her home."

"Mom, I have a cat. I doubt RahRah and Fluffy are going to do well together. You asked for her, why don't you take her to your house?"

Another sneeze provided her mother's answer.

"Harlan?"

"No pets allowed in my building. Guess you'll have to help RahRah and Fluffy make friends with each other."

Maybelle cut Sarah's answer off. "Enough discussion. I want to go to the hospital."

"I do, too, Mom, but I need to take Fluffy and RahRah home first."

"Harlan, will you please take Sarah to her house? She's right about needing to drop Fluffy and RahRah off. I don't want them to have to stay in my car while we're in the hospital."

"Maybelle, I'll be glad to do that, but why don't I take you in my car straight to the hospital while Sarah uses your car to take RahRah and Fluffy home?"

"Thank you, Harlan. George wouldn't be there if it weren't for me."

"Mom, you didn't attack Mr. Rogers. How can you blame yourself? You're the one who found him and probably saved his life."

"Sarah, if I'd been willing to talk to him, he wouldn't have been in that hall. We would have stayed in the fellowship hall and I'd eventually let him apologize to me."

"I think you were the one who owed him an apology." Sarah clamped her mouth shut. There was nothing more to say. While she didn't blame her mother, Sarah agreed a different course of events might have produced different results. Had Mr. Rogers been in the big room or had she followed him into the hall, he might not have been attacked. Then again, if her mother had been in the hall with him, she might have been injured, too.

Maybe it was her own guilt, but like her mother, Sarah felt a need to get to the hospital as quickly as possible. She only hoped, when she got home, the carriage house would still be in one piece. Whether she left Fluffy and RahRah in two rooms or together, it probably wasn't going to be pretty.

CHAPTER FORTY-FOUR

At the hospital, Sarah was directed to the surgical waiting room. Her mother and Harlan were sitting together while Cliff paced in front of them. Thomas sat in a corner, isolated from the other waiting families. From the stack of *Food & Wine* and *Southern Living* magazines in the chair next to him, Sarah had a pretty good idea what Thomas had been doing.

"Thank you for coming. It will mean a lot to Uncle George to know you cared. Isn't that right, Cliff?"

Cliff grunted an acquiescence but didn't sit.

"Excuse my brother. Since we got here, he's been pacing incessantly."

"I understand. I'm so sorry," Maybelle said. "When George wanted to talk, I should have listened. If I had, he wouldn't be in surgery now."

Sarah again assured her mother it wasn't her fault. "Are they having to relieve the pressure on his brain?"

Cliff stopped walking. "They're not operating on his head."

"But all that blood."

"Only a laceration. Head wounds bleed badly, but he only needed a few stitches for that. They think he was pushed or hit from behind. When he put his arm out to break his fall, he either got twisted up with his own feet or rammed his arm into some of the equipment in those boxes, smashing the shoulder of his dominant arm. Right now, they're pinning it. He'll have a long recovery, but he'll make it."

Maybelle sat in a chair and put her face into her hands. When she lifted her head up, Sarah could see wet lines where her tears fell. "I'm so relieved. Don't you boys worry. I'll help him when he gets out of here."

Cliff clumsily put a hand on Maybelle's shoulder. "I'm sure you will. I bet he'll like that."

"Even if he doesn't, I'll be there for him."

Harlan grinned. "How could he not appreciate the attention? I bet he'll be tickled pink."

They were all laughing at the image of Mr. Rogers and his bow tie tickled pink when the doctor joined them.

Cliff jumped into the doctor's private space. "Is my uncle okay? Can we see him?"

The doctor held up his hands in a push-back motion. "Which of you are the family?"

"All of us," Maybelle said.

The doctor laughed. "No, really."

Cliff and Thomas identified themselves, and the doctor invited them to join him in one of the patient/doctor meeting rooms. He held his hand out so Cliff and Thomas could precede him, but Harlan blocked him from following them.

"Is he really okay?"

"Yes, but HIPAA prohibits me from going into any

detail with an unauthorized person. I'm sorry. Excuse me, now."

Harlan stepped to the side and let him pass. Once the doctor was gone, Harlan turned back to Maybelle and Sarah. "What do we know?"

Sarah wrinkled her brow. "I don't understand. What are you talking about?"

"I'm taking a leaf out of your book and trying to help you do the professionals' work for them. So what do we know?"

Maybelle nodded. "I get it. We know I didn't kill Lance or attack George, no matter what Chief Gerard thinks."

"We know lots of people went in and out of the hallway where George was attacked." Sarah thought for a moment. "And we know that was also true that day at Lance's office."

"Who are our suspects? Is there anyone we can put in both locations?"

Sarah smiled. She was getting into this mental exercise. "You're off the hook because you weren't seen at the bank on the day Lance was killed."

"That's probably true, but we'll never know who went in or out of the alley entrance. The tape didn't record anything."

"What? I thought they had state-of-the-art cameras?" Sarah stared in disbelief at Harlan. "I know you said they were having some problems, but wasn't the lab able to retrieve the film?"

"No. The feed on that one camera was corrupted."

"Corrupted or deliberately damaged?"

"They're not sure, yet."

"So," Maybelle said, "there isn't a record of any of the alley comings and goings or that the door was open."

"I'm sorry, Maybelle. I've been nagging Dwayne for access to the tape, but he kept saying it was at the lab. When we were in the fellowship hall, he told me they just got the report back that the lab can't restore the tape."

"Where does that put my mother, Harlan?"

"Back to square one. That's why we need to figure out who the suspects in both incidents are. Besides the two of you, who do we know for sure was at the bank and attended the Blessing of the Beasts?"

Maybelle and Sarah started making a list of who they had seen in both places: "Eloise, Bailey, Cliff, the teller who was promoted to Eloise's spot. Don't forget Thomas. Eloise saw him there."

"There probably are others we haven't even thought about because we don't personally know them. Harlan, there are even some people who are so obvious we haven't considered them as suspects."

"Like who, Sarah?"

"Alvin Robinson met the chief here today because he already was here. He was moonlighting doing security work during the service."

Harlan snapped his fingers. He put his hand up to his mouth in thought. "And he was doing the same thing at the bank the day Lance was murdered. What do we know about him, except he recently moved here from Mobile?"

"Other than seeming like a real nice guy, I don't know anything else about him. Do you, Harlan?" Sarah asked.

"Not really."

"But let's get back to my point about others we don't know. Just like Mom and I didn't see Thomas Howell in the bank, there could have been others either in the lobby or who went in and out of Lance's office who were here with a pet today."

"Or maybe without a pet," Maybelle suggested.

"Right. Harlan, is there any chance we can see the tapes made from the different bank lobby camera angles? That way we could see if any other suspects jump out at us."

"I'll try to see what I can do. Chief Gerard didn't mention them."

"You do think they pulled the tapes, don't you?"

Harlan grimaced. "I hope so. They run on either a forty-eight- or seventy-two-hour continuous loop feed, so if they didn't pull them, they've been taped over again by now."

As what Harlan said sunk in, Sarah glanced across the waiting room and saw Cliff.

"I'm glad the three of you are still here. This HIPAA stuff is for the birds. I didn't think anything could be worse than OSHA standards, but it is."

Sarah looked around the waiting room. "Where's Thomas?"

"He had to go back to Birmingham. The doctor said Uncle George would sleep for a while, but I'm going to sit with him for a bit. There's no need for the three of you to stick around, but, Sarah and Maybelle, I want to thank you again. Uncle George lost a lot of blood from his head laceration, but because of the two of you, it turned out to be relatively minor. If he lay there bleeding much longer, this story could have been quite different."

Cliff knelt in front of Maybelle's chair. "You don't have to beat yourself up for not talking to him. You were his angel."

Maybelle blushed as he stood. "Do you know when George will be allowed to go home?"

"The arm is going to be a problem. It's a bad break and, even with pinning, at his age, there's no guarantee he'll get full mobility back. Instead of sending him home, he'll be released from here to a rehab center. We'll have to see how things go from there." He frowned. "My brother might get his wish after all."

CHAPTER FORTY-FIVE

By the spring in her mother's step and her once-again insistence upon being called Maybelle, Sarah knew her mother was no longer fretting as deeply about Mr. Rogers. For that matter, Sarah felt relieved, too. He might be set in his ways and, truth be told, a little kooky, but he was her neighborhood kook.

Calmed down, Maybelle insisted she wanted to go home rather than spend the night in Wheaton. Sarah tried to argue her out of her decision, but her mother was adamant. "Sarah, you have a regular menagerie at your house. I wouldn't sleep a wink because I'd be sneezing all night."

Rather than continuing the fight or suggesting she follow her home to make sure Maybelle got there okay, Sarah offered up a little white lie. She told her mother that, with everything that had happened, she wanted to check in on Emily in Birmingham. Her mother's acceptance of Sarah's rationale for driving to Birmingham belied her true state of mind.

While Sarah and a sneezing Maybelle were at the carriage house, Sarah walked Fluffy and made sure

Fluffy and RahRah were in separate rooms, with fresh water and food. She decided more extensive introductions between the two would wait until she returned from following Maybelle to Birmingham.

As her mother put her key in her door, Sarah could tell she again was subdued. Sarah made a joke, but her mother didn't laugh. Sarah hated seeing her mother devoid of her sense of humor. "What's wrong, Mom?"

"I guess I'm still upset about everything that happened last night and today."

Sarah followed her mother into Maybelle's living room. Although Sarah favored modern furniture and fixtures, this very traditionally decorated room was Sarah's favorite in her mother's home. She loved knowing the mahogany furniture and Capodimonte lamps once belonged to her grandmother and great-grandmother and that there were touches of Maybelle scattered throughout, too. "Aren't you the one who taught me not to kid a kidder? Are you worried about Mr. Rogers being in the hospital?"

"No, I'm dreading when they release him. George is a proud man and he's not going to like being in a rehab hospital or perhaps having to go to assisted living." Maybelle turned on the lamps in the living room. "It's a fear most of us have."

Sarah was confused. "I haven't given much thought to it for either you or me."

Her mother laughed. "One day you will. You'll wake up and wonder where the years went. How you suddenly have children as old as you feel on the inside. And on the day that happens, you'll have a moment of fear about how much time the future holds and if you'll be able to enjoy it."

Maybelle grabbed a pillow lying flat on the couch, fluffed it, and repositioned it in the corner of the couch. "That's better."

She sat in the barrel chair, which was angled so she could see the couch clearly.

"Is it?" Sarah gazed at her mother, wondering if Maybelle would give her another glimpse within her soul. The sound of the front door opening destroyed any chance of that happening.

"Hello!" Emily called.

"Mom and I are in the living room."

Emily joined them. She dropped her backpack on the floor and threw her jacket on it. From the quickness of her movements and the tense lines crossing her forehead, Sarah knew something had happened. "What's going on?"

Emily pulled a check out of the pocket of her jeans. "Thomas came back from the hospital and fired me."

"Why? You've been doing such a good job for him."

Emily sat on the couch and grabbed the pillow her mother had just fluffed. She ran her fingers over the pillow's cording. "Thomas came into the kitchen as we were putting the last touches on tonight's dinner service. He asked everyone a few questions about the evening meal and told them about the Blessing of the Beasts and what happened to his uncle."

"Was he upset?"

"Not enough that he didn't ask questions about the dinner service first."

"Figures."

"You got that right. Anyway, after he told us his uncle would eventually be okay, he asked to speak to Grace and me for a moment. He led us to a corner of the kitchen, away from the other employees, and told us he didn't think things were working out. Grace pointed out that meal service and sales were up since we took over the kitchen. He acknowledged that but said the incident with Anne and now my mother and sister being involved with his uncle's attack put our working relationship in a bad light. Consequently, he thought it best we sever our relationship immediately."

Maybelle leaned forward. "What! What did you say to him?"

"Nothing. I was flabbergasted. Before I got any words out, he pulled two checks from his pocket and announced they covered what we had worked plus severance pay. Grace and I looked at the amounts on the checks, and I challenged them as not reflecting what we agreed upon."

"What did he say?"

"He reminded me we never reached the contract stage and he didn't see how, under the circumstances, we could do so now."

Emily held up the check again. "He knew what he was doing. He had these checks fully made out before he came into the kitchen. I was so mad, I almost threw it back in his face, but then I remembered what you said about getting a contract and decided to hold on to it."

Emily made a noise somewhere between a snort and a laugh. "You might as well say I told you so."

"I won't."

"You should. Do you know, I think he expected me to throw the check back at him rather than accepting it? He got the weirdest expression on his face when

I shoved it into my pocket. I can't believe for the past two weeks I shared so many of Marcus's and my secrets, tricks, and shortcuts. How could I have been so stupid?"

"Emily, this may sound strange, but, considering everything I've been hearing, do you have your phone?"

"Sure. In my backpack. Why?"

"I know you bank from your phone. Deposit that check right now and call Grace to do the same. This way, you'll be ahead of the game if Thomas stops payment on the checks or is a little short on cash in his account."

Emily pulled her phone from her backpack. She called Grace and then opened her banking app, snapped a picture, and deposited the check. "You know what's even more ironic? He gave Grace one week of severance pay, but he paid me for two."

"Probably for all those secrets you shared."

Emily hit her head. "I was such a fool."

"In more ways than one," Maybelle chimed in. "Seems to me this is a closed chapter, but you have some things to address back in Wheaton. How long are you going to be a fool about those things?"

"Not very long." Emily stood, picked up her jacket and backpack, and gave her mother a kiss.

Once Emily left, Sarah was ready to rehash everything, but Maybelle hushed her. "Past history. It's not worth dwelling on. Eventually, he'll get his due—perhaps from his uncle."

Sarah wondered what her mother was planning to

discuss with Mr. Rogers once he felt better, but she didn't dare ask.

"Sarah, thanks for caring enough to follow me home, but it's time for you to go back to Wheaton, too." Maybelle turned off the lamp, kissed Sarah, and left the room. Alone, Sarah realized her mother had just graciously kicked her out. She took the hint.

Chapter Forty-six

As Sarah drove back from Birmingham, she realized the sun would set soon. Considering everything that had happened, she didn't feel like immediately going home, but driving aimlessly seemed pointless. Ahead, she saw the highway turnoff to reach the bluff. That seemed the perfect place to go.

Cliff had told her she had an open invitation, but she'd felt funny going there since the day they went out on the boat. She didn't want it to seem like she was trying to be more than friends. With him staying with Mr. Rogers at the hospital, she didn't have to worry about running into him.

For a moment, she felt bad about leaving RahRah and Fluffy alone even longer but quickly disregarded that thought. She needed "me" time. This way, she could enjoy the beauty of the sunset from her absolute favorite place and use the few moments of solitude to think about everything that had transpired during the past week.

As she rounded the curve to park near Cliff's house, she saw that his truck was parked next to his cabin. Apparently, he hadn't stayed at the hospital too long.

She guessed Mr. Good Guy's devotion to sitting with his uncle was lip service for their benefit.

Sarah was about to turn around and leave, but she'd come this far. She might as well watch the sunset from the bluff. Sarah thought about parking and not admitting to Cliff she was even there, but if he looked out and saw her sitting on the bluff, he would think she was being rude.

Consequently, she parked and approached the cabin. As she reached the top of the wood-hewn stairs, she saw another car parked on the cabin's far side. Sarah thought again about turning back and leaving, but, accusing herself of never being spontaneous, she forced herself to approach the front window and door. She was about to knock when the sound of voices caught her attention.

Sarah moved closer to the picture window and tried to peek inside the room. Although she couldn't tell who the voices belonged to, there was no question in her mind that an argument was going on and that the voices were male. Uncertain where the men were, she questioned if she could simply back off the porch without being seen. The problem, as she saw the shadow of two men at the edge of the room, was whether the tinted view of the room she had through the window was the same from inside the cabin.

Now she wished she had taken the cabin tour instead of the boat ride. She paused when she heard them bantering Lance's name. At that moment, the two arguing men stepped into full view of the window. From where she stood, their faces were shadowed, but she assumed from his build that the taller and huskier one was Cliff.

As she watched, the smaller man shoved Cliff. Cliff stumbled backward but didn't hit back. Instead, he regained his footing, stepped forward, and yelled something about "your stupid Ponzi scheme" at the man. The other man grabbed a vase from the small table he stood near and threw it at Cliff. It missed.

This time, Cliff responded. He dove at the man and pushed him toward the small table. The table went over, but still the little man stayed on his feet. He was a scrapper.

As their fight brought the men closer to the window, Sarah knew she had to leave now. Before she could move, the black suited man tripped and fell. The larger man froze, looking straight at Sarah. Recognition came over his face while, at the same time, Sarah realized she'd been wrong. The man wasn't Cliff.

It was Thomas. She was surprised the glass between them didn't melt from the intensity of his look as she knew he'd recognized her. At that moment, the other man, who she now could see was Bailey, hit Thomas again from behind. He started to fall but caught himself on something below the window out of Sarah's view. What she could see was him straightening up with something in his hand. Moving forward, Thomas swung the object at Bailey, hitting him in the head. For a moment, Bailey stood perfectly still then crumpled to the ground. He didn't move again, even when Thomas pressed against his neck checking for a pulse.

Sarah wasn't sure if she'd stifled an involuntary scream, but she wasn't going to wait to find out. She started to run back to her car, but she was too late. She heard the front door open and footsteps behind her. Adrenaline pumped her to run faster, willing herself to get to her car and not lose time looking back. It wasn't enough. He caught her, jerking her arm so hard she yelped in pain. Tears filled her eyes from the agony caused by the sheer force with which he wrenched her around to face him. Her vision cleared, and the rage on Thomas's face made her cringe in fear.

Thomas pulled her back up the stairs to a place on the porch where they could both see into the cabin through the wide-open door. She questioned if Bailey was still alive.

It was as if Thomas read her mind. "He's dead, but, Sarah, it isn't what you think. It was an accident. Surely, you saw us fighting?"

"You're hurting me." She tried to pull away, but he held her arm too tightly.

Thomas didn't respond to her comment. He averted his eyes. "We were fighting over him stealing from the shelter. I wanted Cliff and him to give themselves up. Not for this to happen."

"Cliff and Bailey?"

"That's right. The numbers they gave me to report at Catapalooza seemed low. I know it sounds crazy, but between Uncle George and the money being off, I came out here to see if I could find money or something lying around. If I did, I wanted to give my brother a chance to explain before I raised a stink about them skimming off the top."

She knew he was right about what he'd announced being off, but she also knew he still held her arm. Again, it was as if he was in her mind. He let her go and pointed to her arm. "Sorry about that. I panicked.

I didn't want you running off from here thinking you saw something when it really was something else."

"I don't understand." She rubbed her arm. There were going to be bruise marks where her skin still showed white finger impressions from him holding her. "What made you think if money was missing, it was Cliff and Bailey who shorted the shelter?"

"Because Bailey was the treasurer and, well, since Bailey took over for Lance, Cliff and he not only have been hanging out together a lot, but Cliff seems to have a lot of extra cash. For a guy who went bonkers when his loan was rejected, he sure has a lot of nice toys down by the river."

Sarah couldn't disagree with him on that. She flexed her fingers. Her arm tingled, but she didn't think it was dislocated. "I still don't understand why you came out here, especially when you could have talked to him at the hospital."

"As upset as I was over Uncle George, that was the only thing I could think about. I guess I should have confronted him once we found out Uncle George was going to be okay, but Harlan, your mother, and you were there. I wanted to talk to Cliff privately."

"Even if he was guilty of a crime?"

"Cliff and I don't usually see eye to eye, but he is my brother. I thought I owed it to him to give him a chance to come clean. I hoped I was wrong about him being involved, but if I wasn't, I thought I might be able to convince him to give the shelter back the donated money. It sounds sappy, but I figured if Cliff squared things away with the shelter, no one would have to be the wiser. That's why, when I couldn't get him alone to talk, I came out here. Like I said, I thought he might have stashed some off the money in the cabin or by the boathouse.When I got here, I parked and came in."

"You parked?"

Thomas pointed toward Cliff's truck. "Cliff and I rode to the hospital in his truck. My car is at the church. Because I needed to get back to the hotel, I gave him my keys and took his truck while he stayed with Uncle George. We figured we'd trade our rides back tomorrow. It wasn't until I was already at the door that I realized Bailey was here."

His explanation made sense to Sarah. She hadn't seen Bailey's car, either, until she approached the door.

"When I walked in, I stupidly accused Bailey of playing with the shelter's money. He didn't deny it. Then, thinking about Cliff's loan being called and Emily's being rejected, I made some snide remark about him having his finger in the bank's till, too. That's when we started fighting, and it escalated from words to punches. I grabbed the figurine from the table and swung. I don't know how long you were on the porch, but I know you were there long enough to see me grab the figurine off the bookcase and hit him in self-defense."

"Yes." She bit her lip, realizing she probably had admitted too much.

"Then you saw him fall. I thought, at first, I'd only knocked him out, but when I went to help him, I couldn't find a pulse. That's when I realized I hit him in the temple and killed him. Before I could react beyond that realization, I heard you scream. That's when I got scared."

Sarah backed away.

"Wait." Thomas put his hand on her arm again, only more gently this time. "Please, before you leave. I need to call the police and let them know what's happened out here. Cliff doesn't have a landline and my phone is dead. Would you mind calling the police for me with your phone?"

He released her arm and looked back through the doorway. "Please? I've got to report this. I've got to tell them I didn't mean to kill him."

Thomas turned back toward her. With the hand he had held her with, he ran his fingers through his hair, finally resting it on his forehead. "I've got to tell them it was an accident. That I'm responsible for a horrible accident."

His face contorted. Sarah thought he might burst into tears. Seeing how upset he was, she was convinced her initial reaction to what she'd seen was wrong. He might be flawed, but there was no way this man could possibly mean to hurt her if he was letting her call the police. She pulled her phone from her pocket and stared at it as she typed in her passcode and started to dial 9-1-1. Before she could punch in the final number, Thomas grabbed her phone, dropped it to the ground, and smashed it with his foot. Stunned, she turned to run again, but he was too quick.

CHAPTER FORTY-SEVEN

Yanking her by the hair, he forced her into the cabin and into a straight-backed chair. He let go. Her scalp burned. She partially rose from the chair, but he pushed her back. She fell against the hard wood of the chair. Instinctively, she put her hands behind her and felt for its seat. One hand caught the edge and she plopped hip first onto the chair's seat. She didn't try to get up again because any path of escape was blocked by Thomas towering over her as he reached for the supposedly nonexistent landline sitting on a table next to her. With one tug, he pulled the phone cord from the wall.

"Put your hands in front of you."

Remembering the article she'd read in Harlan's office about how magicians escaped when they were tied up, she crossed her wrists and held her hands out toward Thomas.

"Stop the funny business. Uncross your wrists."

From the way he held the telephone cord, she was afraid if she angered him, he would hit her rather than tie her up. "Sorry." She positioned her hands separately but tightened her muscles while she kept the knuckles from both hands together. As Thomas whipped the cord around her wrists, she pulled her hands slightly toward her chest and prayed that when she relaxed there would be enough of a gap that she could work her hands out.

"Why? Why did you do all of this?"

"Figure it out."

Sarah's mind raced, trying to put two and two together. Nothing fit until she remembered Eloise's comment about not all loan requests being collateralized in the fashion her mother offered for Emily and Marcus and the words she'd just overheard about a Ponzi scheme. With Bailey on the floor, what Emily said about corners being cut in the kitchen, and Thomas stiffing Emily on her six months' guaranteed salary, there had to be a monetary connection with the hotel.

She took a stab at it, hoping to distract Thomas while she loosened her hands. "It's the hotel, isn't it?"

"You are the bright one. I could tell that at lunch. You didn't want your sister to have anything to do with my kitchen or me, did you?"

Sarah thought she better humor him. "Not without a contract. I thought you were a man with a purpose, so she needed to protect herself. All I could do was be the voice of reason and try to keep her from acting without thinking." She shook her head. "Little good I did on that one."

He laughed.

"You played Emily like a fiddle until you got everything you wanted from her, right? Were you playing Bailey and Cliff, too?"

Thomas didn't laugh again. "Cliff? That boy scout? No. The only one who had his finger in the till was Bailey."

"At the shelter and the bank? Did he short the shelter or did you both do that?"

He whistled. "You're smarter than you look. So you know the shelter really was being shorted?"

"At Catapalooza, you announced we'd only made a tad over twenty thousand. I knew that couldn't be right because I personally collected twenty thousand in corporate sponsorships. Most things were donated, so once cash ticket sales and other private donations were factored in, our bottom line had to be higher." She felt the cord give slightly.

"It was, but Bailey got greedy. Stop fidgeting."

Sarah stilled her hands and glanced toward where Bailey lay. "Sorry, I'm nervous. You said he got greedy. Did you want some of that money for the hotel?"

"Not from the money raised for the shelter. Too obvious. See how easily even you figured out the numbers were off when I announced the figure he'd given me."

"From what I understood, he was a real numbers person. If it was that obvious, what did he want the money so badly for that he took the chance of others noticing he'd sloughed off the top?"

Thomas smiled. "To fund his Ponzi scheme."

"I don't understand."

"With Lance looking the other way, Bailey started a pyramid or Ponzi scheme using construction-related loan money. He denied a loan and then waited a few days and called the people and told them he'd found some new silent investors for them who, without worrying so much about compliance rules as his bank did, were willing to give them a short-term loan at a point above the going interest rate until they secured a mortgage or loan from another source. As each one paid the loan back, he skimmed from the top and lent the money out again."

"But how did he know the people would be able to pay him back?"

"Easy. He only did it with customers whose credit and resources should have been approved to begin with. Only, this time, his pipeline broke down. He was desperate and thought he could use the cash from YipYeow to pay off his present obligation. Once he lined up a new investor, he planned to announce an error occurred when the cash was counted so the shelter earned more money than previously stated."

"But how are you and the hotel involved?" Even as the words came out of her mouth, she realized it must have something to do with creative financing Bailey arranged for the hotel.

"The Howellian has run in the red since it opened because of cost overruns, but I knew I could turn everything around if I could just get more capital. Lance did part of the hotel's initial financing without collateral, so I went back to him for an additional loan."

"But he passed you off to Bailey?"

"That's right. He was too busy with the city council duties to handle my loan request, but he told Bailey to treat me like family. Instead, Bailey turned my application down. Said I was too extended and the assets didn't justify any further loan from the bank. In fact, he threatened that the bank might have to foreclose if I didn't keep making my payments as due. I panicked.

I went to my uncle and he refused to invest in the hotel or loan me any money. Told me the hotel was my folly and he wanted nothing to do with it. He wouldn't throw good money after bad."

"Is that when you threatened to put him in a retirement home?"

"I never threatened him. I was trying to explain what his house was worth if we sold it or changed it into our own restaurant or bed-and-breakfast. He asked where I thought he was going to go while I transformed his home and I mentioned a retirement home. He freaked. Told me I was an ungrateful lout and kicked me out. Desperate, I went back to the bank to talk with Bailey again. He repeated the bank couldn't grant me the loan, but then he offered me a way to not only borrow the money but have a portion of it forgiven."

"I don't understand. When Emily and Marcus's request was turned down, Lance told us there were a multitude of new compliance rules. This doesn't sound like a deal that would meet any of them." She felt one of the cords loosen ever so slightly.

"It wasn't. Bailey offered me a private loan from a group of investors. I'd get the money and wouldn't have to put the hotel up as collateral if I used my family and personal connections to influence a few of the city council members to delay some votes. I said that didn't sound legit, but Bailey explained the bank was going to reject some loan applications, but like he was doing with me, he would then offer the applicant a short-term loan like he was doing with me."

"But why did he need you to delay construction permit approvals or votes for a week or two?"

"To give Bailey time to reject the bank application and then run his private deal without the person having to start over at the council. It created a temporary annoyance to the borrower, which he would aim at the council, but, in the end, the applicant got his permit and money, Bailey got his piece of the action, and the bad taste with the council would be forgotten once everyone got what they wanted." Thinking of Marcus and Emily and how excited they were when the loan and permits came through, she knew Thomas was right.

"I didn't have a choice. I tried working through Anne first, but she was impossible to deal with. Then I realized Lance was an easy target. All it took was a little flattery and a few dinners and it was easy to plant questions in his mind that made him ask for information or take an action that delayed something being on the agenda for a week or two."

Sarah moved her hand a little more. She needed to keep Thomas talking. "It sounds like a good system, but what happened?"

"Bailey made a mistake."

"What?"

Thomas paced in front of her. She kept working on her hands.

"He denied loans to your sister and Cliff. Bailey's deals were tied to accounting entries made at certain times during the month based upon his constant turnover of funds. Not knowing the family histories, he didn't realize your sister and my brother were the wrong ones to turn down to keep the pipeline going. Those two, plus a construction loan that wasn't granted elsewhere, quickly resulted in him not having enough money in the account before the month's closing date."

He stopped pacing and stood in front of her. One hand was almost loose, but it needed another few wiggles, which she couldn't do if he was staring at her.

"But couldn't he temporarily transfer money from some other account?"

"Maybe, but he was scared. Eloise had already raised reconciliation questions, but Lance was too busy to address them. When Cliff and your mother confronted Lance and he reviewed the applications, he realized something was off. He called Bailey at city hall on his cell and told him to hurry back. We ran into each other in the alley as I was about to knock and sneak in to say a quick 'Hi' to Lance. Lance let us both in, but I didn't stay because it was obvious Lance wanted to talk to Bailey."

"And you went through the lobby?

"Yes."

"Where was Eloise?"

"I don't know. She wasn't at her desk when I came out of Lance's office. I left the bank right after I made my deposit and didn't look for her again."

What he said made sense. It fit with Eloise having left her desk but seeing him at the teller's counter. Thomas turned away from her and she tugged at her hand. It gave. She kept her hands close together. "When did you learn Lance was dead?"

"At the same time as you. Two plus two added up to Bailey probably being the last person in there before your mother found Lance."

"But why didn't you say anything to anyone?"

"I couldn't. Bailey threatened if I went to the police

or talked to Harlan, he'd take the hotel away from me. I went along with him because he assured me he'd make everything right financially for both of us, including forgiving my loan."

"He was going to use the money we raised for the animal shelter?"

"No. Jane, the one who once was in business with your sister and Marcus, came to him for prefinancing authorization because she wanted to be able to buy a Main Street property to open a restaurant if the zoning changed. Bailey figured if we sold her my uncle's house and he, instead of the bank, did the financing, he could use her down payment to reconcile all the bank accounts. Only problem was my uncle didn't want to sell when I broached it or even scared him with my car."

"You were the one who almost hit him on the night of the planning meeting?"

"Sarah, I never got close enough to hit him. I only wanted to scare Uncle George so Cliff and I could work on him about moving out. I was desperate. Bailey said it was now or never to close the deal."

"What about at the church? Did you hit your uncle to scare him then, too?"

"That wasn't me. It was Bailey. You've got to believe me. I had no idea he'd hurt Uncle George."

"And today?" She nodded toward where Bailey lay, while she eased her other hand out of the cord.

"Once I realized he'd skimmed off the top of the shelter's money and might be trying to use that, I called him when I knew Cliff was staying longer at the hospital and asked him to meet me here and talk it all out. I urged him to return the shelter's money.

He refused. One thing led to another and, as you know, I struck him with the figurine."

"I believe you. Why don't you let me go and we'll call the police? I'll tell them I saw the fight and you had to defend yourself."

He gazed into her eyes. "It's too late for that. You'd always know the truth."

Chapter Forty-eight

The hair on Sarah's neck prickled. Her hopes of talking Thomas out of doing anything drastic were quickly fading. "I promise. I won't say anything."

"That's a promise you can't keep. You're a nice girl. It will eat at you and eventually come out. I can't take that chance."

She tried to keep him talking, but he didn't take the bait. Instead, he went over to Bailey and used his handkerchief to pick the figurine up from the floor. He wiped it clean and then, wrapped in his handkerchief, carried it to where she sat. She didn't know what to do. If she lunged at him, he'd strike her with the figurine and if she sat still, but he grabbed her again, he'd see her loose hands.

She nodded toward Bailey. "What about him?"

Thomas turned his head for a moment, and she pressed her hands closer together so if he pulled her arm, she could keep them from coming apart. "It's a shame. They're going to think you got a lucky hit in and killed him."

She sat up straight and calmly stared him in the eyes. "No one is ever going to believe I killed him."

"You're right. Especially if you're here to tell them." He glanced around the cabin. "Considering how hard Cliff worked on this place, it's a shame it's going to burn with Bailey and you in it."

"What?"

"With all his toys, there's plenty of tinder and gasoline around here. It isn't going to be too difficult to start a fire."

"Fire only works in books. I don't think that's the way to go here."

He laughed. "I always said you were spunky. And what, in your opinion, is the way to go?"

Sarah stalled. She looked out the window, hoping the view of the bluff and water would give her an idea or at least a final moment of peace. What she saw almost made her gasp. Cliff was standing on the porch. Sarah turned her head away from the window, hoping Thomas wouldn't look in that direction, but she spoke as loudly as she could. "Well, I'm a cook of convenience. I never try to make a dish from scratch by myself. I always get help. I think you're in the same position."

"I don't know what you're saying."

"Only that going it alone doesn't usually work well. Remember that night we had the planning meeting, I was going to whip up brownies from a mix, but Marcus and Jacob made those delicious cookies and petits fours while Emily and Grace worked together on the puffs. What I served was far better than if I'd tried to do it alone."

Sarah was afraid to look toward the window, but she hoped Cliff had heard her meandering thoughts and specific message to call for help through the open door.

"That's it. Get on the floor."

When Sarah didn't move, Thomas reached for her hair again. As he bent toward her, Cliff burst through the door and knocked his brother away from Sarah. Thomas twisted free and swung at his brother. Cliff took the punch and staggered sideways. When Thomas went to swing at him again, Sarah lunged forward, using her hands and body weight to topple the leg he was braced on out from under him. She fell in a heap on the ground. Thomas stumbled and tripped over Bailey. Cliff charged and pinned his brother as a siren was heard in the distance.

Sarah smiled. Not only did Cliff listen well, he was a pretty good guy.

CHAPTER FORTY-NINE

On Tuesday night, the "Closed for Special Party" sign on the Southwind Pub's door said it all. It was truly a celebration in so many ways. The party buffet, which Marcus and Emily, cooking together again, had put out was fantastic. Not only did it feature all the foods on the pub menu but also a few main dishes from their proposed fine-dining establishment. Once the city council had agreed on a replacement, who most of the members believed understood Lance's vision for Wheaton, it had voted five to four in favor of rezoning. Its newest member, Eloise, had been the swing vote allowing the restaurant in the big house to become a reality. Unfortunately, Jane was opening a competing restaurant in Mr. Rogers's house.

Cliff had brought them this news when he stopped by the office to check on Sarah and tell them Jane was buying his uncle's house. Apparently, even though Mr. Rogers was ashamed and believed Thomas should serve time, he also felt he owed it to his late sister to make sure Thomas had legal representation. Selling the house was the only way he could afford to do that for his nephew and still have enough money to take care of himself.

Because Maybelle visited him daily, Sarah knew the doctors had made Mr. Rogers understand that once he was released from the rehab center, an independent living apartment would be easier to maneuver than the big house. He'd balked at their recommendation until Maybelle suggested, and Sarah agreed, that Sarah would keep Fluffy, so he could visit her whenever he wanted. So far, RahRah was ignoring but tolerating Fluffy's presence.

When Mr. Rogers contacted Jane, she'd jumped at the chance to make an offer without a realtor involved. With the bank approving her financing, a no-brainer with the nice payout she'd received from Marcus and Emily for her ownership piece of the original Southwind, her opening a restaurant right across Main Street was a done deal.

Sarah waited for the waiter to serve her glass of wine and Harlan's scotch. She took a sip of her pinot grigio. "What will happen to the Howellian now, Harlan?"

"It will be foreclosed on by the bank and sold. Some chain will probably take it over and run it well. Unless, of course, Marcus and Emily want to make a go of it."

Sarah held her wine and watched her sister and Marcus working the room, together. "Not them. It may become competition for them again in the future, but they'll take that on, under whatever it's rebranded. If they never hear the name Howellian again, it won't be too soon."

Harlan lifted his glass and clinked it against hers.

"I'll drink to that. Too bad they can't relax tonight and enjoy this more."

"Believe me, they are enjoying every moment of this evening." After all, for Marcus and Emily, this was fun but also their livelihood.

Sarah also was delighted to see her mother smiling. Not being Chief Gerard's top suspect agreed with Maybelle. She and Eloise had their heads together at a table planning something. One thing that came out of the horror of the past few weeks was the friendship between the two. Sarah wondered if her mother would loosen Eloise up or if Eloise would figure out a way to tame her mother's impulses.

"Harlan, I want to say thank you to you, too. You've really been there for my family and me."

It was Sarah who blushed when Harlan acknowledged her appreciation. "I'm not going anywhere. I'm here for you."

For Sarah, this party was a celebration of life. She couldn't believe how far she'd come since her divorce. Not only was she comfortable living in the carriage house and working for Harlan, able to say she had enough money in the bank to be secure and, if she wanted, take some college classes; but, free from the rat, she had three great guys in her life: Harlan, Cliff, and RahRah.

Recipes

Sarah's Sweet Potato Puffs
the Convenient Way

1 teaspoon brown sugar
½ teaspoon chili powder
¼ teaspoon cumin
¼ teaspoon salt
Dash or two of cayenne depending on
  your love of spice
1 20-ounce bag sweet potato puffs

Preheat the oven to 400° F.

Mix the brown sugar, chili powder, cumin, salt, and cayenne together.

After spraying a baking sheet with nonstick cooking spray, empty the bag of frozen sweet potato puffs on it. Lightly spray the puffs with the nonstick cooking spray and then sprinkle them with the spice mixture. Toss the puffs until well-coated with the spices and bake 20–22 minutes. Voilà!

Makes 4 small servings.

CLASSIC WINE SPRITZER

Classic wine spritzers mix chilled wine, ice, and either club soda or sparkling water. Chill wine 30 minutes to one hour. Place ice (small pieces are preferred to large cubes) into glass. Depending upon strength desired, add three to six ounces of white wine. Fill remainder of glass with club soda or sparkling water. Garnish with lemon or lime slice, if desired.

HOWELLIAN CATNIP

This drink uses a dash of chilled white wine (fruity preferred), ½ cup ice, and the remainder of the glass is filled with chilled Sprite, 7UP, or any type of lemon-lime soda. The Howellian Catnip also has a touch of food coloring (optional). It gets its name because it barely contains a taste of wine. (Although having only a nip of wine makes the Howellian Catnip an economically savvy drink, it should not be served to children.)